Read the entire Wicked series:

Wicked

Witch & Curse

Wicked 2

Legacy & Spellbound

wicked

Resurrection

Nancy Holder & Debbie Viguié

SIMON PULSE

NEW YORK LONDON TORONTO SYDNEY

SIMON PULSE
An imprint of Simon & Schuster Children's Publishing Division
1230 Avenue of the Americas, New York, NY 10020
Copyright © 2009 by Nancy Holder and Debbie Viguié
All rights reserved, including the right of reproduction
in whole or in part in any form.
SIMON PULSE and colophon are registered trademarks of
Simon & Schuster, Inc.
Designed by Ann Zeak
The text of this book was set in Aldine 401BT.
Manufactured in the United States of America
First Simon Pulse paperback edition July 2009
10 9 8 7 6 5 4 3 2 1
Library of Congress Cataloging-in-Publication Data
Holder, Nancy.
Resurrection / Nancy Holder, Debbie Viguié. — 1st Simon Pulse ed.
p. cm. — (Wicked)
Summary: A threat more powerful and frightening than anything
they have faced before looms over the Cahors witches as both the
Deveraux and Cahors family lines face extinction, and Cahors family
secrets are revealed.
ISBN: 978-1-4169-7227-3 (alk. paper)
[1. Witches—Fiction. 2. Warlocks—Fiction. 3. Magic—Fiction.
4. Good and evil—Fiction.] I. Viguié, Debbie. II. Title.
PZ7.H70326Res 2009
[Fic]—dc22   2008050194

To all the fans who wanted this book so badly. Thank you so much, from the bottom of our hearts. Blessed be.
—Nancy Holder and Debbie Viguié

ACKNOWLEDGMENTS

Thank you, Debbie, for being my friend, my creative partner, and my rock. And thank you, Michael del Rosario. You are our champion. This book is for you both, and for my daughter, Belle, who is living proof that magic and miracles are what we're made of.

—N. H.

Thank you to Nancy, the best cowriter/friend that anyone could ever ask for. A special thanks to a great editor, Michael del Rosario, for his belief in this book. Finally, thank you to those people in my life who have always encouraged me: my husband; my parents; my sisters; and Schrodinger, the little black cat who sat on my lap and "helped" me type.

—D. V.

PROLOGUE

Are you going to Scarborough Fair?
Parsley, sage, rosemary and thyme,
Remember me to one who lives there,
For she once was a true love of mine.

Tell her to make me a cambric shirt,
Parsley, sage, rosemary and thyme,
Without any seam nor needlework,
And then she'll be a true love of mine.

Tell her to wash it in yonder dry well,
Parsley, sage, rosemary and thyme,
Which never sprung water nor rain ever fell,
And then she'll be a true love of mine.

Tell her to dry it on yonder thorn,
Parsley, sage, rosemary and thyme,
Which never bore blossom since Adam was born,
And then she'll be a true love of mine.

Ask her to do me this courtesy,
Parsley, sage, rosemary and thyme,
And ask for a like favour from me,
And then she'll be a true love of mine.

Have you been to Scarborough Fair?
Parsley, sage, rosemary and thyme,
Remember me to one who lives there,
For he once was a true love of mine.

Ask him to find me an acre of land,
Parsley, sage, rosemary and thyme,
Between the salt water and the seastrand,
For then he'll be a true love of mine.

Ask him to plough it with a lamb's horn,
Parsley, sage, rosemary and thyme,
And sow it all over with one peppercorn,
For then he'll be a true love of mine.

Ask him to reap it with a sickle of leather,
Parsley, sage, rosemary and thyme,
And gather it up with a rope made of heather,
For then he'll be a true love of mine.

When he has done and finished his work,
Parsley, sage, rosemary and thyme,
Ask him to come for his cambric shirt,
For then he'll be a true love of mine.

If you say that you can't, then I shall reply,
Parsley, sage, rosemary and thyme,
Oh, let me know that at least you will try,
Or you'll never be a true love of mine.

Love imposes impossible tasks,
Parsley, sage, rosemary and thyme,
But none more than any heart would ask,
I must know you're a true love of mine.

Part One
Melchior

In the time of the end, kings and lords shall be laid low and their treasures given to those who will never understand their power nor know until it is too late the terrible things that they behold and the curse that is upon them.

—ancient Celtic prophecy

ONE

GOLD

☾

Dancing, spinning all around
Wounded now we've gone to ground
But Deveraux power still remains
And where we are, darkness reigns

An uneasy peace on Cahors lies
We dare not dance 'neath moonlit skies
We fear the dark that creeps outside
Not half as much as the one we hide

Medieval France: Fantasme, Pandion, Jean, and Isabeau

Thrum, thrum, thrum.

Fate loosed Fantasme, ancient falcon, powerful familiar of House Deveraux, upon the wind. The bells around his talons jingled like a temple dancer's anklets as he soared high above the wooded lands of France. He smelled the heat of Pandion, the hawk familiar of the Cahors; if one could say that a falcon smiles, Fantasme grinned in lustful anticipation. The son of his master, Duc Laurent, would soon bed the daughter of House Cahors. Perhaps Fantasme would take their familiar in the same way. Or *peut-être* he would simply rip her to shreds.

Thrum, thrum, thrum . . .

Below, the beaters threshed out the serfs, smashing the branches of the oak trees with poles in order to flush the unwilling sacrifices from their wretched hidey-holes. Other, lesser game would serve as for the great feast before the marriage of Jean de Deveraux and Isabeau of the Cahors—venison, pork, poultry. Ancient enemies, joined in matrimony—the result of decades of plotting, planning, and assassination.

The Deveraux asserted that a century before, Nicolette of the Cahors had poisoned Elijah, son of the most powerful warlock family in all of France, and buried his body in a ditch.

It was claimed in turn by House Cahors that Elijah had lured their witch princess to the festivities at Scarborough, and there had hacked her to pieces.

Neither claim was ever proven, but Fantasme knew that one hundred years later, history was about to repeat itself. A Deveraux and a Cahors bound together? More likely they would bleed each other in their sleep.

Below, fine young Jean raised his arm, his signal for Fantasme to return. Farther back in the hunting party, Jean's mistress, Karienne, rode alone, knowing she would soon be sent away.

Thrum, thrum, thrum: teardrops on leather; heartbeats; and the sly chuckle of unseen forces, who were, once again, about to set the families at each other's throats.

In a castle some leagues beyond, the hawk Pandion jingled her bells in protest, hobbled to her perch when she would rather be searching for game. She smelled Fantasme in the wind, and she would sooner slice his eyes open with her talons than see him at the marriage.

Dressed in yards of black veils chased with silver, Catherine, witch queen of the Cahors, prepared her daughter, Isabeau, for marriage to Jean de Deveraux— steadied her with sacrifices, raising bloody hands to their Goddess, while Isabeau wept with fear and hatred. She would marry Jean, but she would not keep him long.

Unless the Deveraux revealed the secret of the Black Fire to the Cahors, the proud warlock dynasty would be murdered in their beds before the year was dead. Catherine had sworn it; and Isabeau was her mother's child, raised to obey no husband and lord, only her liege lady, author of her birth. Despite the presence of Isabeau's father, Robert, women ruled in

House Cahors. Men were for getting children, and not much else. Dispensable, and pitiful.

The Present: Jer, Without Her

"Holly," Jer Deveraux whispered as he drifted in darkness. And loneliness. And in dreams. . . .

Are you going to Scarborough Fair?

If we could turn back time; if we could go back; if there was something I could have done differently . . . The path not taken . . .

His life was nothing but regret. There was no joy in it, only pain.

If I could see her again before I die . . . but if I can't, I would rather die . . .

Holly Cathers. Holly of the Cahors. You have bewitched me. Ruined me.

By the Horned God, damn you, love me still. I beg this of you.

Thrum, thrum, thrum, the beating of his heart, the fluttering of his soul.

Seattle: Dr. Nigel Temar and Hecate

It was hard to believe that it had all started with a cat. Not just any cat either, but the resurrected familiar of a witch. The zombie cat that he had found in the ruins of a house, hissing and spitting and trapped under debris, had been the greatest gift he had ever received.

Gold

He had taken the feline, and studied it. He knew little about magic but much about science, and with the cat he was sure that he could bring his greatest dream to fruition. A lifetime of searching, and the answers he needed were trapped inside the tiny feline body.

Perhaps most amazing of all, he had discovered that the creature could not be rekilled. No matter what happened, it revived, just as angry, just as miraculous. *Curiosity killed the cat, but satisfaction brought him back.* He had no idea what had actually killed it, although from the violent reaction to water dishes, he guessed it had something to do with drowning. However, the doctor knew it wasn't satisfaction that had brought the hellcat back. Months of study had finally paid off: Two days before, he had finally replicated the resurrection—but with science, not magic. Now he had two angry revivified cats in his lab, and he couldn't be happier.

Around him Seattle smoldered in ruins. The destruction caused by Michael Deveraux in his battle with Holly Cathers and her cousins had ensured that the city would be years recovering, if ever. Thousands were dead or missing, victims of unnatural storms and fiendish creatures. Yet still people wanted to carry on as usual, lying to themselves, pretending that the stuff of their nightmares wasn't a reality.

But as he walked to his office in one of the few buildings left intact at the University of Washington at

Seattle, Dr. Nigel Temar's thoughts were not on the victims. They weren't even on the two dead cats waiting for him in his lab. Nor were they on the twisted metal debris that once had been classrooms, or the gaping crater where the chemistry building had once stood, or the hundreds of impromptu memorials set up to honor students who had lost their lives there.

No, his thoughts were on one student only. Kari Hardwicke had been one of his grad students, and hers was the only presence he longed for, hers the only absence he felt.

He entered his building and made his way down three flights of stairs to his basement office. He unlocked the door, flicked on the lights, and quickly locked the door again behind himself. An unearthly yowling met his ears, and he smiled at the cat that was throwing himself against the bars of its cage. The other one glared sullenly from its enclosure, still not entirely used to its seemingly uncomfortable life-after-death.

All those months working so closely with Kari, prepping lectures, grading papers, discussing mythology. All he had wanted to do was take her in his arms and share with her the real secrets of his research. He might have given into the temptation, too, if it hadn't been for her ill-timed affair with the brooding warlock Jeraud Deveraux.

Nigel was nothing, though, if not patient. He

knew how to watch and to wait. He'd known when the warlock's passion had waned. He'd watched Kari's vain attempts to recapture her lover's interest.

Then something had happened that he couldn't have foreseen. Kari had gotten involved in an age-old feud between the warring houses of Deveraux and Cahors. He had lost track of her a couple of months back, but he felt confident that he could find her.

He swept a place clear of papers on his desk and then gently set down a laptop, *her* laptop—which he had finally managed to locate, beneath a huge pile of rubble that had once been the tiny office she'd shared with two other teaching assistants.

"Kari, dear, you won't believe what I've achieved," he whispered as he stroked the case a moment; then he opened up the clamshell and hit the power button. He hoped he would be able to show it to her soon. If only he could find her.

An hour later he had scanned all her documents, skimmed through e-mail, and even launched her Instant Messenger. Although there was an address book, he realized he didn't know what names he should be looking for. Finally he started hitting her Web site favorites.

It took a while, but he finally found the site he was looking for. It was a Wicca site, nothing too interesting, but it had a forum that Kari had posted in. He was able to view a string of communication between Kari and a user named Circle Lady. Recognizing that name, he opened her Instant Messenger and fired off a note to Circle Lady, who appeared to be offline. Then he returned to the Web site and sent a message to her there.

A moment later, the Instant Messenger pinged, and he turned to it with a flare of hope. He was disappointed to see that the response was not from Circle Lady, but someone calling themselves English Rose. He sent a brief response.

"Hi."

A moment later English Rose accused: *"You're not Kari."*

"No, but I'm looking for her," he typed without hesitation.

"I'm looking for Circle Lady," came the unhelpful reply.

"Maybe they're in the same place?" he suggested.

"Goddess forbid . . . Kari's dead."

He stared for a moment at the screen as the words registered. His stomach twisted; his heart felt numb. Dead? He should have known, should have felt it. For a long time he stared at the screen.

And then the yowling of the cats penetrated his fog of grief. There were worse things than dying. There was *staying dead.*

"Are you sure?"

"Yes, I'm sorry."

"How long ago?"

"A couple of days."

"Where is the body?"

He waited for the answer to this most important question. It was slow in coming, and for a minute he wondered if English Rose had decided not to tell him.

"It hasn't been . . . recovered . . . yet."

He caught his breath. Blinked.

"Kari," he whispered. "Don't go. Don't leave." He realized he was talking to her soul. Or trying to. Did he believe in such things?

"I think we need to talk," he told English Rose.

In the end she wouldn't give him her phone number, so he gave her his university extension and waited impatiently for the phone to ring. When it finally did, he was actually a little surprised that his caller did in fact seem to be from England.

Coy as she had been in giving him her phone number, he was not surprised that she didn't seem willing to reveal anything else. He took another deep breath. He needed her to find Kari, and if she was right and Kari was dead, then time was of the essence.

"I know Kari was in over her head. She was caught up in the middle of a coven war that destroyed half of Seattle," he said.

"It didn't do much for London, either," she snorted.

Nigel closed his eyes. So, London it was. He tried to stay focused, make plans, behave like a scientist. "I need help transporting her body back here . . . for a proper burial in her hometown," he said.

"Then I suggest you contact the local authorities. However, you might want to wait a few more days."

"Ah, yes, the business of recovering the body."

"Yes, quite."

He could hear the suspicion in her tone. Of course, if he'd known about dead bodies before the police and had not contacted them, he'd be suspicious of people who asked questions too.

He decided to gamble. Tenuous as the link was, English Rose was the only connection he had to Kari. "The problem is, you see, I need the body to be preserved as best as possible. The family wants an open casket."

"Why don't we drop the games," the woman said.

He sensed she had made a decision about him. Or was willing to. "Gladly. You first. You could tell me who you are."

"English Rose is as good a name as any. And you, professor?"

"Since I can only call you by your screen name, how about I give you mine. I'm generally known as Dr. Frankenstein."

He could hear her suck in her breath. "I think I understand you, Doctor. What you want, however, will be tricky."

"I don't care how it is done. All that I care about is retrieving the body quickly. I can pay you well for your time and your services."

"In that case, I think we can work something out. Although I'm more interested in information than in money."

He had gotten her attention, that was for sure. Although the cat he had found had been clearly resurrected by magic, he had been fairly sure that most witches didn't possess such knowledge of resurrection.

And now he was certain of it.

Outside Cologne, Germany:
Holly, Pablo, Armand, Alex, and the Temple of the Air

Holly thought that she must not have a heart anymore, because if she did, it would have broken long ago. She had walked away from everyone she cared about: Amanda, Nicole, Uncle Richard, Jer, and Owen, Nicole's baby. Well, Jer had walked away from all of them, leaving without a word. Nicole had been giving birth to Owen, and Holly had been forced to choose her destiny.

Her cousin Alex Carruthers had invited her to join forces with him to rout out more strongholds of the

Supreme Coven, bitter enemies of both the Mother Coven and Holly's people as well. The Mother Coven, made up of female and male witches who worshipped the Goddess, had tried to force Holly to claim allegiance. After she had reluctantly acquiesced, the Mother Coven had twice failed to protect Holly's coven against attacks from their bitterest enemies, the Deveraux.

Because of that, Holly had chosen to go with Alex. Amanda, Tommy, Richard, and Nicole all wanted peace. And they deserved it. They had done their bit for Coventry, as it were.

Philippe, the French male witch aligned with the Goddess, would have been willing to continue the fight, except that he was in thrall to Nicole, and so his first loyalty lay with her . . . and with the child, who might or might not be his. Nicole had been with him, Eli Deveraux, and her now-dead husband, James Moore. James had betrayed his father, Sir William Moore, leader of the Supreme Coven in London.

James had thought he'd killed his father, but at the last instant, a hideous demon had pushed out of Sir William's corpse like a huge cobra. The memory chilled Holly's blood, and made her wish that she, too, had stayed behind with Nicole and Amanda. Together, her twin cousins and she were the three Ladies of the Lily, said to be very powerful. Of the three, she possessed the most magical power . . . purchased at terrible prices. Parts of her soul were dark now, as dark as that of any Deveraux or Moore.

Of those who had fought beside her, only Pablo and Armand accompanied her on her new journey, with Alex. Her long-lost cousin was fair-haired and blue-eyed, such a contrast to Jer Deveraux. And in more ways than one: Alex loved Holly. It was obvious in every smile, every look, in how he checked to make sure she was all right after they attacked enclaves and strongholds of warlocks dedicated to the Supreme Coven. How he conjured wine and good food for her, and made pillows and a mattress out of thin air for her, expending valuable magical energy that he might need in their next foray against the enemy.

And speaking of energy . . .

I need a vacation, Holly thought grimly as they trudged along under cover of darkness somewhere in the German countryside. *Holly Cathers, you just defeated your archnemesis, the man who killed your parents and made your life a living hell. What are you going to do?*

Apparently she was going to start the whole process all over again.

She should have chosen to go to Disneyland instead. As the group began to move even more slowly and silently, she wondered if it was too late to change her mind.

There were sixteen of them in total. Besides Holly,

Pablo, and Armand, Alex traveled with a dozen members of his coven, which he called The Temple of the Air. It was a good name. Air was definitely Alex's element, and he could control it in ways that were astonishing.

I wonder what my element is, Holly thought. Her introduction to her witchblood and the legacy that came with it had been a bloodbath, literally. She had never had a chance to explore all the subtleties and niceties of the craft. She had unbelievable power but no idea what she was doing most of the time.

It's probably water, she thought grimly. It would be ironic and morbid. After all, those who loved Cathers witches were doomed to die by drowning. That was how her parents had died, on a rafting trip. *That's what happened to Nicole's cat, Hecate. That's how I killed her.*

Nicole. I wonder how she is. Fire would definitely have to be her cousin Nicole's element. She was always the drama queen, so wild, so passionate. Nicole's twin sister, Amanda, with her practicality and thoughtfulness, was definitely like the earth, a nurturer through and through.

The group came to a halt so suddenly that Holly bumped into Armand hard enough to make them both stumble. The moon slid out from behind the low-hanging clouds, and for a moment she could see the others clearly. Alex was deep in conversation with one of his men, a witch named Stanislaus, who had just returned from scouting ahead.

Rumor had it that there was an outpost of the Supreme Coven nearby, one renowned for dark magic and evil purposes. Although Alex had once lectured Jer that there was no need for covens, or even families, to fight, it wasn't entirely true. Evil was evil, and Alex insisted that it had to be dealt with to make the world a safer place for all of them.

Except I am evil, Holly thought. It was the brooding fear that she always tried to push out of her mind. Sometimes at night she dreamed that the reason Jer didn't want to be with her wasn't because of his terrible scars or his own black heart, but because of hers.

You're not evil, Pablo said, popping quietly into her head.

Thanks, she said, too tired to yell at him for reading her mind. It was the young boy's special talent, one they had put to good use while spying on the enemy. But she found it disconcerting that he knew her secret thoughts.

Alex finished consulting with Stanislaus and turned toward her, his face eager and his eyes alight. "We've got 'em," he announced.

"Oh, goody," Holly said, under her breath.

Pablo looked at her sharply, but Alex had missed her sarcasm.

"We're going to take them now," Alex continued, looking keen and fresh. His blond hair glowed in the moonlight, and his blue eyes gleamed. He grinned at her. "You ready?"

"Now?" Holly asked, stunned. "Shouldn't we plan or prepare or hold circle or something first?"

"No time," Alex said impatiently. "We have the advantage of surprise. If we don't strike now, we risk losing that."

Armand and Pablo looked as uneasy as she felt. She was sure that Alex had never seemed more confident, though. Reluctantly she nodded agreement. All she really wanted was to find a nice soft bed to crawl into. If he thought that they should go in, that was what they'd do. After all, she'd had less warning than this before a fight.

Holly cast a spell that muffled their movements as they continued on their way, walking closely together. In a valley below, a large black-and-white structure with a shingled silo dominated a crisscross maze of animal pens. Holly blinked in surprise. A barn?

"Are you sure we're in the right place?" she asked Alex.

"Not all branches of the Supreme Coven have the audacity of the London one," he said. "Some prefer to remain much more anonymous."

Holly shook her head as she stared at the wooden

structure. Pablo and Armand gazed impassively at her, and she couldn't begin to guess what they were thinking.

An owl hooted as Stanislaus led them around the west side of the barn, away from the main doors. Inside, horses chuffed and stamped in their stalls. Did the animals sense that death was about to rain down upon their owners?

Rickety doors in the ground looked like the entrance to a root cellar of some sort. Several of Alex's covenates were already at work, silently punching holes in the wards that she could see shimmering in the air. Their presence helped calm her nerves and focus her mind. Suddenly the serene barn was instead a fortress of evil giving lodging to her enemies.

The enemies of my House, and my friends, she thought. *I shall give them no mercy. None.*

As the wards came free, she realized that she was beginning to sound more and more like her ancestress Isabeau. The only daughter of a bloodthirsty, merciless witch, Isabeau had been trained from birth to be hard and unforgiving.

Maeve and Janet, two of Alex's female covenates, threw open the doors. Alex hurled himself down a flight of stone stairs dripping with broken wards. Holly lunged after him, and the blood began to sing in her veins. She could hear shouts below her, and she conjured fireballs in each hand.

The first warlock came into view, a tall, thin man wearing black pajamas.

"*Verdammt!*" he bellowed, lunging toward Alex.

Slightly above Alex on the stairs, Holly threw one of her fireballs into his face. The man screamed, collapsing and rolling to the bottom of the stairs. He blazed, and she did nothing to help him.

Maeve, Janet, and Stanislaus clattered around Holly and down the stairs. Alex leaped over the burning man, then turned and held a hand out to Holly. She sailed over the warlock, who had stopped struggling.

"To the right!" Pablo shouted.

Holly and Alex turned to the right and found themselves inside a large cavernous space. At least two dozen warlocks were rushing toward them. Some cast wards; one came at her with a sword; others pulled out revolvers and submachine guns.

Holly laughed as she knocked her adversary's sword aside with a wave of her hand. A moment later the room rocked with explosions, and then walls of flame. The smoke made her cough and choke, until Alex conjured a shield around them, a bubble. He grinned at her, and she threw back her head in wanton pleasure.

And then it was over. The fire died, revealing the carnage. Holly looked down at the scorched bodies of her enemies, and she couldn't help but feel disappointed. That had been far too easy.

Gold

It was barely midnight when they locked the cellar, replaced the wards around it, and melted into the night. It had happened so quickly it was almost as if Holly had dreamed the whole thing.

"There's a great hotel in Cologne," Alex said. "I've stayed in it before. It's just a short walk."

Great, more walking. Holly was really starting to wish for a magic broom. In her mind she remembered past fights, when she had conjured spectral warhorses to ride into battle.

A spectral warhorse would mean she wouldn't have to walk anymore. She sighed. It would also take more concentration and strength than she was capable of. The adrenaline from the short skirmish had drained out of her the moment it was over. So she put her head down and kept walking, forcing one foot in front of the other. And when she looked up again, they were in the city.

Even her exhausted brain couldn't help but marvel at the beauty of historic marble buildings juxtaposed with soaring skyscrapers of neon and glass. Cologne sparkled with bustle and lights.

On their left they passed an ancient Gothic cathedral of ornate double spires, stained-glass windows, and elaborate friezes of saints. Holly paused, moved by its beauty. She had never seen anything like it in her life.

I wish witches had structures like that, she thought. *Beautiful places where we could gather to worship, and the tourists could take pictures and brag about having been there.*

"This is Cologne Cathedral," Alex told her in hushed tones. "The bodies of the Three Wise Men are said to rest inside it." He took her hand. She let him.

"Do you believe that there were three wise men?" she asked.

"Most men are fools," he replied, smiling faintly. "They throw away their power . . . and their chances for happiness."

He's talking about Jer, she thought with a flip of her stomach.

Suddenly Pablo made a choking sound. He staggered and then fell, crashing to his knees. She let go of Alex's hand and dropped down next to Pablo.

"Pablo!" she shouted, grabbing his arm. His eyes had rolled backward in his head, and only the whites showed.

"Phil—ippe," he gasped, then collapsed onto the street.

London: Rose

Rose was thrilled with the contact from Dr. Frankenstein. She still didn't know his real name, but she could find out easily enough. It didn't bring her any closer to finding Sasha, but if she could learn what he knew about reanimating the dead, it would be well worth her time and efforts.

Luna, the high priestess of the Mother Coven, had personally asked Rose to search for Sasha. Rose's special talent was finding people, especially those she had met before. Yet, despite all her skill, she had been unable to find the woman who had once been Michael Deveraux's wife, before she had escaped him and lost herself in the Mother Coven.

The last time Rose had seen Sasha, the woman had been a member of Holly's coven. Luna herself had sent them to Rose. Rose's home served as a Mother Coven safe house, and when she had sheltered the Cathers Coven, Kari Hardwicke had also been with them. She remembered the younger woman as being flighty and frightened—not of witchblood, and not really even a borrower of magical power. Just . . . angry, and anxious to get out of the terrible war she'd stumbled into.

The Mother Coven would not approve of Rose's bargain with Dr. Frankenstein, so she would have to be careful in deciding who among her witchly friends she could trust. The Mother Coven frowned on ambition. They saw it as a warlock trait. In the coven every witch had their role, their place, which they were carefully prepared for. Unlike the members of the Supreme Coven, they were strongly encouraged to pick a specialty and not to learn much outside their roles. As a result, only a very few in the Mother Coven had a broad base of power, or the knowledge or skill to challenge Luna, their high priestess.

Rose had no desire to challenge the high priestess, but she was tired of feeling as if she lived in a cage. She was a safe house keeper, a person locater, nothing more. If she could learn Dr. Frankenstein's secrets, though . . . She pushed the thought from her mind. One step at a time. She still had to figure out how to retrieve Kari's body.

It took two days to gather the witches she needed and another day to make sure that they could sufficiently break the wards around the former Supreme Coven headquarters to get inside. They went at night and dressed in dark clothing.

What they found inside was a nightmare. Bodies of humans and demons were lying broken and lifeless in crumpled piles, limbs askew as though flung by giant hands. The stench was unbearable, and Rose struggled not to vomit.

"By the Goddess," Sarah, a young witch, breathed in horror.

"I didn't know there were so many women warlocks in the Supreme Coven," a male witch, Kyle, muttered as he flipped over yet another body and Rose shook her head.

"Neither did I," Rose said grimly. Finding Kari

was turning out to be a lot harder than she had anticipated.

Finally, an hour later, Rose gazed down on a familiar form. It took a moment for Rose to be sure it was her. Bodies often looked very different when the spark of life was gone. Additionally, someone had slit this woman's throat, and her face was covered in blood.

"It's her," Rose said, at last.

Sarah wove a spell of invisibility around the body before Kyle stooped to pick her up.

"Light as a feather, stiff as a board," he joked.

Sarah wrinkled her nose, and Rose shook her head. "Let's get out of here," Rose ordered them tersely.

"I feel tainted," Sarah said with a shiver as they started back to the entrance, picking their way around bodies. "To think that I've stood on Supreme Coven soil . . ."

"It is very disturbing," Kyle added, serious for a moment.

Once outside they all breathed easier. A few minutes later they reached their destination without mishap. The Supreme Coven had clearly abandoned London. That should be cause for rejoicing.

When they were safely inside Rose's home, they laid Kari out on the living room floor. Her face was mottled and gray, and maggots crawled in the deep slash across her throat.

"Decomposition has advanced," Kyle said. "This isn't going to be easy."

"Do what you can," Rose instructed. Kyle was the only witch she knew who loved dead things. His skills with preserving bodies were often called upon for ceremonies and rites, and if the occasional preservation seemed odd, he never asked questions.

"If we remove the organs, this will be easier," he ventured, lifting one of Kari's arms and inspecting her fingertips.

"Like mummification?" Sarah asked.

"I was going more for taxidermy, but yeah," he said, lowering her arm and frowning at the gaping hole in her chest.

"No, the family would like her as intact as possible," Rose said. She couldn't help but wonder if Dr. Frankenstein would be able to reanimate a body that had been dead several days and was as badly damaged as this one. If he could, his would be a secret worth knowing.

"I'll need the usual," Kyle said. "Salt, myrrh, amber." He made a face. "This isn't going to be easy."

Four hours later, it was done. Kari was as well preserved as possible. Rose and Kyle placed her in a large box, and Sarah went to work putting a glamour on it, so that no one would see the body inside.

When it was done, Rose dialed the number she

had for the doctor, and when he answered, she said, "We're ready to ship. Please give me the address."

Seattle: Dr. Temar and Hecate

Inside his laboratory Dr. Temar carefully, reverently opened the plain wooden box. Inside he saw what appeared to be dozens of gilded dried herbs and flowers. They were beautiful, delicate, and completely unreal. This was the glamour that English Rose had placed upon the crate to make sure that anyone who opened it would not see the body that was inside. He muttered a few words under his breath, ones she had told him would break the illusion.

The air seemed to shimmer for a moment, light traced the outlines of the flowers, and then they faded and he saw the beautiful face of Kari. The witches had been true to their word. Although she had now been dead a couple of weeks, her body was in a state of preservation, though it was far from perfect.

Something had exploded in her chest, shredding flesh and bone until there was not much left intact. Her throat had also been cut, a jagged line passing over the jugular. He had prepared himself for what he might see, but he couldn't stop the tears that fell from his eyes and wet her lifeless cheeks.

"Kari, I swear I will bring you back," he vowed.

Inside their cages the cats screamed.

Avalon: Eli

Eli Deveraux walked the beaches of the island of Avalon like one in a dream. After the battle at the Supreme Coven headquarters in London, he had somehow ended up at Avalon. He still wasn't sure how or why. What he did know was that he was different.

He was stronger, more powerful. He could feel the vitality that he had taken from his father, Michael Deveraux, and from his rival, James Moore, when he had killed them that night. It had been Wind Moon; anyone who killed a witch or warlock on Wind Moon gained their power.

He turned, and without lifting a finger or uttering a single syllable he set an oak tree on fire. Then just as easily he put it out with a sudden violent wind. He seemed to have control over three of the elements now, but the fourth, water, eluded him. As did a way off the island.

At least he wasn't in too much of a hurry. From his past experiences on the island he knew where everything was, including the kitchens and the larders. Most of the island's demonic inhabitants seemed to have disappeared. Whether they had gone to aid their masters in the fight or had fled at the first opportunity, he wasn't sure. Either way, he walked the island mostly undisturbed, watching the waves crash on the sand, the rushes wave in the wind. Towering rocks gazed down on him like castle turrets, and sea birds cawed.

With the island almost entirely deserted, though, it was easier to feel . . . something. Nicole had told him that there was a presence on the island. He had never felt it before, when he had come there to rescue her, but he could feel it now. It was as though something were watching him, peeping out at him through the cracks and crevices, through time itself. Whatever it was, the evil that emanated from it freaked out even him . . . and he was just about as evil as they came.

He had been there for a month, and every day he scryed for Nicole, trying to find her. Every day he found nothing. He refused to believe that she was dead. Somehow he was sure that if she was, he would feel it, would know somehow. Even if the baby wasn't his. With the magic now at his disposal it would take some incredibly powerful wards to hide her forever.

He combed every inch of the island, turning over rocks, feeling along the crevices of ruined stone walls, looking for something that might have belonged to her. A personal object could serve as the basis of a finder's spell. All he could find were things of James's that she might have touched—a jeweled goblet; James's clothes, left behind. He found a cache of

James's backup athames—ritual knives used in magic ceremonies.

He spent undue amounts of time in the bedroom where Nicole had been kept a prisoner. It was decorated in the style of warlocks who worshipped the God—with carved images of Pan, and the great, leering face of the Horned One.

He tore the bed apart—the very bed where James had forced Nicole—and pounded it in anger with his fists. He found the hidden cavity in the headboard. It was empty, but he sensed that powerful magical objects had once lain inside. His blood froze as he recalled the stories he had heard from his father, of the silent bargain the Deveraux and Cahors had made—the secret of the Black Fire in exchange for a son of both their blood. James had possessed the magical ability to force Nicole to carry his child. Had he done it?

Eli's imagination clawed at him, tormenting him as each day on the island dragged past. He became obsessed with the marriage room; he scoured every inch; then, one day in despair, he stood in the center and turned slowly, eyes closed.

"Open my eyes that I might see the treasure that belonged to my lady," he whispered. He winced as he thought about how much it sounded like a prayer to the Goddess. In many ways Nicole was his Goddess.

And after everything that had happened, she should have been the lady to his lord. He grit his teeth as he thought again of James marrying her, taking her. His fingernails dug into his palms until he could feel blood oozing out. The drops hit the floor, a fitting sacrifice.

"Take my blood in this hour, grant me a prize from my lady's bower."

He opened his eyes and continued to turn, hoping to see something, anything, that could have belonged to her. And slowly he tilted his head up, and as though compelled, he lifted his eyes to the ceiling. It was ornately carved with symbols of the Horned God.

And there, in the dead center of the ceiling, was the glint of something round, something metal.

He lifted his hand and willed it to come to him. It came free easily, as though it had been long waiting for just such a call, and fell into his hand. It was a thin ring of gold with a tiny circumference. He wondered if it would even fit Nicole's pinky finger. He closed his hand around it, and let his blood cover it.

That night he tried his seeking spell one last time, but with the gold ring as the focus of it. "From this ring give me power to see the woman newly a mother, and tell me then where I might find this lady who holds the heart and mind."

A woman's scream pierced the night. He jumped

to his feet and whirled around. His heart slammed against his ribs as he wondered if somehow he had managed to bring Nicole to him.

There was another scream, and he realized it was outside; he ran as fast as he could, conjuring fireballs to light his way. A third scream—it was coming from the cave where he and Nicole had hidden when they'd been trying to escape the island.

The cries grew fainter; fear spurred him to put on a fresh burst of speed. What if he hadn't brought her to him? What if he was about to see what was happening to her right now?

Then: silence.

He swore to himself as he ran the last one hundred feet before bursting into the cave. He stopped at what he saw. A spectral woman lay there, trembling with pain and exhaustion, a newborn baby upon her breast.

Nicole? No, it wasn't she; it was someone else. From the style of her clothes she had been dead a long, long time. The ring, then, must have belonged to her. He sank to his knees in rage as disappointment ripped through him.

Then the ghost woman turned and looked at him.

He blinked, and so did she.

"Can you see me?" he asked her.

Her brow furrowed, and he realized she couldn't

understand him. He held up his hand slowly. He pointed first to her, then to his eyes, and then to his own chest.

She nodded. Her eyes were wide, young, and incredibly gentle. He knew he had never seen her before, yet something about her seemed so . . . familiar.

He pointed again to himself. "Eli."

She smiled faintly at him before pointing to herself. "Mary."

A shiver went up his spine and a terrible fear raced through him. Slowly he lifted his finger and pointed at the baby she clutched.

Her smile widened and she looked down at the child. "Jesus."

And suddenly the entire cave changed. Everywhere he looked he saw animals and people. Mary and her child were the center of attention. He turned to where the entrance to the cave was. He didn't trust his legs to hold his weight, but he figured he could try to crawl free. Only, standing at the mouth of the cave were men of great power and wealth. Their clothes were bejeweled. They carried with them boxes. He could feel the magical energy coming off them, crackling powerfully.

They strode by him without noticing. No one there except for Mary seemed to see him. Her ring— he guessed it must be hers—and his spell must have created some sort of portal between their times. He turned back to watch as the Magi—that must be who they were—laid their gifts at her feet.

He remembered the legends and he watched as they laid down gold, frankincense, myrrh . . . and silver. And that was when he realized.

There were four of them.

TWO

PARSLEY

☾

Searching, searching we will find
Poisons to harm body and mind
But strength we gather as we wait
Eager to seal our enemies' fate

Hidden things all around
Taunt us, call us to be found
We shall seek though we might die
Heaven and hell, earth and sky

Medieval France: Jean, Karienne, and Isabeau

"I shall never leave you," Jean whispered to Karienne as he removed his ritual robe and came, for the last time, to her bed. She smelled the blood of sacrificial victims on him, and gazed overhead at the mural of the pit of hell where his ancestors resided, and then she felt his heat and his strength as he shivered with a deliciousness that, for the moment, outweighed her sorrow. Yes, he must put her aside, but she had his love. And the love of the son of the most powerful warlock family in all of Coventry was the bridal trousseau she would bring to the castle of the count, who was to become her husband. Thus had Jean assured her protection in the lonely years to come.

"Once I have a son on Isabeau, I will murder her," Jean promised her. "Then I will come for you."

"Swear an oath on your soul," she begged as he lay down and covered her.

His eyes glowed with evil, and he laughed. "Wench, you know by now that I have no soul."

The Present: Holly, Without Him

Holly jerked from a dream, and rolled over in the darkness. Her heart was pounding and her face was wet with tears. She had been dreaming about Jer again. She could almost feel his lips on her closed eyes, her cheeks, her lips.

He is dead to me, she told herself. But the truth was, there was a tiny part of her soul that flared whenever she dreamed of him, thought of him. Then, and only then, did she feel fully alive.

But their love lay in ashes, and she knew it. It was as dead as that part of her heart.

In the Forever Place, Damaged

In the mystical greenwood beyond space and time, Fantasme flew, carrying a tincture of the essence of the Cahors' witch's soul. He screeched in triumph.

From the other side of that eternal forest, Pandion gave chase.

Outside Cologne, Germany: Pablo

Pablo, the little witch boy who could read minds, called out in searing terror to his covenate Philippe again, and again, although he lay unconscious.

And although he was in thrall and in love, and wished to take no part in warfare, Philippe answered.

One Month Later, North Berwick, Scotland: Nicole, Amanda, Tommy, Richard, Owen

Nicole Anderson-Moore had a warlock for a lawyer. If her twin sister, Amanda, hadn't been bouncing a fireball menacingly on her fingertips, Nicole might have laughed. As it was, she looked him dead in the eye and asked, "And what makes you my attorney?"

Derek Jeffries smiled at Nicole, seemingly paying no attention to Amanda and his own impending doom. "I'm from the firm Hackem, Hackem, and Derringer. We represent the Moore estate."

Even the mention of that name was enough to make Nicole feel sick.

"How did you find us?" the girls' father, Richard, demanded.

It was a good question, one that Nicole would

dearly love to have answered. For the past two months they had been on the run, moving from place to place, never staying anywhere for more than a night or two. It was hard on them all, but they had each wanted to get as far away from the ruin of the Supreme Coven headquarters in London as they could. They had made it only as far as Scotland, unsure how safe public transportation was and whether or not they should attempt to return home to Seattle.

"One of the services our law firm provides to practitioners is tracking of relatives upon the death of one of our clients. Upon the deaths of Sir William and his two named heirs, the family finder spell immediately engaged. As James Moore's widow, Nicole is the closest living family member."

No matter what I do, I can't escape James, Nicole thought bitterly. *Or, apparently, his lawyers.*

"So, all you'd have to do to find Holly is kill us?" Amanda asked, eyes narrowed.

Holly, their cousin and high priestess, had been gone since right after the battle.

"It's not quite that simple. First you would have to retain the firm as your attorneys. Then you would need to draft up a will or something of that nature. Then we could magically attach your relatives either in the order of your preference or in the order of nearest relation. So, as you can plainly see, you and your precious Holly are fine."

Parsley

"Except that you've already declared yourself as Nicole's lawyer," Richard growled.

Derek smiled. "Well, there is that. I guess she'll just have to postpone writing her will. As her legal representative, however, I wouldn't advise that. Now that she has a child to look after, a will is imperative to ensure that the child is provided for and that suitable guardians are appointed."

Nicole forced herself to smile. "I wouldn't worry about Owen; he's very well looked after."

Derek flashed her an oily professional smile. "I don't doubt it."

"So, what now?" she asked.

"I've come to take you home."

"To Seattle?" Tommy asked hopefully.

"No, to Scarborough."

"What's in Scarborough?" Amanda asked suspiciously.

"The ancestral home of her *late* husband."

Nicole burned under his stare. "Don't look at me that way. I didn't kill him."

"No, you managed to get one of your lovers, Eli Deveraux, to do it. I must say, very old-school of you."

"Don't you dare think I planned that," Nicole spat.

"And don't mistake my admiration for condemnation," Derek said.

My life is way too complicated, Nicole thought. The

39

baby cried, and she was grateful to be able to focus on him for a moment. She could still feel Derek's eyes on her. She wondered briefly if his firm's family finder spell would be able to determine if James was her baby's father.

She shook her head. She wouldn't give Derek the satisfaction of hearing her voice her own confusion on that topic. No matter how many times she went over it in her head, though, she still couldn't puzzle it out. The first eight months of the pregnancy were hazy, almost like half memories from a dream. She couldn't even figure out who the father could be. Eli, James, her beloved Philippe. The timing just didn't make sense. And then there had been the thing, the *presence*, in her room when she was James's prisoner on the lost island of Avalon.

She looked deep into her son's eyes and wondered how she had come to be in some twisted paranormal version of *Mamma Mia!* More than anything, though, she wished that Philippe were there. A week after Holly, Armand, and Pablo had taken off with Alex Carruthers to find lost Cahors relatives and battle evil, Philippe had received a psychic distress call from Pablo. Afraid for the little boy, Philippe had left in the middle of the night and had promised to return as soon as he could. She hadn't heard a thing from him since. She sighed heavily and turned her attention back to Derek.

Parsley

"In addition to lands, there are rather extensive financial holdings. We'll go over it all on the way," he said.

I want Philippe, she thought as Owen snuggled against her.

A private jet and two helicopter rides later, they had arrived at the mansion that belonged to their enemies. It was getting dark when they finally stood at the gates that led to the drive. Still they could make out the hulking structure, and Nicole did her best to ignore the sense of evil that was coming off it.

Derek entered an alarm code and the gate unlocked. He swung it outward and then took a step backward.

"After you, Mrs. Moore," he said, his tone lightly mocking.

It took all of Nicole's willpower not to lob a fireball at his head. Instead she ducked him a mocking curtsy and said, "No, after you. I insist."

Derek shook his head. "Unfortunately, it doesn't quite work that way."

"I think you need to explain yourself," Amanda interjected, moving more closely to her twin.

"My firm has represented the Moore family for generations. I myself was the chief liaison for the last five years, and I have entered these gates many times."

"So, enter them now," Tommy said. He raised his chin and folded his arms, as if challenging the powerful warlock.

41

"I'm afraid it's not that simple. Sir William Moore and all who went before him were very powerful men. They were, however, not stupid men. The only safe way to enter these premises is at the invitation of a Moore."

Nicole had a sinking feeling in her stomach.

"And, like it or not, you seem to be the only one left alive," Derek finished, pinning Nicole with his eyes. They were warlock eyes: hard, cold, with an almost reptilian gleam in them. Everything she knew told her not to trust him. There was something else she saw there, though, that convinced her he was telling the truth.

"Is there a magic password?" she asked, briefly allowing herself to be amused at the thought.

"If it's 'open sesame,' we're leaving," Amanda said.

"No, you should be able to walk right on in. Then you will need to invite each of the rest of us by name."

"What are we, vampires now? I thought we were witches," Tommy said with a roll of his eyes.

"I would never speak lightly of the Cursed Ones, and you would do well to follow my example," Derek said pointedly.

"Oh, man, it was a joke. Are you kidding me about vampires?" Tommy groaned.

Derek didn't answer but returned his attention to Nicole.

She took a deep breath and stepped forward. She had expected . . . something . . . alarms, demons appearing out of portals . . . maybe an earthquake. Instead there was nothing. She turned and looked suspiciously at Derek, just in time to catch him sigh in apparent relief.

"Voilà," she said, throwing her hands up into the air. For a moment she wasn't Nicole the witch or Nicole the mother or Nicole the unwilling bride. She was just Nicole, drama queen.

Amanda smirked at least. The others just stared.

"So, I just call you by name?"

"That's it," Derek said.

She realized she didn't remember his last name. It was on the business card she had stuffed in her pocket, but she didn't feel like giving him the satisfaction of reaching for it.

"Okay, Lawyer Derek, come on in."

He stepped forward and joined her. Nothing happened. Nicole didn't relax, though. What if it was some terrible trick and only Moores or warlocks could enter? Could she really risk any of the others? She sucked in her breath. She teetered for the moment on the brink of indecision. She could run back to them and they could run as far away as they could.

She knew they'd never be able to hide from the spell the cursed lawyers were using, though. And so far, no harm had come to them. *And in the home of our enemy would be the last place they would look for us, ma petite,* a female voice with a strong French accent whispered in her head. Isabeau, their long dead ancestress, come to impart some of her wisdom or enforce her will.

Nicole looked at the people she loved. Her sister, Amanda; Tommy, Amanda's soul mate; their father, Richard; and little baby Owen cradled in his arms. It was a terrible choice, but in the end it was easy. She gambled with the only life she could.

"Tommy Nagai, I invite you to come here," she said, her voice shaking.

He stepped forward boldly, slipping out of Amanda's grasp. A glance at his steely eyes told Nicole that he knew full well why she had called him first.

He stepped forward, and a bolt of lightning flashed across the sky. Nicole dropped to the ground and threw up a protective shield around them both. Thunder rolled and fat drops of rain suddenly began to splatter down.

"It's just a storm," Derek said. "Bad timing."

Nothing else happened, but the skies opened up and the rain began to pour down in earnest. The rest of them might have been able to stand in the rain and debate this, but Owen needed to get out of the freezing wet.

Parsley

"Richard Anderson, I invite you to come in. Owen Anderson-Moore, I invite you to come in. Amanda Anderson, I invite you to come in."

And a moment later they were all racing beside her up the drive to the house that stood with dark windows gaping at them like so many hideous mouths waiting to devour them.

Just let them try, Nicole thought grimly as they pounded up the front steps and onto the porch.

Derek produced a key and opened the massive front door. Nicole expected it to creak as it opened, but it gave way smoothly. They tumbled inside the foyer and stood for a moment, dripping on the marble floor as they took in their surroundings.

Derek snapped on the lights, and a chandelier above their heads came to life and showed them a massive staircase rising up three stories, and passageways to the right and left.

Tommy whistled. "Where's the butler?"

"All Sir Richard's servants were damned creatures. When he . . . died . . . they were taken back to hell."

Nicole noticed the hesitation. It was something that had been plaguing her. She wasn't really sure Sir William was dead. After all, she had watched a demon erupt from his body and escape the massacre at the Supreme Coven. More than the other warlocks that might be searching for them, she worried about that creature. Was it Sir William's true face? And, if so, how long before he came home to reclaim what was his? She shivered.

"You should change into some dry clothes," Derek said, noticing and mistaking the cause.

The others fanned out, turning on lights as they went. Nicole wanted to tell them to be careful. Who knew what wards or magic booby traps might be in place. She was tired, though, and a change of clothes did seem in order. She picked up the backpack she had dropped upon entering the house, and turned to the right. The first door opened into a bathroom, and she used it to change.

Ten minutes later she found everyone congregated in the kitchen. Amanda was perched on a countertop holding Owen, with Tommy leaning against her. Richard was pacing, and Derek had spread some papers out on one of the countertops. Nicole moved over to him.

He handed her a pen and slid the first paper in her direction. "No matter what world we live in, paperwork is still a pain," he joked.

Nicole glanced down at the paper. "The whole thing is fine print," she noticed.

He chuckled. "You can take your time and read it all if you like. Actually this is all the mundane paperwork. We'll save the special parts for last."

"Great," Nicole said with a sigh as she began to skim the document.

"It isn't right, what happened to you," Derek said suddenly, his voice softer.

Nicole winced. "What, I'm supposed to believe you're a warlock with a heart of gold?"

He smiled, and she fought back a chill. "Like everything in life, there is a spectrum. Think about witches. On the one hand you have the noble, selfless creature of great virtue."

Nicole nodded, her thoughts instantly flying to Anne-Louise Montrachet.

"On the other hand you have power-mad half-insane witches who embrace the dark in their search for power."

In her mind Nicole saw Holly, and she flushed and refused to meet his gaze.

"So it is with our side. There is the epitome of the warlock, someone completely evil like Sir William, and on the other hand there are those of us who sacrifice for the power to make the lives of others better."

"You make it sound so noble," Amanda mocked from her perch.

He shrugged.

"So, you're one of those better warlocks?" Nicole asked.

His smile turned darker. "I wouldn't go that far." He glanced sideways at Amanda. "And you can tell your boy toy not to even think about coming after me with an ice pick."

Nicole shuddered. It was a reference to how her covenates had killed the warlocks guarding the entrance to the Supreme Coven's London headquarters prior to the battle.

Richard stepped forward and purred, "No, we leave those kinds of toys for the grown men. You know the thing about magic? It's only a good defense against other magic."

It wasn't entirely true, but there was enough truth to it that, combined with the reputation her father had earned as a warrior, it made Derek flinch.

"Dad, he's trying to be nice," Nicole said with a sigh. "Like it or not, he's sort of our lawyer for now. And something tells me that's the real altar he sacrifices on."

Derek inclined his head. "Well spotted, Lady Moore."

It's a compliment; just accept it, Nicole thought to herself, forcing a smile onto her lips.

Pembrokeshire, Wales: Jer

The dolphins breached in a semicircle as Jeraud Deveraux broke the surface of the chilly, turbulent sea. They chattered at him with their happy faces, squeeing in their language; he knew there were warlocks who could converse with animals, but he was not one of them.

He knew that those beloved of Cahors witches were cursed to die by drowning. He was not one of those, either. Otherwise, the hours he had spent swimming against the current would surely have dragged him under and ended the life he wished so thoroughly to be rid of.

Yet, despite his bitterness, he found comfort in the frigid waters. His face and body were a melting ruin of scars caused by the Black Fire, the magical secret weapon of House Deveraux, once again lost. Swimming with the dolphins, he could forget the pain that continually racked his body, inside and out; on land each movement brought searing pain, even a year later. And the dolphins didn't care that he was a monster, so hideous that he had refused to be joined in thrall with Holly Cathers, the only woman he had ever loved.

No. That's not the only reason, and you well know it.

Of course he was lying to himself. He was a Deveraux, and through the centuries the Deveraux warlocks had based their survival on deceit. Holly was tainted, as he was. She had made terrible deals with the darkness to keep her people safe. The goodness in her was shadowy, and as icy as the waters he swam in. Mix her magic with his, and the world would quake.

It doesn't matter. I don't love her anymore. That died when she agreed to go with Alex Carruthers and his damn Temple of the Air. Smarmy bastard. He and I swore one of us would die on Wind Moon. Holly dismissed our bad blood as testosterone poisoning, but if I'd had the Black Fire, I'd have used it against him then.

If I had it now, I would hunt him down and light him up like a torch.

No, I wouldn't. She made her choice. I'll let her live with it. If there's anything left of the Holly who once loved me, she'll realize soon enough that she has made a mistake.

Besides, Jeraud Deveraux didn't know how to conjure the Black Fire. His father, Michael Deveraux, who had conjured the Black Fire that had disfigured Jer, was dead. Jer's brother, Eli, who had helped Michael create the fire, had turned on their father and killed him in the last battle at the Supreme Coven headquarters in London. He'd gone missing and was presumed dead.

He's alive. I know it. And I'll find him.

The ocean rumbled as if in disapproval. Clouds rolled in, obscuring the sun, symbol of warlock virility. Jer had cast runes and performed finder's spells for three straight months, and still there was no sign of Eli. Better, perhaps, to let the dead bury the dead. Michael and Eli had cast their lot in with the Horned God, and the world was better off without them.

And what of me? To what power do I owe my allegiance now? Warlock blood pulsed through his veins; he wasn't some male witch obligated to the Goddess. Like Alex Carruthers.

His mother, however, had joined the Goddess's temple. And Holly believed there was good in him. He had turned his back on his male relatives. . . .

And look where it has gotten me.

As it began to rain, raindrops shooting past him like bullets, he dove beneath the surface. The dolphins joined him, sleek and untroubled. He wished he could lose himself in the sea forever. He wished that by drowning he would know that Holly had actually loved him.

It's over for me. For us. I'm . . . free.

A dolphin nosed him, as if to remind him that he was a land creature and should soon return. Once he would have found joy in communion with such a magical creature, but delight and happiness had been burned out of him.

He swam back toward the coast and found purchase in the breakers, trudging naked onto the rocky shore. The sharp shells sliced the scars of the soles of his feet, but unlike the rest of his body, most of the nerve endings in the bottoms of his feet were dead.

Someone was watching him. He felt it before he saw anyone; he murmured a few words in Latin, and a dot on the cliffs above him telescoped in his mind. Eve, the warlock sent by Sir William Moore to kill Michael Deveraux. Eli had robbed her of her target, and she was cast adrift, as Jer was. She was one of the only people he knew who didn't flinch when she looked at him.

She reminded him of Kari, when they'd first become lovers. Driven, ambitious, lustful. He wasn't sure she knew what love was.

Of course, he didn't know, either.

He could tell that she knew he'd spotted her; she began making her way down a narrow path. He went to his small white towel and began to dry off, averting his gaze at the sight of his gnarled hands; his fingers were swollen lumps of scar tissue. It was remarkable—perhaps miraculous, or simply ironic— that Black Fire hadn't touched his groin. A waste, from his point of view.

He was fully dressed by the time Eve reached him. She was wearing a black fisherman's sweater and black jeans. She had let her short hair grow, and her huge eyes in her delicate face gave her an elfin appearance. But there was nothing dainty about Eve. She was a trained assassin, and she had nearly taken him, Jer, down in her eagerness to please her master, Sir William Moore.

Despite her protestations to the contrary, Jer assumed she was still Sir William's willing servant. Moore had transformed into a hideous demon and had vanished during the battle, and as with Eli, Jer hadn't seen him since. But this was the third time Eve and Jer had crossed paths—and each time, he'd braced himself for an attack. None had come.

Maybe the third time is the charm.

"Good morning," she said to him in her upper-class British accent.

"What do you want?" Jer's voice was flat and cold.

"By the God, you're testy today." She smiled faintly at him. "Seen your brother?"

"If I had, I wouldn't tell you. I'm betting Sir William is turning up the heat. Wants payback for the massacre."

She began to shake her head, then sighed heavily and crossed her arms. As she moved her weight, he felt a stir of desire, and efficiently and magically quelled it.

"Actually, this time I have come from the Supreme Coven, but not from Sir William. No one's seen him. And since James Moore, his son and heir, is dead, it's been declared that House Moore sits on the throne of bones no longer."

She uncrossed her arms and inclined her head, a

gesture of deference. The wind ruffled her hair as seagulls wheeled across the sun, casting shadows on her face.

"I've been authorized to offer the throne to you," she declared. Then she gazed up at him and smiled. "The Temple of the Air's got us on the run."

He stared at her. "Are you serious? I took part in the attack."

She moved closer to him, and he smelled fresh soap and soft skin. Felt her body heat. "Come *on*, Jer. We're warlocks. There's no such thing as loyalty. Only enlightened self-interest."

"Well, I'm not interested."

Her smile played on her mouth. There was a dimple on either side of her mouth. He hadn't noticed them before. "Maybe Eli would be interested."

"Ask him. If you find him," Jer said. He wondered if that had been Eli's plan all along. What had Michael felt, when he'd realized his son was about to murder him? Pride, no doubt, that his older son was as ruthless as he.

"Perhaps we could sweeten the pot," Eve ventured, laying a hand on his forearm. His chest tightened. No one touched him anymore.

"I would rather die," he said frankly, brushing past her.

"That can be arranged too." The seagulls nearly drowned her out.

He stopped walking. "Are they that afraid of her?"

"Are you?'

He resumed his pace. There would be tea at the inn where he was staying. And a fire.

He was cold.

Outside Warsaw, Poland:
Holly, Alex, Pablo, Armand, and the Temple of the Air

Pablo recovered from his psychic fright, and the Temple of the Air moved on. Alex quizzed him repeatedly about what had caused his collapse, but Pablo didn't know. Alex accused him of lying. But why should he lie?

Pablo knew that Holly Cathers was worried. It didn't take a psychic to read the tension in her face, the fear in her eyes. Being psychic, though, he did know that it wasn't for herself or him or Armand, or Philippe, or even Alex Carruthers that she was worried. No, her thoughts were with her cousins Nicole and Amanda. She had every reason to be afraid for them. And Pablo had every reason to be worried about her.

The decision to join with Alex and his Temple of the Air had been a mistake. He and Armand had come with Holly in the hope of fighting evil and making a difference. Some days Pablo wished that he had never heard of the Goddess, had never known another's thoughts. He would have given everything to spend his childhood fishing instead of fighting.

But there was going to be more fighting, a lot of it. When he had regained consciousness in the hotel room in Cologne, the only thing he knew was that he had seen the future. He couldn't remember what it was, but it scared him. Holly had told him that he had called out for Philippe, but he had no memory of it. As always these days, when Pablo thought of Philippe, he closed his eyes and said a brief prayer for his coven leader.

He missed Philippe, but more than that he missed Richard Anderson. Whenever the world went crazy, Richard slipped away to a peaceful place in his mind where he relived his memories of fishing with his father. Richard didn't know it, but Pablo had gone with him several times into those memories, and although he had never even held a fishing pole, he now believed it to be the epitome of tranquility. *Someday I will go fishing,* he promised himself.

All Holly wanted in the world was to go to bed and wake up from the nightmare she was living. Ever since the battle in London, she felt as though she were spinning out of control. Everything that she had believed, clung to, seemed to be turned upside down. She had believed when it was all over there would be rest, peace, and that she and Jer would be together. None of that had happened.

Life was more stressful than ever, and Jer was

nowhere to be found. She didn't regret her choice to join with Alex Carruthers and his Temple of the Air, but she wished she could have known what was in store for her. She had thought when he said they would continue to fight evil that they would be wiping out small dark covens. Instead she had discovered that the Supreme Coven headquarters in London that had been destroyed at such great cost was just one of many such headquarters around the world. In fact, it hadn't even been the central one, or the largest one, or even the most evil one.

"Just one small stronghold among many," she muttered.

"What?" Alex asked as he walked into the room.

She shook her head. "Have you found any Cahors?" she asked, gesturing to the map he held in his hand. The promise of finding other long-lost family members had helped her make the decision to join with Alex.

"No, but I did find another warlock coven we can take care of," he said, smiling.

Holly sighed. So far they had taken out half a dozen small covens without taking any casualties to themselves or Alex's followers. They were beginning to rack up quite a body count, and yet they still seemed no closer to finding other Cahors.

Alex sat down beside her. "Don't worry; we'll find them. For now, though, we have a job to do."

"Can't we just skip this one?" she asked.

His eyes turned dark. "No, we can't. Look, every time we take out one of these covens, we're striking a blow at the Supreme Coven. Look how much chaos they're responsible for, and how much death. How many have you alone lost because of them?"

Too many, Holly thought, as the faces floated in her mind. She saw her parents, Tina, Barbara, Marie-Claire, Eddie, Kialish, Dan, Silvana, Tante Cecile, Josh, Sasha, Kari, Alonzo, José Luis, whom she had never even met, and Hecate, whom she herself had drowned. She might as well add Jer to that list. He was as lost to her as he would have been if he were dead.

Alex kissed her. Although she did not resist him, she did not return it. She knew what his plans were for her, for *them.* She needed time, though. Maybe one day he would kiss her and she wouldn't think of Jer. She couldn't help but think of the members of Alex's coven—she couldn't think of it yet as *her* coven—who would willingly share his kiss and his bed. Still, she, Pablo, and Armand had had very little contact with Alex's followers, even though they were all traveling together.

The Temple of the Air, at least those members who had come with them, was a dozen strong and a mix of male and female. They weren't rude to Holly, Pablo, and Armand, but neither were they welcoming. It was sometimes easy to forget they were even there, since they kept their distance. Alex had chosen to spend more and more of his time with Holly. She, in turn, had stayed close to Pablo and Armand. Them she knew and trusted, and that was important, especially when her whole world was chaos.

"Cheer up, Holly. I have some news you will really like," Alex said, breaking through her thoughts.

"What?"

"I've found another Supreme Coven headquarters, and after we wipe out this coven, we're heading there next. Together we have the power to destroy it."

Holly took a deep breath. "Where?"

Alex conjured a globe, and it spun slowly in the air in front of her. On it she saw a red dot. She could hear her high school geography teacher shouting in her head, but she was too tired for guessing games or trying to remember something that seemed so long ago. She looked at Alex questioningly.

He smiled. "It's in Bombay."

Paris: Eli

Cloaked in invisibility, dressed for the winter chill in jeans and a thick black hoodie, Eli shielded the flame of his black candle as he threw salt and hare's blood into the wind and recited a spell in the old tongue to find the One Who Is Lost. A trio of oblivious German tourists passed him; a nun in a black-and-white habit paused, tilting her head, as if trying to detect the source of her sudden unease.

Yes, I made a blood sacrifice on your hallowed ground, he silently taunted her. *What of it? Your religion is steeped in blood sacrifice.*

His thoughts instantly returned to Mary, and he winced. Seeing her in that cave had led him to find a boat that was hidden in there. He had returned in the morning, afraid of what he would find, but her image had faded. He had tried not to think of the boat as some gift magically left across time for him, but it was hard, especially when he had searched that cave his second day on the island.

Occult energy rippled along his skin like an aura. He had been learning more and more to harness his newfound powers. Surely, armed with that, he could find one witch and her child.

He glided unseen in the weak sunlight as he walked along the rooftop of Notre Dame Cathedral. The ancient city of Paris sprawled beneath him, white marble and skyscraper, and endless traffic. Snowy fog wound around the base of the Eiffel Tower and bathed the Seine. He'd had a sense—a hope—that Nicole and her baby had fled there.

That baby might be mine, he thought, clenching his fists inside his hoodie. *And they are in danger.*

Parsley

All of Holly's covenates were on the hit list of the Supreme Coven. They'd gotten past the wards at London headquarters and had taken out innumerable warlocks. Now Holly and Alex were on the rampage, seeking out warlock covens and destroying them. As far as Eli could tell, Nicole and the baby weren't with them. At least Holly had that much sense.

I have to find them, before the Supreme Coven does. He was sick with fear. Sick, and astonished with himself. His ambitious, cruel father hadn't raised him to believe in such mundane fantasies as love. Eli was a Deveraux warlock, consecrated to the Horned God, and it was obvious even to him that this consuming worry was wrongheaded and harmful. He was so distracted that any number of his enemies could have snuck up on him at that very moment, and he wouldn't even have noticed if one of them had cut him down.

Which is why I have to find her.

Although the city sparkled, and sun glinted off the windshields of the thousands of cars, trucks, and buses barreling down the narrow Parisian streets, no telltale red glow revealed the object of his finder's spell: Nicole Anderson Moore, widow of James, and daughter-in-law of Sir William. And her child.

That child is mine. It has to be. Because Nicole is mine.

She has to be.

He placed his palms on the battlement of the cathedral, and listened to the blood roaring in his ears. Magic thrummed through him. Once, he had been very skilled at watching and waiting. But no more.

No more.

Frustrated, he trudged back to his hotel room. He slammed the door and flopped onto the bed. With a huff, he tried to decide what to do next.

As Philippe knelt inside Notre Dame Cathedral, he realized he had never felt so alone. He lit two white candles and prayed fervently as he stared into their twin flames. Each represented a group of people he was desperate to find. He prayed to find them both, but he would be happy if he could at least find one.

He had been a fool to leave Nicole's side. When he had gotten the distress call from Pablo, though, it had been one of the most vivid, terrifying moments of his life, and it had awakened him out of a deep sleep. It had taken him a couple of weeks, but he had at last tracked the group to Cologne. After that, though, it was as if they had simply vanished.

When he had finally given up, he had tried to return to Nicole's side, only to discover that for some reason he could not find her. He should have been able to find his lady; they were in thrall to each other, and that was an unbreakable bond. Something dark seemed to be hiding her from his sight. Something dark crossed his mind, and the flame of his candles were snuffed by an unseen hand.

Eli woke with a shout. Sweat ran off his body in sheets and he was shaking uncontrollably. *The Hunchback of Notre Dame* was on his TV, but in French. He didn't know how he'd fallen asleep or how the set had turned on, but it was two in the afternoon and he'd been out for at least half an hour. He felt completely drained in a way he never had before. He had pushed himself to the brink of exhaustion before, but it had been nothing like this. He felt as though all the life had gone out of him, only to suddenly be restored. It terrified him.

He stood up and walked around the room, stretching his limbs and conjuring a few small magics. Everything seemed to be functioning, but he couldn't shake the feeling that he had lost something.

"Apparently just my sanity," he said to himself.

He'd assumed his search spell would have yielded results by now. After all, he was an extremely powerful warlock. Maybe Nicole didn't want him to find her. The thought wounded him to the quick, which was almost as irritating as his failed magic.

"I demand an answer," he grumbled to the chilly air.

Magic crackled. On the TV screen a close-up shot of Notre Dame Cathedral flashed; then the TV abruptly turned off.

Eli stared for a moment, surprised. He knew better than to look for a rational explanation. Magic was in the air; he could feel it. Apparently the next stop on his quest would take him inside one of the most famous of Parisian landmarks. Ironic, given that he'd spent the morning on top of it.

"Why'd it have to be a church?" he sighed.

Eli had been practicing dark magic long enough to know that no matter what you did or who you sacrificed, sometimes you still didn't get what you wanted. As he stood in the back of Notre Dame and stared at all the people who had lit candles and were praying fervently in front of them, he speculated that in many ways all religions were alike. All of them left the practitioner with unanswered questions, unfound objects, and bitter disappointments to temper the joys. They also instilled in their worshippers a love of ritual. The people who knelt in prayer in front of their candles reminded him of many a night he had spent doing almost the exact same thing.

He still wasn't sure what he was doing inside the cathedral, or what it was he was meant to find. Still, the message had been very clear. He walked for a few minutes, taking in the ancient stone and the sheer size of the building. Finally, with nothing better to do, he took a candle for himself, lit it, and, choosing a place somewhat away from the other supplicants, knelt before the candle, a smile twisting his lips.

A few minutes later an older man knelt next to him. His lips moved in silent prayer, and Eli fought the urge to make his own prayers—to the Horned God—audible. It would be amusing but in the end pointless, as it would bring him no closer to finding Nicole.

A flash of silver in the old man's hands caught Eli's attention. He turned his head slightly, expecting to see a rosary—but saw instead a pentagram. The man looked up and met Eli's eyes.

"That's a symbol of witchcraft," Eli said mildly, purposefully choosing to call it that and not Wicca.

"Not always. It was a Christian symbol for a long, long time. It represents the five wounds of Christ and the five senses of man."

"I've never heard such a thing."

"Few have. But where I come from, young man, there are Christians not so ignorant of their heritage. They know who they are and what they're looking for."

The hair on the back of Eli's neck lifted. Something about the old man unnerved him as nothing else had since he was a child. Eli knew he was a messenger, but from whom?

The young warlock licked his suddenly dry lips. "And where is this *magical* place?"

"Bombay," the old man said before returning to his prayers.

Bombay. That's where I need to go. Eli knelt a moment more before snuffing out his candle.

THREE

CLOVE

Laughing now as witches die
Deveraux power is on the rise
Horned God sustain us and renew
Blood feuds that are old and true

Dancing, dancing in our minds
Reflections of the past behind
What secrets must now be told
Or all is lost to waters cold

House Moore, Scarborough: Amanda

The corridors dripped with blood, and the walls expanded, contracted, lub-dub, lub-dub, lub-dub. It was a living thing, with a beating heart, and no one else knew. And as soon as she woke up, she would forget.

Amanda swayed as she descended the circular stairs toward the basement, deep, deep down in the earth, where the secrets were buried, where the dangers grew in the dark like mushrooms.

"Amanda, don't come alone." The voice was inhuman,

slithery, and cold. The words formed before her like black snowflakes, then burst apart and shattered. "You know what to bring.

"What I want."

Beneath her feet, the floor rippled like lizard skin . . .

Amanda woke up with a jerk. Panting, she flicked on the lamp on her nightstand and cringed at the sight of the leering faces supporting the green and red canopy of her four-poster bed. The Green Man, with his intense hollow eyes and face-splitting smile, tongue extended, adorned each of the four ebony posts. The image was everywhere; was she surprised that she dreamed about Moore House night after night?

The problem was, she couldn't remember any of those dreams. And no one else seemed to be having them.

She was wearing her light pink cow footie pajamas—Nicole and Owen had them too, although Owen's were yellow—and she was glad for the extra layer of warmth as she climbed down from the bed and padded across the black marble floor. She opened the massive bank of curtains with the silk pull. Weak lavender and cream light poured through the leaded panes of the windows. Another night over, and she was glad about it, even though witches favored the hours when the moon held sway.

She crossed back to her bed and felt under the pillow for the charm she had placed there. A small dream catcher woven with silver threads gleamed in her hand. Pieces of blue and green aventurine dangled from black and silver ribbons. Black and silver were the colors of the ancient Cahors family, the noble French family whose witchblood ran in Amanda's, Nicole's, and Holly's veins. Their branch of the family went by the name of Cathers, and the three cousins had learned of the connection two years before, when Holly Cathers, their cousin, had lost both her parents to drowning.

We'd thought it was an accident then. We know better now.

She placed the dream catcher in a small silver box. Blue aventurine was a multipurpose healing stone that increased visionary powers. Green was called the Stone of Heaven, for healing, protection, and guidance on new adventures.

Then she placed the box under her arm, picked up her flashlight from the nightstand, and tiptoed out of her room. Across the hall Tommy's door was closed. They weren't sharing a bedroom yet, which made it easier for her to conduct her research into the nature of her bad dreams.

We're in thrall. We should be doing this together, she thought guiltily as she tiptoed past his door and down the hall. Nicole's door was shut as well. Amanda's tiny nephew, Owen, would be asleep in his cradle beside Nicole's bed. Richard, who was Nicole's father and Owen's grandfather, slept in an adjoining room.

Amanda knew there was an MP5 submachine gun beside his bed, in addition to the many magical charms she, Nicole, and Tommy had filled his bedroom with.

Ever since moving in a month before, they'd had endless discussions about whether or not they should stay in the house. She, Amanda, had wanted to leave, and Tommy, the lord to her lady, had agreed with her. But Nicole felt Owen would be safest there. Thanks to Lawyer Derek, Nicole had confirmed that spells designed to protect the house against intruders clearly did not apply to her or Owen—or any of those whom Nicole had invited across the threshold.

But that could be a trap too.

Nicole had made a good case for staying, at least until they pulled themselves together—after the battle at the London headquarters of the Supreme Coven. They didn't know what the future held; they couldn't protect Owen if they were on the run. They had to live somewhere. They had warded and charmed the house with layers and layers of white magic. And yet . . .

And yet.

Amanda wondered if Nicole wanted to stay in the house in case Philippe was trying to come to her. He had left shortly after Owen's birth, promising to check in daily until he found Holly and the others. They had still been on the run then; he had disappeared before they had moved into James Moore's mansion. It would be easier for a magic spell to pinpoint their location if they were not a moving target.

It wasn't like Philippe to leave Nicole; they were thrallmates, and their first loyalty was to each other. Pablo's magical distress call had clearly alarmed him. Maybe Pablo's crisis was directly connected to Nicole's and Owen's safety.

Amanda prayed to the Goddess every hour to keep him safe and to aid him on his quest. But as the days and weeks passed without word from him, she grew increasingly troubled.

Amanda could reach only two conclusions. Either someone was preventing him from communicating with them or he was dead. She shuddered as she even let the thought enter her mind.

Powerful magic permeated Moore House, of that, Amanda was certain. And if she could use it to discover what had happened to Philippe, she would. Which was one of the few good arguments *she* could make for staying in the house.

Her flashlight beam played over the ancestral portraits of the Moore family, many of them centuries old. A frisson of anxiety shot up her spine at the sight of so many evil warlocks, male and female, staring down at her. Conjuring a sphere of light to chase away the shadows would cost—magic always had a price— and many of the sections of the centuries-old house weren't wired for electricity. If they stayed, they would have to do something about that.

She stopped at the landing and studied the circular staircase. There had been stairs in her dream. She remembered that much.

She gritted her teeth and went down the stairs to the main floor, where heavy brocade curtains kept out the dawn. Defiantly she pulled them open, and gazed out at the gardens of the house. Topiary trees shaped like falcons and lions posed against a vast field of browned grass and mazes of privet hedges. A marble statue of Pan, an aspect of the Horned God, held a set of faun's pipes to his mouth. Water trickled from the pipes into a reflecting pool, where, despite the cold weather, water lilies floated.

Where was Sir William now? Did the demon he had become retain his personality? Would he be back?

Amanda crossed the great room in the dark, deliberately avoiding the suits of armor standing at attention, the mosaic-like displays of weaponry covering the walls. The Moores' past was England's past, where might made right—hundreds of battles won and fought, for land, honor, and power.

That's still going on, she thought as she finally reached her destination, the kitchen. She found the light switch and flicked it, revealing a luxurious blend of old and new: marble floors and stone arches encasing fine mahogany cabinets, granite countertops, and the latest in appliances.

She set the box with the dream catcher down beside the stove and selected a shiny copper pot from the hanging profusion above her head. She filled it with blessed water and added salt, putting it on to boil over the gas. Then she turned on the electric kettle to make tea.

Once the water on the stove had begun to bubble, she wafted the dream catcher over the water and chanted in Latin, "Reveal to me, all that I see; unravel the seams of my dreams."

She pulled out of a drawer a plain five-by-seven notebook she had bought in the village grocery store, and flipped open to a new page, which she dated August 1. She grabbed up an equally nondescript pen and held it over the paper, waiting for images to materialize and rise from the gossamer threads. First came the blurry faces of Tommy and the others, as she had expected; she always dreamed about them. Next a few random memories of the day—sweeping a floor, making a grilled cheese sandwich, and playing with Owen.

And at last, fillips of nonsensical images that she prayed held the keys to her nightmares, and the house:

a lily—symbol of the three Ladies of the Lily—
    she, Nicole, and Holly
a hulking black demon with fangs of burning

embers and black reptilian eyes—Sir William?
His dead son, James?
a crystal key—hmm, white magic? A revelation?
a rabbit—fertility. Owen?

And then there was nothing more. She waited, surprised. Dozens, sometimes hundreds, of images rose from the dream catcher. Since implementing the ritual, she had never listed fewer than thirty-nine—a magical number, as it was thirteen times three. Four was . . . wrong.

She recited the incantation again.

The water in the pot bubbled and spat, hissing like a cat. She moved back slightly to avoid being scalded. Steam clouded her vision for an instant, and then image after image rose from the pot, swirling and changing into other images. Hastily she scribbled them down: *a blue eye; a sweet smile; Owen's face; a holly branch; water (an ocean? lake?) a pyramid; a yellow flower; a blue robe with gold; a ravine; a bus driving past a castle; more flowers; shadows; trees; sunlight . . .*

About a minute later the water had boiled away, and she had filled three pages. As her tea steeped, she murmured incantations over the dream catcher, cleansing it of the previous night's bounty and preparing it to snare the coming night's new dreams. Then she prayed to the Goddess in her incarnation as Athena for insight into the meaning of the images. Many witches insisted that every dream held secret codes and messages from the unconscious, designed to instruct and protect.

When Holly had ruled the coven, she had instructed them to stay away from dreamwork. They'd had enough going on in their waking lives to keep them busy, and she'd felt that their enemies might try to attack them magically through their dreams and nightmares. But Holly wasn't there.

We have no idea where she is either.

Amanda's father had suggested they stay off one another's radar unless there was an urgent need to communicate. The fewer people who knew where they were, the better.

But what about Philippe?

She sighed and went to the refrigerator to start breakfast. Amanda, always the good, quiet sister and covenate, the one who made breakfast and cleaned up afterward. Amanda, who only recently had learned to voice her opinions and stand up—shakily—for what she believed in.

Amanda.

She cocked her head. Had someone called her name? She listened, then shrugged and opened the fridge. Eggs, milk, and bread. She'd make French toast. Nicole loved it, and of course she was breast-feeding

Owen, so she needed a lot of calories. He was vora-
cious.

She carried the ingredients to the counter and
turned to get out a mixing bowl. She walked past a
double stainless steel sink abutting a ceramic splash
guard of green and red falcons, and above that was a
mahogany cabinet where she kept some dried herbs
and some pacifiers for Owen. For a split second the
faint image of a

door

whispered

across her peripheral vision.

She frowned and looked around, then studied the
sinks, the tiles, the cabinets. Holding the egg carton
against her chest, she said aloud, "Did I just see something?"

There was no answer. There was nothing out of
place. A sense of soothing calm washed over her, and
she gave her head a little shake. Everything was fine.
They were safe.

She began breakfast.

Seattle, 1971: Daniel and Marie-Claire Cathers

"You're in a black mood," Marie-Claire said, pouting.

Daniel Cathers sighed as he turned to look at his
sister. She wore a long black dress with a halter style
top. Silver bracelets shimmered on her tiny wrists. She

had draped herself across the living room couch, and the contrast with its stark white was stunning.

"You'll ruin my party," she went on.

"Must everything always be about you?" he snapped.

"Yes," she said with a shrug of her pale shoulders.

Marie-Claire had always been vain and selfish. He had come to terms with that years before. She was beautiful, and she had used it as an excuse not to have to be anything else.

He turned, determined not to argue with her. He knew from experience it would gain him nothing. She rose fluidly and placed a hand on his arm. When he turned back, he was surprised to see her brow furrowed. She was nervous.

"It's just, Richard is coming tonight and I want everything to be perfect," she said.

Daniel smiled. "Ah, the man of the hour," he mocked.

She flushed. "Don't call him that," she snapped.

He couldn't stop himself from needling her. After all, she was his sister. Fair game. "Yes, I'm sorry, you've been actually going out with him for more than two weeks."

"For your information we've been dating for three months," she said, her eyes flashing angrily.

Something in their depths stopped him. "You're serious about him, aren't you?"

She nodded, eyes wide.

"He's crazy, a troublemaker, not exactly what I'd call husband material."

"I see things differently."

"And what about him?"

"He already asked me to marry him."

"Oh, now I see! And you haven't told Mom yet. This ought to be good," Daniel said, with a lazy, lop-sided grin. In his mind he could already hear the earful Marie-Claire had waiting for her.

"I plan to tell her tonight," she informed him.

Daniel sighed. "You know, he's probably going to get drafted any day now."

Marie-Claire raised her chin. "So?"

"So, what if he doesn't come back?"

"He'll come back." She didn't look as sure as she sounded. Her little bracelets jingled as she folded her arms across her chest.

"What if you don't want him when he does? I mean, even if you managed to wait for him, he could come back from Vietnam with pieces missing."

She slapped him. Despite the sting—or perhaps because of it—his respect for her increased. Maybe she was growing up after all. Still he had a problem seeing his sister as a wife. He gave her a thin smile and left the room.

He climbed the stairs to his bedroom, locked the door, and sat down at his desk. He opened his drawer, reached underneath the tray that held pens and paper clips, and extracted what he was looking for. It was an ancient manuscript, bound in skin. He unwrapped the black silk cloth that protected it. The cloth itself was beautifully embroidered in a silver thread with a hawk and lilies.

With a shudder he opened the book and continued reading where he had left off. The manuscript was in old French. Daniel had a gift with languages. He had been able to read and write in French since he was six. Even though this was an ancient version, he found he had no trouble reading it and understanding its meaning.

That was how, earlier that day, he had discovered that he was a witch.

If he was being honest with himself, he had to admit that it hadn't come as a complete surprise. There had always been something different about his family. They all seemed to possess the ability to sense things before they happened, and he had had more than one dream that had come true. When his father had died a couple of years before, his mother—who had always been the strong, overbearing parent—had only become worse. She had also taken to muttering a lot and seemed to spend endless hours alone in the attic. He had surprised her up there one day, and she had hastily shoved something into an old trunk before yelling at him to get out.

That "something" was the book he now perused. The whole thing read like some twisted fairy tale. Only instead of one evil witch, there was a whole family. Their name was Deveraux, and according to the book they were warlocks instead of witches, but he had yet to figure out exactly what the distinction was.

A scratching sound outside his door made him jump. He twisted in his chair but saw only his closed door. Whatever had made the noise seemed to stop. Cautiously he turned back to the book, and a moment later he heard running footsteps in the hall.

"Very funny, Marie!" he shouted.

The scratching sound came again, and he stood up and threw the door open. The hall was empty. The hairs on the back of his neck raised and he broke out into a cold sweat. "Damn book is getting to me," he muttered before closing the door.

Suddenly his room shook violently, throwing him to the ground, and insane laughter filled the air. Sudden, overwhelming pain seized the bones of his rib cage. He rolled over onto his back and pressed his hands against his sides. He looked up, and a small white face swam before his eyes.

"Marie?"

"Not Marie, not Marie. Only me, only me," something answered in a singsong voice.

His vision cleared just in time to see a small green

scaly creature about a foot tall, with pointed eyes and a large sharp nose, hop on spindly legs onto his chair and with skeletal fingers slammed the book closed. It wore no clothes, and its pointed head was bald.

Then it scampered off the chair and scooted under his bed.

Daniel struggled to a sitting position, grunting in pain. He searched wildly around for a weapon, but there was nothing.

"Who are you?" he asked, speaking to the air as he scanned the room.

"Cacoph. My name, my name, oh, Daniel of the Cahors!"

"My last name is Cathers. What are you?" Daniel shouted even as he struggled to calm his mind. He crawled to the bed and raised the edge of the bedspread. Bracing for an attack, he looked under the bed.

"What kind of witch are you that you don't know an imp?" The thing—Cacoph—hissed, baring its teeth at him.

"I'm not a witch. My mother—"

Cacoph screamed and launched itself. Daniel tried to twist out of the way but Cacoph landed on his chest, grabbed hold of his shirt, and leaned in so its face was an inch away. It smelled like rotten grass.

"She dabbles, she plays. She wishes the knowledge to bring your father back from the dead. But it is not for her. She is not a true Cahors. She is not of the blood. You are, but I won't tell you, either! I don't answer to your kind!" Cacoph ended with a shriek.

The imp slammed its fist into Daniel's injured ribs, and Daniel screamed in pain. "My master will kill you and your children and your children's children."

"I don't have any children!" Daniel bellowed as he tried to throw Cacoph off him. It just dug its claws into him until he writhed in pain.

"No?" the thing asked, cocking its head to the side. "Then my master will kill you someday in front of your children and then will wipe out all Cahors everywhere."

"There are no more Cahors. They all died a long time ago!"

"I think not," the imp said, foaming at the mouth. "But they all will."

It sunk its teeth into Daniel's shoulder, and it was as though a thousand needles were pricking and tearing at him. Suddenly he heard himself shouting in French at the top of his lungs, *"Tais toi!"*

The imp's eyes went wide for a moment, and then it vanished in a cloud of smoke. Daniel dragged himself to his feet and made it to the bathroom, where he locked the door before stripping off his shirt. Blood was coating his shoulder and much of his chest, and he grunted as he tried to clean the wound.

Clove

There was a knock on the bathroom door followed by his sister's voice. "Hey, are you okay?"

He choked back a curse. He was most certainly not okay, but not for anything would he drag Marie into this world of witches and imps and insanity.

"Fine," he said through gritted teeth.

"Are you sure?" she asked, her voice hesitant and an edge of fear creeping into it.

He clenched his jaw, then exhaled to steady himself. "Fine. I just tripped and banged my shoulder. I'll be okay in a couple of minutes."

"Do you want me to get you some ice?" she asked.

He hesitated for a moment. "Yes, that would be great."

He listened as her feet retreated down the hallway toward the stairs. She was so rarely helpful. She must have known he was hiding something.

"This is one secret you'll never get from me," he vowed.

When she returned with the dark blue ice pack, he managed to open the door partway and accept it without revealing the jagged wounds on his shoulder.

"Thanks," he said, managing a grimace.

She was trying to look inside the bathroom. "Anything else?"

"No. Just get ready for your party."

She started to turn away, and another thought

struck him. "But when you see Mom, tell her I'd like to talk to her."

She narrowed her eyes. "You won't tell her about Richard and me?"

"No, no, I'll leave that for you."

"Groovy."

By the time he had finished cleaning up and had changed clothes, there was half an hour left before guests were supposed to arrive. He tried to tell himself it hadn't happened. He'd imagined it. But the cuts on his body proved otherwise.

So he tried to force it away, compartmentalize it, save it for later. He immersed himself in the normalcy of the moment, or what passed for normalcy. Marie-Claire's birthday parties were always over the top, and this one was shaping up to be no exception. A sparkling disco ball twirled from the ceiling of their finished basement, above the portable wooden floor she'd rented. The Bee Gees were blaring through the house. Spiral glow-in-the-dark garlands hung from the rafters, and she had set out lava lamps on card tables covered with tie-dyed tablecloths and fuchsia napkins. Then she changed her shoes for ridiculous high platforms and added some sparkle to her eyes and cheeks.

While she was upstairs putting the finishing touches on her supercurled hair, he forced himself to go through a stack of vinyl albums in the living room, hoping he could slip some Jethro Tull into her relentlessly superficial musical selections. But his hands were shaking. He thought he was going to be sick. He kept stopping and checking under the sofa, the chairs. Opening closet doors and peering inside.

Something attacked me. Something from hell.

Then his mother walked in, and he felt the tension in the room soar sky-high.

"What is it, Daniel?" she asked, her eyes hard and glittering.

She knows, he realized.

"Should be an interesting party tonight," he said, trying to maintain.

"Yes. Marie will no doubt have a flock of her boyfriends here." She appeared to use the term loosely.

He set down the Jefferson Airplane record and gave her his full attention. "That bothers you?"

"They bother me. I want her to fall in love with someone who practices . . ." She stopped herself short and looked at him warily. He didn't know if she was trying to pull information out of him or if she'd honestly said too much.

"Practices what?" he said.

"Nothing," his mother murmured quickly, turning away.

"Witchcraft?" he pressed.

She jerked and turned back toward him, her face pale.

"That's right. I know," he said. "You know I can read old French."

"Let me explain," she said.

Inside him something felt like a wolf leaping forward for the kill. His mother never thought she had to explain herself. It was as though he could feel her fear, her weakness.

"Don't, Mom. I think it's pretty self-explanatory. You found a book about Dad's family. Now you think you're some kind of powerful witch who can *really* control your kids. Maybe even defy gravity. Or stop the aging process."

She smiled thinly, a bit of the wolf coming out in her. "You have no idea what I can make happen."

He rose. "Yeah, I kind of do." He unbuttoned his shirt and showed her the bandages. "Did you send that thing into my room to stop me from reading your book?"

"Oh, my God, honey," she gasped. "What— what—?"

Her reaction surprised him. And frightened him. If she *hadn't* sent that thing into his room, who had?

"Mom," he said, "it's not just a book. It's dangerous. There's a reason it was lost. Stop. Stop it now."

"Don't tell me what to do," she retorted, sounding more the child than the parent. "You can't stop me practicing the Old Religion." Her gaze traveled again to his shoulder. "Tell me again how this happened. What thing was in your room?" She thought a moment. "Was it an imp?"

"What are you going to do if you really get mad at me, conjure up something with bigger teeth?" He was quaking. "Marie!" he shouted. He had to warn her.

"Stop it," she ground out. "She doesn't know."

"Marie!" he yelled.

Then his mother turned and pointed at the door. "Get *out*," she growled. "Get out or I *will* hurt you."

Once again she was his mother, the woman who was always in control, who never backed down from anyone.

He felt himself shudder, and he wanted to back down like the good little boy he had always been. Instead he narrowed his eyes and stared deep into hers and enunciated every word.

"Stop or I'll tell her."

"She won't believe you," she replied, raising her chin. "Trust me on that."

The front door opened. She was throwing him out. Fine. *Fine.*

He turned and walked to the door.

That was the last time he spoke to his mother.

And as far as he knew, Marie never knew about any

of it. He heard from friends that Richard came back from Vietnam and that Richard and Marie got married. But he wasn't invited to the wedding, and after a while he almost forgot about the book, and the imp, and his own family.

Then he got married himself, and had a little girl. Named Holly.

And I loved you, baby, and I didn't want to put witch-blood into your veins. I denied it; I never told you. I was so afraid, and then you started showing us your gifts. On the river trip your mother and I fought because I had never told her, either. I'm so sorry. I wanted so badly to give you a normal life that I didn't prepare you. Didn't reveal our family legacy. And then I died . . .

Those who love a Cahors are doomed to die by drowning, and yes, I was a witch, but I loved you so much
so much
so much
Holly . . . forgive me . . . if only I could turn back the clock.

En route to Bombay:
Holly, Armand, Pablo, Alex, and the Temple of the Air

Holly sat up with a gasp. "Daddy?"

The darkness pressed in around her, and as she came fully awake, she remembered. He was dead, drowned in the rafting trip long before she had learned who she was. He and her mother and her best friend had been the first people she'd lost in this hellish war. For a moment, though, he had seemed so near. It was almost as though she could still smell his aftershave lingering in the air around her.

It wouldn't be the first time she had had a dream vision of him. She lay back down and tried to still her thoughts, desperate to remember something, anything, of the dream, or visitation, or whatever it had been.

Bits and pieces of it came back to her, but they didn't all make sense. After trying for several minutes, she finally got up and decided to take a short walk outside the house where they had found lodging for the evening. She stepped carefully so as not to disturb anyone else. When she reached the front door, she found it unlocked. *Someone else must be awake.*

She slipped outside and breathed in deeply of the cold, clear air. High above, the moon seemed to wink at her. She used to love staring at the moon. So much had happened, though, that it was hard to take joy in it. It just made her think of the Goddess to whom she had sacrificed so much, and who had in turn taken so many and who had eroded away parts of Holly's own soul.

She became slowly aware of the presence of another. Finally she turned to see Armand. He stood, tall and silent in the night like some harbinger.

"You're awake," she said.

"There was something in the house," he said simply.

89

"Near me?" she asked.

"*Sí.*"

"What was it?"

"I thought perhaps it was a demon," Armand said with an uneasy shrug.

Holly nodded. Armand was the one who had freed her when she herself had been possessed by hundreds of demons in the Dreamtime. She knew that it had taken every bit of knowledge and strength he had to do it. He had always been quiet and thoughtful, but he had lately become more withdrawn. It had been easy to overlook because she knew she'd been more withdrawn as well. One of the reasons she had agreed to join this pilgrimage was because Alex had held out the hope of being able to heal the damage to her mind and soul from all the fighting, all the death, *all the things that I sacrificed to protect my covenates*.

"And?" she asked.

"It wasn't. I think you were receiving a visit, although I know it wasn't the Goddess."

Tears stung her eyes, and impulsively she threw her arms around his neck. "Thank you," she whispered. "It was my father."

He put his arms around her and just held her for a moment. It felt good to touch another human being, someone who understood, someone who didn't ask anything of her.

Clove

Mumbai: Anne-Louise Montrachet

Ten miles from my luxury hotel, and I'm in an unbelievable slum, Anne-Louise thought as she passed under the low threshold into the old warlock's hovel. She was dressed in a sari of deep blue trimmed with gold, and she inhaled the pungent odor of sandalwood incense as she shuffled through a floral carpet of pastel bell weed petals and fragrant gardenias. Sitar music thrummed, vibrating against the potent magical emanations in the air. The earthy room hung in gloom, despite the beautiful twilight outside that washed the poverty-stricken alley with the promise of better days.

Ever since waking from her dream vision that had told her that Alex Carruthers was an imposter, she had been searching for the Cathers witches in vain. The Mother Coven did not know where they were, and she wasn't about to share her information with anyone other than the three girls. Whisper, the cat goddess who had guided her through her visions, waited in the hotel room while she ventured out in search of a man who might be able to help her.

The wizened old man was sitting on a red silk cushion, wearing dozens of bead necklaces around his neck and nothing more than a dhoti, a traditional saronglike skirt. His feet were bare. His left eye was milky white; the lid drooped over his right eye.

Although he was bald, his long white beard coiled in his lap like an albino snake.

Anne-Marie knelt on the dirt floor at his feet, offering a hamper of dried fruits and fresh mangoes. *I pray the Goddess has brought me to my answers.* She pressed her palms together and dipped her head.

"Great Swami, divine seer," she began, "thank you for agreeing to meet with me."

"Tipping the scales," he whispered in heavily accented English. "Must be righted." His shaking hand reached forward, trembling along the skin of the nearest mango like a spider. He grabbed it and cackled gleefully. "Balance."

She remained silent, waiting for more. He bit into the mango without peeling it; fragrant juice ran down his chin. He flashed her a toothless grin and rocked back and forth. Then he dropped the mango into his lap and reached for another.

"Sir," she ventured, "we were to speak of the witches I seek. Holly, Amanda, and Nicole." They had exchanged written letters.

"Bargain." He wagged his finger at her as he sniffed at the mango. "Balance."

Il est fou. He's crazy. Another dead end, she thought, disappointment flooding through her. She had been certain the runes had told her to travel to India— to Bombay, now known as Mumbai. Her crystal ball had led her to this man, Swami Mukherjee.

And yet . . . magical power occasionally caused the appearance of madness. If she could get through to him, communicate with him . . .

"Sir, these women are in terrible danger," she said. "I must find them."

He nodded. "Temple of the Sun, you are looking there. But . . . balance, Frenchie!"

Temple of the Sun? "As in Machu Picchu?" she asked him. "The Pyramid of the Sun, in Peru?"

He burst into gales of laughter. Beneath her knees and shins the ground jiggled slightly. His doing? Earthquake? She tensed, and looked at him to see if he had felt it too. To her surprise he threw his arms around himself and began to whimper.

"Silence!" he whispered, shaking his head. "Too much, too much!"

He leaped to his feet; the two mangoes tumbled to the ground and bounced like tennis balls. The hamper of dried fruit tipped over. A strip of plastic webbing snapped from the roof of bamboo poles and matting, and flapped down onto Anne-Louise's head like a pennant.

"Swami Mukherjee," she said, reaching for him as he backed away, shaking his head. "We should get out of here."

He began to babble. Unsteadily she rose, glancing

up as a pole dislodged and almost hit her on the shoulder. Grabbing for his hand, she was thrown back to the floor as the hut shook hard. Another piece of plastic swooped over her face, obscuring her vision. The floor rolled like an ocean wave, and he screamed.

"Swami!" she cried, pushing the plastic away as she sat up—

—just in time to watch the floor split down the center, becoming two islands separated by a chasm boiling with smoke. With one final shriek Swami Mukherjee disappeared into the smoky void, and Anne-Louise teetered on the edge.

"*Ma Déesse!*" she cried as she began to fall in after him.

"*Alors!*" shouted a man as a strong arm wrapped around her wrist. Then someone dragged her backward as smoke billowed out of the pit, clogging her throat and searing her eyes.

The man urged her outside, murmuring magic spells she recognized as that peculiar brand of Catholicism and White Magic favored by male European witches. She finally recognized his voice before her burning eyes could see him.

"You are Philippe, of the Spanish Coven," she said, doubling over and coughing hard.

"*Oui.*"

He dashed back into the hovel. She saw and felt

the pearly luminescence of magic permeating the air. She heard him swear in guttural French.

Then he reappeared. "Gone," he said. He added his magic to hers as she cleared her lungs and eyes with a healing spell.

"Are you searching for the Three as well?" she asked. "Holly, Amanda, and Nicole?"

He ran his hands through his hair as he nodded. "For Holly originally. I had a message from my covenates that there was great danger. I went to find them but could not. And now I have lost Amanda and Nicole and the baby as well," he said, the desperation in his eyes painfully clear.

People in street clothes had begun running toward the swami's hut. Together, Philippe and Anne-Louise moved into an adjacent alley, watching as each conjured restoration spells designed to aid the swami, if indeed he could still be helped.

After an hour of futile searching, the locals gave up. Philippe led the way back into the hut, and they stared down at the place where the fissure had occurred. The dirt floor was sealed once more, and there was no evidence that it had ever split apart.

"Nicole had a baby?" Anne-Louise ventured.

"*Oui.*" His voice shook; he was distraught, barely keeping himself under control.

"Perhaps the . . . father of that baby wove powerful

magic around it, to protect it. Perhaps anyone who tries to find it is dealt with harshly."

He was silent for a long time. As she gazed at him, a muscle jumped in his cheek. His jaw was clamped, and his gaze was stony and troubled.

"I have reason to believe that I am the father," he replied.

She wrapped her small hand around his larger one. "Then it might be Alex Carruthers who is keeping you from them," she said. "I had a vision, and I know he's an imposter. He's not the cousin of Holly, Amanda, and Nicole."

He jerked. "He's not? Then who is he?"

She took a deep breath. "I don't know." Then she looked down at the remains of a mango, flattened into a pulp. "Obviously he doesn't want us to find out."

"That won't stop me," he declared.

"Nor I." They smiled thinly at each other.

Scarborough: Nicole and Owen

Nicole was bored. She smiled as she realized how long it had been since she had felt that emotion. What once would have been annoying now seemed like a luxury. Amanda and Tommy had gone into town for supplies, and her dad was getting in some target practice—and, she suspected, double-checking the perimeter booby traps he had set in place. No matter how many wards, light or dark, were protecting a place, her dad always gave it a special real-world makeover too.

That left her and Owen puttering around the house, and it felt almost normal. If she closed her eyes, she could almost make herself believe that she was a normal woman with a normal baby and a normal husband, who would be coming home from work soon. She would cook him dinner, spaghetti, one of the only things she could make that was edible. Then they would play together before putting the baby to bed. Maybe there would even be some time for cuddling in front of the television before bedtime. It sounded so deliciously boring that it made her want to cry.

She scooped Owen up into her arms and even whispered to him "Daddy's coming soon," just to see how it would feel.

Owen smiled at her. As he did, she felt her own smile slipping. Something didn't seem right. Suddenly he opened his mouth wide and said, "Yes."

She gasped and nearly dropped him. He started to laugh, high and wild laughter, and she hastened to put him down on the couch. He just stared at her and continued to laugh.

"Stop it, Owen!"

He just laughed louder. She shuddered and pressed her hands over her ears. She tried to think of a spell that would mute his voice, but every bit of magical knowledge seemed to fly out of her head.

Owen raised his tiny hands into the air and closed them into fists as though he were trying to catch her fleeing thoughts. And then his powder blue footsy pajamas shimmered and turned into black robes. Symbols that she couldn't understand appeared in black smoke in the air around him, winking in and out of existence.

"Stop it!" she shouted over and over again, terrified to touch him and not even able to remember how to throw up a shield around her or him.

Suddenly behind her she heard a deep male voice boom, "Owen, no!"

The moment seemed to shatter into a thousand pieces. The black smoke disappeared, his blue footsy pajamas were once again covering him, and everything Nicole had ever learned about magic flooded her mind. Owen scrunched up his tiny face and started to cry as Richard strode forward and picked him up.

"Thanks, Dad," Nicole said. "I don't know—"

He shook his head. "Let's talk about it when someone's asleep."

She looked at her son and couldn't help but remember the way he had looked at her when he was laughing. "That sounds like a good idea."

An hour later Tommy and Amanda came home. Nicole called them onto the grounds as usual, and the two of them came into the house laughing and tickling each other. Tommy was singing "Scarborough Fair" at the top of his lungs.

When Nicole looked at him oddly, he shrugged. "Hey, since we live here, I figure I should actually learn the words to the song."

"It's not the national anthem," Amanda said, rolling her eyes.

"No, it's like the town-al anthem."

"That's not even a word," Amanda said, punching him in the shoulder.

"How do you know? Have you looked it up?"

Richard came into the kitchen, his face grim. "Family conference."

The laughter died on Amanda's and Tommy's lips, and Nicole was sorry for it. As much as she sometimes wished she could have a normal life, she would have given anything for Amanda and Tommy to live in happiness and peace somewhere far from fighting.

Tommy looked uncertain, and then began to edge toward the door.

"Stay," Richard commanded.

Tommy moved back, face serious but eyes alight. *If he's not family at this point, I don't know who could be,* Nicole thought.

"Owen's upstairs asleep. A little while ago we had a bit of a problem with him," Richard began.

"Is he okay?" Amanda burst out.

Richard held up his hand. "Near as we can tell, he's fine . . . now."

"What happened?" Tommy asked.

Nicole took a deep breath and then described everything she had seen and felt. The others listened intently. Amanda kept getting paler, and by the end of the recital her hands were shaking.

"Wow," Tommy said when she'd finished.

"Yeah, wow," Nicole echoed.

"What does it mean?" Richard asked bluntly.

None of the three magic users had an answer for him. They fidgeted uncomfortably under his gaze.

Finally Tommy took a stab at it. "Well, the baby's, like, manifesting magic early. And babies get all they need from their mothers . . ." He flushed and trailed off.

"You mean like milk?" Nicole asked.

"It makes sense if you think about it," Amanda said, staring fixedly at the kitchen counter. "Everything he needs to live he leeched off you when he was inside you, and to some extent he's still doing that."

"So, when he starts to do magic, he's pulling it from her until he's old enough to take care of himself in that regard?" Richard asked.

Tommy and Amanda nodded, but Nicole wasn't

buying it. "I felt like he was sucking it out of me, but the things he was doing—I can't do them. I can do small glamours, yes, but I can't change my clothes! And those signs and symbols in the air, I don't know any of them and I didn't get a happy feeling off them in general."

"Maybe they're coming from his father," Tommy ventured.

The room went completely silent. It was so quiet the silence seemed to roar in Nicole's ears. There was the question again. Who was the baby's father? If those symbols really had been dark magics, and Owen really was getting them from his father, that ruled out Philippe. She shuddered and wrapped her arms around herself, wishing she didn't feel so sick inside.

"Does that mean the father is nearby?" Amanda asked quietly.

Nicole heard Owen's "Yes" from earlier echoing around in her head. She silently prayed to the Goddess, *Please, please, don't let Daddy come home!*

"Maybe he's not just pulling from his parents," Richard suggested. "It could have come from another magic user close by."

Amanda shook her head. "I don't think so. We weren't that far away, and I didn't feel a thing. Did you?" she asked, turning to Tommy.

"Nothing," he agreed.

"What if he was getting it from the house?" Nicole asked.

"That's impossible," Amanda blurted.

Nicole stared at her twin. She had the feeling Amanda was hiding something. She thought about calling her out then and there, but she knew her sister. Amanda usually didn't keep secrets without a reason. Nicole thought maybe she should wait and try to talk to her alone first. After all, they were the Ladies of the Lily. She just really wished she knew where the third lady was. If ever they could have used Holly, it was now.

Suddenly Richard's demeanor changed. "Meeting adjourned; he's awake."

"I didn't hear anything," Tommy said.

"I didn't feel anything," Amanda chimed in.

Suddenly over the baby monitor on the far counter they could hear Owen start to coo.

"Dad, you sure you're not psychic?" Nicole asked suspiciously.

He smiled. "Nope. Just years of practice with kids."

Nicole went upstairs to get Owen, and Amanda excused herself. She had to get away from the others so she could have some time to think. Could it be possible that Owen was somehow channeling the energies of the house? It made her sick just to think of it, but it made sense. The house seemed to be calling to her sometimes. If it was, couldn't it also be reaching out to Owen?

She shook her head. If so, then why them? Nicole and Tommy didn't seem to be affected by the house. She turned toward the stairway. She would go to her room for just a few minutes. There she could think in peace.

Amanda.

She stopped. She could have sworn someone had just called her name. She knew, though, that it hadn't been the voice of any of her family members. *Who's there?* she thought, trying to reach out with her mind.

Help me.

Her heart began to pound and fear knifed through her. She wasn't in any position to help anybody. She could barely keep herself together. *I can't.*

Yes, you can. I need you, Amanda.

She bit her lip to keep from screaming. The voice seemed to be both outside her head and inside it at the same time. She put her foot on the bottom rung of the stair.

No!

Taking a deep breath, she raced up the stairs, a faint wail bouncing off the walls around her. *Can't, can't, can't.* She made it to the top of the stairs and kept going until she was locked inside her room.

She turned around and started for her bed but came to a shuddering halt. There, on top of her bedspread, were a pile of dead flies. The hundreds of bodies spelled out the words *"Help Me!"*

FOUR

BASIL

☾

With lies we spin webs of power
Traps awaiting the crucial hour
What care we for oaths and signs
When temptation is the sweetest wine

Old things, new things; all remains
Blood we give from our own veins
But rest is not for us meant
Penance for the lives we've spent.

Mumbai: Eli

Fantasme, the exquisite falcon familiar that had served House Deveraux for nearly a thousand years, wheeled above the Tower of Silence, where the corpse of a young girl rotted in the sun. Eli had watched the pallbearers carrying it into the stone structure. Hanging vines and brilliant purple and pink flowers cluttered the base of the carved stone turret and spilled over the path to the entrance. The Zoroastrians, who were the Magi mentioned in the Christian Bible, believed that

all living things—including the earth, water, and fire—
must be separated from dead, putrefying flesh, and
they laid out their deceased in towers. But a chemi-
cal in Indian animal feed had killed off nearly all the
vultures in the country. The bodies were left to rot in
the sun, a process that took much longer than being
devoured by vultures—and created anguish in the
Zoroastrian community.

Fantasme was eager to lend a hand, and Eli was
glad to give him whatever he wanted. The Moores
had held him hostage and tortured him, promising
him unending torment if the Deveraux didn't share
the secret of conjuring the Black Fire with them. The
Deveraux never had.

Fantasme dive-bombed into the tower, and Eli
returned his attention to his finder's spell. A tiny
black falcon shape hovered above his open palm like
the arrow of a compass. He was searching, as always,
for Nicole. By the way the bird fluttered and changed
direction, he knew someone was nearby. He didn't
think it was Nicole herself but, rather, someone who
was connected to her.

Beneath his feet the ground rumbled. He frowned
and looked down, trying to remember if India was
known for earthquakes. It rumbled again. He murmured
a protection spell around himself and kept going.

The earth was still as he walked onto the sidewalk

of the main thoroughfare, where his driver was waiting. The man snapped to attention at the sight of his employer and opened the back door of his boring but serviceable Mercedes. Eli nodded and climbed inside. He looked out the tinted window and saw Fantasme circling high in the air. Not everyone could see him; he blurred in and out of this reality and the magical greenwood, where he endlessly pursued Pandion, the hawk of the Cahors.

Eli sat back against the heavily embroidered draperies covering the leather seat. The driver worshipped Ganesha, Remover of Obstacles and Patron of Letters. There was a small statue of the elephant God glued to the dash. Eli wondered how one prayed to him, and if he would answer the prayers of a warlock. Eli had been raised to revere the Horned God, who loved sacrifices best. Eli's father had made countless sacrifices to get what he wanted—including Nicole's mother and, Eli suspected, both of Holly's parents as well.

He ground his teeth at the thought of the bitch. Since birth he had been taught that love and loyalty were illusions designed to keep the powerless in their places. But now that he had seen Sasha Deveraux, his mother, and had heard her side of what had happened between her and Eli's father, Eli realized that he had loved her all his life, and hated her for deserting them.

Through a bizarre rift, Sasha and Eli had been flung back into the time of Isabeau Cahors and Jean Deveraux. Sasha had sustained mortal injuries, and Isabeau had told her that if she stayed in the past—where she had not been hurt—she could live out her days. Would she dabble in time-changing magic there, and alter the present?

That would be the kind of thing a well-meaning witch would attempt, no matter that she might harm her own loved ones, or make them cease to exist altogether. Witches who worshipped White Magic ascribed to the notion of the greater good—the needs of the group overruling the desires and, yes, even the fate, of an individual—any individual. It was no wonder that worship of the Horned God had spread like wildfire during the Middle Ages, when the Catholic Church abused peasant and noble alike. "The greater good" were simply code words for oppression.

Where was witchdom when Nicole was forced to marry James Moore? They couldn't be bothered to attempt a rescue, until Holly Cathers turned to the darkness for help. No lily white Lady of the Lily, that one. Her soul was divided now, up for grabs between the Goddess and the Horned God. It would be interesting to see who wound up with it.

The streets of Mumbai sailed past, and Eli sighed heavily as he watched the little falcon hover above his open palm. The driver was occupied with the traffic—how could such poor people afford so many vehicles?—but even so, Eli made it invisible.

Suddenly it pointed to the right.

"Pull over," Eli ordered the driver.

"Yes, sir." The driver's upper-class English accent reminded Eli of James Moore.

Eli murmured a few words and made motions in the air to push a gaudy little truck and a swarm of bicycles out of the Mercedes's path. Back in the day, when the Deveraux lived in a majestic castle in France, nobles simply ran peasants over if they were in the way. He didn't want to cause an incident.

And . . . he didn't want to hurt anyone.

He felt a chill. *I'm getting soft.*

As the limo drew toward the curb, a young guy on a bicycle wearing a faded long-sleeved green T-shirt and a pair of khaki trousers sneered and deliberately slowed his pedaling. Eli flicked his fingers, and the bicycle slammed to the ground, rider and all.

Smiling thinly, he said to his driver, "I'll get out here. You find a place to park and wait for me."

"Very well, sir."

The driver waited as Eli hopped out, sauntering around the bicycle and the rider, who was grunting and trying to get up. Eli made a show of stepping around him. He saw several Indians do the same. Then a girl with long hair bent at the man's side and started speaking to him in a language Eli didn't understand. She whipped out a cell phone. Then she saw Eli.

"Excuse me, sir," she said in English. "I noted that you have a car. Would it be possible to transport this man to hospital? He has broken his leg."

Eli paused. *If I do it, maybe she'll have dinner with me. Or more.*

But he didn't want to have dinner with her. He wanted to find Nicole.

Sweat beaded on his brow. *I'm losing it. This is not who I am.*

He responded in French, telling her that the car was unavailable, and suggesting, in addition, that she and the bicyclist both go to hell.

Then he walked off, feeling a little better.

Dover: Jer and Eve

Darklightdarklightdarklight, *the revolving prism of the white lighthouse warned the ships at sea to beware of the bone-shattering rocks tossed upon the coastline, encrusting the shallows beneath the tides. The buoys clanged; the gulls screamed; the purple swells peaked, collapsed, and hid the evidence.*

Beneath their crusted veils of ice, Holly wrapped her arms around Jer and put her mouth over his. He did the same. Their legs tangled, untangled, like mermaid tails. Warm air from her body blew into his mouth, his throat, his lungs. It was too hot;

fire swam through his bloodstream and ignited every cell. Too hot; he moaned and tried to pull away. Then he realized that his arms were tied together, by the traditional black silk cords of warlock handfasting. He tried to tell her, but her mouth was clamped over his.

Like a killing undine, a water elemental, she began to suck the breath out of him. It whooshed out like oxygen in a blaze; creating a suction. He pounded gently on her back, and a shudder went through her.

Then she pulled back and he realized she was laughing. Her dark eyes were half-closed as she shook silently, laughing. She threw back her head and opened her mouth, and the life-giving air she had drawn out of his body bubbled toward the surface—

—the surface, so far away.

The moon rippled above the black water, and grew smaller and dimmer as Jer and Holly sank toward the endless bottom of the sea. He jerked his arms, straining to free himself. He kept his mouth clamped shut and shook his head, trying to signal to her that it was not a game. They were in danger, great danger. He stared at her hard, kicking his legs. A stalk of kelp thrashed behind Holly, rising above her like a monster. It had two yellow reptilian eyes; as it unfolded, they focused on her. Two leaves became a mouth, with fangs—

Still she laughed; still they sank.

The kelp monster began to lower its head toward her; the mouth opened, revealed teeth of sharply honed abalone shells.

They glistened like pearls. A skull gleamed on its long, slimy green tongue.

Eli. *Here he was at last, stripped of all life, like their father. The skull tumbled out of the monster's mouth and swirled end over end.*

"Holly!" Jer shouted. The sound carried, vibrating through the stormy ocean until it hit the rocks and shattered. Sparks flicked toward the moon.

He knew, then, that he was going to die. He had no breath left in his body. He had used the last of it to warn her.

And still she laughed. She laughed as he squirmed in her embrace; then she tugged once, twice, and let go of him. Clinging gracefully to the kelp monster with her left hand, she reached forward and pushed his shoulder with her right. He flailed, trying to grab her. It was clear that she didn't understand.

Why doesn't she need any air?

Then she pushed him again; he sank farther; and she pulled back her right foot and kicked him as hard as she could in the face. He heard a crack; it was his nose, breaking. His blood mushroomed in front of him, creating a crimson barrier that obscured her face. He gasped, sucking in water.

As he looked up at her, she started laughing again.

"Adieu," she said, "mon Jean, mon homme, ma vie . . ."

Her smiled faded, and her face contorted with hatred. And he knew she wasn't Holly; she was Holly's dead ancestress

Basil

Isabeau, who had sworn to kill her husband, Jean, six hundred years before.

"Holly," he said, "it's me. It's Jer. I'm not . . . *Je suis Jean, et tu est ma femme, Isabeau."*

I am Jean, and you are my woman. You are my wife, Isabeau.

"Then you'll die, too!" he screamed, grabbing her ankle. "Die with me!"

"Jer, wake up," Eve said, shaking his shoulders. "It's okay. It's a dream."

He opened his eyes. They were in their attic room in their Dover bed and breakfast. The slanted ceiling dropped at a sharp angle behind her, and the mirror bolted to the wall showed his disfigured face, twisted in a grimace.

She was bending over him, wearing a white silk long-sleeved nightgown that looked like a medieval shift. Beneath his blankets he wore a long thermal T-shirt and a pair of sweatpants. A foghorn broke the silence as he fought to bring himself under control. He heard himself panting. Wind batted the leaded diamond panes. He smelled Eve's floral shampoo, and her body heat diffused the room's chill . . . but not his unease.

"Don't be an idiot," he snapped at her. "We're warlocks. We can kill people in dreams."

"Did you dream that Holly killed you?" she asked. "Again?"

Jer didn't answer. Stonily he lifted the covers off himself, forcing her to straighten and step back. He didn't want Eve comforting him. Or pretending to.

There were two single beds in the rustic wood-and-plaster room; at his request they had pushed them apart, placing a nightstand between them. He noted her laptop on her bed, and the blue glow of the screen. He wondered if she had contacted the Supreme Coven to tell them that they were on the move again. She had sworn not to reveal their location while they traveled together, but when had the word of a warlock ever meant anything?

"Would you like some tea?" she asked him, gesturing to the electric kettle the B&B had provided.

"You Brits. You think you can solve everything with tea." He didn't care that she looked hurt.

"I've left the Coven," she said, gesturing to the laptop.

He laughed harshly. "What did you do, send them a letter of resignation?"

"Now who's being an idiot? Do you think I want an assassin coming after me?"

She led him over to the computer and turned it around so that he could see the screen. An e-mail message was open, front and center over a few other windows, including a picture of a black cat. Warlocks didn't have familiars. Maybe it was just a pet.

The message read:

> If you find either of the Deveraux brothers, assure them they are welcome. The Moore regime has ended, and they did us a favor in ridding us of their father, Michael Deveraux, as well.
> —Bryson Saracenz, for the Supreme Coven

Jer read without comment. He didn't know what to think. He had spent many long months leading his own coven, the Rebel Coven, and he was sure he had operated beneath the Supreme Coven's radar. If they had even heard of the Rebel Coven's existence, they probably (and rightly) had assumed he had formed the Circle to rebel against his father.

Now he was the only survivor. His heart spared a moment for Kari Hardwicke, who had died in the attack on the Supreme Coven. She should never have been a covenate. He'd known it all along, but she'd dazzled him. She'd been a sexy "older woman"—a grad student—as brilliant as she was tenacious. He'd let go of her way before Holly, but he knew Kari had thought that Holly had stolen him away.

"Maybe I should look for Holly," he said. "Instead of Eli."

"No," Eve said quickly. "You should find your

brother. She's nothing but trouble. You need to be with your own."

I could have been in thrall with Holly, he thought, staring through the leaded panes. The moon threw nets of silver over the crashing waves far below. Those who were loved by the Cathers witches were doomed to die by drowning.

Maybe my dreams are wishful thinking.

He watched the water and wished he were free of all this. And free of her.

"Tea's ready," Eve announced. "You drink it black."

"And as hot as possible," he replied. "So it burns as it goes down."

Her hand trembled as she poured the boiling water into a white china cup.

Seattle: Dr. Temar

"Oh, my God," Dr. Temar murmured as he watched the EKG blips on the monitor attached to Kari Hardwicke, who had been dead for months. *She's coming back online,* he thought giddily, because he couldn't make his mind say the real words: *It's finally happening. She's coming back to life.*

He was wearing a pale blue scrub cap, scrubs, booties over his shoes, and gloves, and he glanced from the monitor to the small, still form beneath the sheet on the hospital bed, then back again. The heartbeat was stronger. Should he do a quick EEG scan? He wanted to see her brain wave activity.

He licked his lips and took a step toward her bed. In the dead of night, during a rainstorm, he had moved her shipping crate to the basement of his Queen Anne home. He couldn't guarantee enough privacy at the university. Experimenting on cats was one thing, but if someone had discovered a human body in his lab, how could he have explained it?

His house had been left basically intact during the fires and floods—a few windows had cracked; the attic was destroyed. He put up tarps, and continued his quest.

Sweat broke across his forehead. He was ecstatic, and terrified. For centuries, millennia, science had tried to do what he had done.

And practitioners of magic, too, he thought. *Rose and her people are waiting to hear my results.*

And then, it was done.

She's alive.

His fear evaporated and he raced to her side. Her face was dead white, with slight blue lines running beneath the skin. Her veins. She had never turned the dark purplish black associated with livor mortis. But she wasn't rosy-hued, like a living person.

Maybe she's not going to make it all the way back, he thought anxiously, remembering the cats he hadn't succeeded in resurrecting. He'd named his one success

Osiris, after the Egyptian God who'd risen from the dead.

He didn't want her to be frightened by the five electrodes attached to her body, so he gently pried the two off her shoulders, shifting the layers of gauze to get at the ones on her sides and midsternal areas. He felt her cold skin through his surgical gloves. He had kept the room temperature low to stave off infection.

There, done. He wanted to clean off the jelly and adhesive necessary to make the electrodes work, but he didn't want to startle her. He placed the green, brown, and white discs on the gunmetal gray equipment cart and pulled the sheet back over her body.

Her eyelids fluttered, but her eyes stayed closed. He dropped down to one knee and reached beneath the sheet for her hand. Her fingers jerked and she grabbed him, squeezing hard.

"Kari, it's Nigel." His voice caught. "You were . . . you've been sick. You're in Seattle. You're—you're safe."

She grimaced.

"Are you in pain? I can give you something."

"Headache. Bad. And my . . . heart." Her hand moved in his grasp. He blanched. He didn't want her to find out what had happened to her, not quite yet. He was worried about what the shock would do to her. All his prepared speeches evaporated from his memory.

Basil

"Oh, Kari," he murmured, so in love and filled
with joy that he thought he would faint. "Kari, it's all
right now." He pulled down his surgical mask so that
his face would be the first thing she saw.

"Nightmares," she went on. "Hell." A tear ran
across her temple.

"Are you hungry? Thirsty?"

She turned her head and looked at him. He was
chilled to the bone. Her eyes looked . . . dead. Robotic,
or like a bad computer graphic. There was no spark of
life in them. Had he done something incorrect? The
cats . . .

There's a lot wrong with the cats, his inner voice whispered at him. *And you knew there might be something wrong
with her.*

"You're tired," he said.

Her hand caught in the sheet and pulled it down
over her collarbones, and halfway down her chest.
Thank God he had bandaged her, wrapping layer after
layer of gauze over her torso after he had pieced her
heart back together—and tried to rebuild her rib cage,
gluing the pieces back together like a jigsaw puzzle.

"You had some terrible injuries," he said, remembering his prepared statement. "A friend of yours summoned me. Rose."

Her expression changed. Her mouth smiled.

But her eyes did not.

"Rose, in London. And she helped me bring you back here, to get well. . . . We thought it for the best. And you had some severe wounds," he continued. "You had to have heart surgery. And . . . a few other things."

He wouldn't tell her. Ever. If any of her old friends came looking for her, he would tell them there had been a mistake. She hadn't died.

"I'm free." It was her first sentence. Her smile grew, and he quaked. Her eyes—

"Yes. You're free. Go back to sleep," he urged.

"I . . . nightmare." A shudder went through her.

"It's all right," he said. "I'll be here." He turned around and grabbed the chair he'd placed by her bedside. He'd been so nervous he'd forgotten it was there. He made a show of bringing it near her bed and sitting in it. He smiled at her. "There, you see?"

She said nothing. She glanced down at her chest, then slowly lay back down. He pulled the sheet up to her neck.

"Good?" he asked her.

"Cold," she whispered.

"I'll get a blanket." He pushed back his chair and walked across the lab to an old-fashioned armoire. He heard a rumble of thunder, followed by a crash of lightning. He prayed the floods were really over. He didn't want to have to move her. He wanted her here, safe, warm, protected.

"This will do the trick," he said as he got the fluffy light blue blanket and turned around.

She had gotten out of the bed—he didn't know how she'd done it so fast—and she was wedged in a corner with her arms pressed flat against the wall. She was naked, except for the heavy bandages that covered her from beneath her arms to the bottom of her rib cage.

Hecate and Osiris sat facing her on the floor, gazing up at her. He had no idea how they'd gotten there.

"I died," she said. "I died." Her voice was flat.

"No," he soothed. "That was a bad dream."

"I was in hell."

She gazed down at her chest. "I want to see."

"Later. They're still healing."

She pushed from the wall and staggered forward. He came to her side, still holding the blanket.

"Kari," he began, but she brushed past him, mummy-like. As his grad student, she'd been to his house many times, and she knew the layout. He realized she was headed for the bathroom. He joined her.

"You've had a shock."

She ignored him. She put her hand on the door-knob to the bathroom and stared down at it for a beat, then opened the door and flicked on the light. She turned to the left, staring at herself in the mirror over the sink. She stared at herself with her blank eyes.

"I died." Her voice was flat, emotionless.

"Kari," he began.

"I died." She leaned toward the mirror.

He cleared his throat. "You need to go back to—"

"And I'm still dead."

Scarborough: Tommy, Amanda, Nicole, Owen, and Richard

Tommy stood on the porch of Moore House as Nicole and Amanda built a snowman. Bundled up until he looked like a stuffed animal, Owen was snuggled on Nicole's back, waving his mittened fists.

The steam from Tommy's tea wafted into the gray, snowy air, and he listened to the two sisters laughing and chatting. But their conversation was forced, and the laughter was awkward. They were scared. Maybe even as scared as he was.

Things were not quiet in Moore House. Things were . . . walking. Or waking up.

Beneath bright pink earmuffs Amanda's hair streamed across her shoulders. His heart caught as the sun glinted off it. Then he shut the door and went in search of Richard, who was in the great room, checking his guns. Four Micro Uzis and at least a dozen pistols were arranged in four neat rows on a dark blue tarp that he had spread over the hardwood floor. Boxes of ammunition towered beside them. Tommy was supposed to memorize their makes and models, and which ammo went with which weapon.

But ever since the birth of Owen, Tommy had developed a phobia about guns. Nicole herself had asked her father to put them someplace more secure. Owen was no toddler; he wouldn't be able to get to the guns, much less accidentally shoot one, but Tommy agreed with her. He wished they didn't have them at all.

"Tommy," Richard said, smiling in greeting. He was preoccupied, worried. "I think we need to have another round of target practice. How about now?"

In the months since the five of them had moved into House Moore, Richard had been drilling them on shooting. Tommy didn't like it, but he agreed with Richard that they had to be prepared for anything and stay on alert. But what he wanted most in the world was to take Amanda away from all this and find a tranquil place to grow old together. There had been too much death and mayhem in their lives, and he was done.

"First, sir," Tommy began. He took a deep breath. "Sir, you know that Amanda and I are in thrall. That means there's a special magical bond between us."

Richard cocked his brow and laid down the gun. "Is there something wrong?"

"I think our bond would be strengthened if we got marri—"

The floor beneath his feet vibrated, just a little. He blinked and looked down at his athletic shoes, then back up at Richard. The Vietnam vet set his jaw and rose silently from his chair. The floor vibrated again, a little harder, and Richard grabbed two of the four submachine guns. He was all business as he handed one to Tommy.

It might just be an earthquake, Tommy thought. *Do they have earthquakes in England? Or a sonic boom.* It had never ceased to amaze him that the normal world—the world that knew nothing of witches, or covens, demons, or spells—continued on its path. He wished he were as ignorant.

"You two want to get married?" Richard asked, without looking at Tommy. He was scanning the floor, tracing a visual path with the tip of his gun. He began gliding across the floor, as silent as a snake.

The floor shook again.

"It's coming from the basement," he said over his shoulder. "Is that what you're saying?"

This isn't how I pictured this, Tommy thought, his heart thundering. "Yes."

The veteran soldier had his back to him, his head cocked as he continued to sweep the area with the barrel of his Micro Uzi. "Are you asking me or telling me?"

Tommy swallowed. "Asking."

"You want my blessing?"

"Yes, sir."

Richard half-turned around. He smiled at Tommy, and he looked younger than he had in years. "That's a nice show of respect."

"I respect you," Tommy said simply.

"And I respect you."

They shared a moment. Was that a yes? Unsure, Tommy cleared his throat. "They're in the front yard. If something's going to happen—"

Richard nodded. "Go to them. Take them to the caretaker's cottage. And, son, the answer's yes."

Like all the other outbuildings, the cottage stood empty. According to the lawyer, upon the death of James Moore all of the servants had vanished overnight. Literally.

Tommy nodded and hurried to be abreast with Richard. The black-and-white marble felt more substantial than the wood. Richard reached out and clasped him on the shoulder, and Tommy smiled briefly, then headed for the door. Richard crept past the stairway. Behind it there was a door to the basement, with a plain set of stone steps leading down into the darkness.

The boiler's down there, Tommy thought. *Maybe there's something wrong with it. What if it blows up?*

He was five feet from the door when the marble squares ahead of him suddenly buckled and cracked, as if someone had placed too heavy a weight on top of them. Tommy reared back, aiming his weapon. His mind flashed ahead to an image of Nicole, Owen, and Amanda coming toward the door, and being hit by stray bullets.

"Richard!" he shouted.

"On it." Richard hastened to get up beside him, and the two fanned the area with their weapons.

"If they come through the door—Amanda, I mean—"

"Get them. Tell them to make sure their magical wards are intact. Something's in the house."

Tommy darted to the right, gasping as he passed into frigid air that turned his breath to mist. Then the air shimmered a deep purplish green, extending the length of the foyer. It was blocking him from the door.

"Amanda!" he shouted; then regretted calling out. He didn't know where Richard was, and he didn't want to alert anything to their presence.

"Come back, son," Richard bellowed, but Tommy stayed where he was. The purple-green light danced like sparks along his skin. It was thickening, like a sheet of ice.

"Tommy!" Richard shouted.

If Tommy hadn't shouted for Amanda, he would have retreated. Shaking, he made his mind still and called to her: *Stay away. Run.*

Basil

The light hardened. He realized only then that it was coating his face, too, and if it closed up his mouth and nose—

Richard grabbed his shoulder and yanked him backward. Tommy wiped his mouth and eyes, spitting on the floor; then he looked back up to see the purple pulsating and changing color to a deep, vibrant red.

"What the hell is it?" Richard said.

"A portal?" Tommy took another step back.

There was a huge roar, and the crimson light shattered. The house rocked on its foundations, throwing Tommy and Richard to the floor. The marble began to crack as a fissure formed, separating the foyer into two jagged halves. Tommy and Richard rolled toward the stairway as smoke and steam erupted from the crevice, followed by the shrill scream of some kind of animal—

—or demon.

"Go, go, go!" Richard shouted, and Tommy went on automatic, scrambling up the stairs after Richard as the staircase itself tore from the wall and began to wobble like a gyroscope. Then fire shot straight up out of the hole, followed by another inhuman shriek.

His legs spread wide apart in a fight for balance, Tommy grabbed on to the wooden railing of the banister and aimed his Micro Uzi with one hand. Beside him, Richard swore.

"If you see the door open, stop," he said. So Richard

was worried about the girls and the baby being shot by accident—

Stay away, Tommy called out to Amanda in his mind. *Danger!*

Marble squares shot into the air, smacking the cathedral ceiling overhead, crashing down and shattering. Flames licked the walls, singeing the ancient portraits.

Then something red and leathery burst through the fissure. It was a lizardlike head, at least as long as Richard was tall, and its green, glowing eyes were the size of the kitchen table. Its snout was elongated, and as Tommy aimed his weapon, preparing to fire, it opened its long jaw, exposing dozens of fangs, and fire shot out of its mouth.

"It's a dragon," he shouted, so Richard could hear him. Despite everything he had seen—demons devouring his loved ones, a sea monster rising from the sea—something in him refused to believe what he was seeing. *A dragon. Oh, God.*

It screeched again, and then fixed its eyes on the two men. More of the floor gave way as the dragon pushed its enormous body through the floor. Two long wings unfurled, and its neck telescoped, smashing into the walls of the foyer. Cracks bulleted up the wooden walls and split them apart. Large chunks of the ceiling rained down like bombs.

Basil

The dragon threw back its head again as it slammed against what was left of the ceiling. Snow sprinkled down. Tommy was thrown to his knees, and Richard grabbed his arm.

"Let's go," he said, dragging him up the stairs. Tommy followed, his mind on the front door and Amanda, outside with Owen.

"We should open fire," he bellowed at Richard.

"It hasn't attacked. No need to provoke it," Richard replied.

Tommy! Help us!

It was Amanda. He heard her as clearly as if she were running beside him.

He heard a whoosh; it was the dragon, spouting another geyser of fire.

Outside the house.

He stopped, pivoted, and shot off rounds from his Micro Uzi. The smoke was so thick that he couldn't tell if he had hit the dragon's body, but its head slammed back through the ceiling as a stream of fire rocketed Tommy's way. He flattened himself on the swaying staircase and covered his head with his hands. Stinging heat ran along his skin. He stayed as he was, praying that he wasn't simply giving the dragon a better target.

Richard's weapon kept firing. Tommy felt the hard metal of his own Uzi and contracted his chest, drawing it out from underneath him. Although he couldn't make himself look up, he aimed it in the direction of the heat. He was afraid the flames would burn the eyes right out of his skull.

The noise was deafening; his eardrums shut down until he could hear nothing but a soft pounding he realized was his heartbeat. Then the staircase tilted forward and he started to slide. He reached his hand forward and splayed his fingers, hoping he would snag one of the railings. If he didn't, he'd go flying directly into the path of the creature's mouth. Maybe by the time the dragon munched him, he'd be fried to a crisp.

His hand made contact with something hot; his skin sizzled and he grimaced. Then his shoulder slammed into a piece of burning wood and he cried out. The space in front of him was devilishly hot.

Then someone grabbed his right ankle and yanked him backward. He assumed it was Richard. Then he was hoisted up by his shoulders to his feet. His center of gravity was wildly out of whack because he was hanging at a strange angle—the staircase had fallen over. He scrabbled for purchase, and managed to get toeholds on the stair. Cautiously he opened his eyes . . . to a wall of smoke.

If Richard was talking to him, he couldn't hear him. Nor could he see him. When his arm was jerked to the left, he blindly turned, struggling to keep his footing, trying to grip the railing without letting go of his Uzi. His burned fingers were stiff, and he swore as he felt the weapon go.

Richard pushed against Tommy's back as the two climbed the stairs like it was a ladder, his feet slipping and sliding. More than once he hung in the air, and Richard pushed his feet back onto the stairs. He had a moment of giddy hysteria when he imagined they were going through a fun house. Then they at last stepped onto an even surface—a landing—then forward a few feet—and up another flight of stairs, this set solid and upright.

Cold air washed down on him, and then snow, soothing his hands and prickling his face. A blast of wind told him they were outside, and he forced his eyes open. They stood on the slate roof of House Moore, wind and snow dervishing around them, as the huge red dragon burst from the front of the house and rose into the air. Its huge scarlet wings flapped with such force that it drew flames out of the house. Snow flurried around it in a vortex as it raised and lowered its enormous wings.

Beside him, Richard raised his Micro Uzi, tracing its trajectory. Then he lowered it with a frustrated shake of his head and turned. His mouth moved, but Tommy didn't hear a word he said. Tommy squinted, then shook his head and pointed to his ears.

Richard gestured forward, and Tommy gave him a thumbs-up. Together they crab walked along the side of the roof, past turrets and gables, chimneys and skylights—none broken—silhouetted by the flames, until they reached the front edge of the section that had been ruined. Tommy looked down. There was no sign of Amanda, Nicole, or Owen.

There were several ways to get down from the roof; as he recalled, there was an old rusty ladder that ran down to the second story, and from there, more stone steps. They found it handily; Tommy scaled it, sending out his thoughts to Amanda, receiving no sense of her anywhere. He had no idea how he managed to move so fast—adrenaline, magic.

Soon they were racing down the gravel path that led to the caretaker's cottage. Amanda burst out through the front door and caught Tommy in her arms. They held each other for an instant; then Tommy looked past her to see Nicole on the threshold, with Owen in her arms.

"We need to call the fire department," Tommy mouthed. He didn't know if he was speaking or yelling.

Then the tiny baby stretched out his hand. Nicole's mouth dropped open, and she spoke. Amanda pulled gently away from Tommy and looked in the direction of the mansion. Her face lit up.

Basil

Tommy turned, and looked.

House Moore was no longer on fire. A few wisps of gray steam were all that were left of the masses of flames and cauldrons of smoke. And instead of serious destruction of the front part of the house, ancient stonework had replaced the wood that must have burned away. The country house looked as if it had been built over an ancient castle, which the fire had now revealed.

Amanda said something. He stared at her blankly. She waved her hands and moved her lips.

". . . castle," Amanda said. He could hear her again. "Do you think it was there all along?"

"Did you see the dragon?" he asked her. His ears were still ringing.

She smiled faintly. "How could I miss it?"

"How did it get here?" Richard said, giving Amanda a tight hug, then moving on to Nicole and his grandchild. "They say that every castle has a dragon in the dungeon."

Tommy closed his eyes and staggered a little. Now that the crisis had passed, his nerves were beginning to take over. Amanda slid her arm around his waist.

"Come into the cottage and sit down," she urged him.

"I thought I'd lost you," he said in a rush. "I thought

I'd never see you again." Tears welled in his eyes. "Amanda Anderson, will you marry me?"

She stared at him, openmouthed. And then she shrieked with happiness and threw her arms around him.

Part Two
Balthasar

☾

And the Deceiver who nearly destroyed us all will come again and this time his wrath will not be checked and the whole world will burn for him.

——Gospel of Balthasar

FIVE

FRANKINCENSE

☾

Twisting, turning through the year
Death and carnage do we cheer
We close our fists and we find
Our enemies torn, body and mind

Seasons change and we sing
For all the good that they bring
But we also shed a tear
For they also bring us fear

Scarborough: Tommy, Amanda, Nicole, Owen, and Richard

Richard didn't trust the lawyer Derek as far as
he could throw him. So he sat in the kitchen and
watched as the warlock presented stacks of papers to
Nicole. The incident with the dragon had rattled all
of them a lot more than they were admitting to one
another. It had served as a grim reminder that none
of them was safe.

Which was why Nicole was making out her will.

"So, in the event of your death you have your

father, your sister and her fiancé, and Philippe who could raise Owen. Which order do you want those put in?" Derek asked.

"What do you mean?" Nicole asked, looking confused.

"He wants to know which of us is your first pick to raise Owen," Richard explained.

His daughter looked at him with anxious eyes that nearly broke his heart. "Why do I have to choose?"

"It's just the way this is done," Derek said, and to his credit, his voice still sounded patient even after three hours.

Nicole looked like she was going to cry. Richard sighed. "Sweetie, it's not a popularity contest. None of us is going to take the order personally," he said.

She seemed to brighten at that. "Okay, then, that order. First dad, then Amanda and Tommy, and then Philippe."

"Great. Now, given that you are a witch and that the first three are here with you and the last one is . . . um . . . missing for now, who do you want as your backup?" Derek asked.

Nicole put her head down onto the kitchen table. "Aren't those enough?"

"Ordinarily, yes. But you are far from ordinary. Even for a witch, you are extraordinary. Frankly, it's a miracle you're still alive."

"Thanks," she groaned.

"I'm putting a family locater spell on the will so that if all of you should die in the same incident . . ."

"You can say battle," Richard informed him grimly.

Derek winced. "As Nicole's legal representative, I do not want to hear about any battles or any other activities that might break the law of either of our countries."

"So, trying to be an officer of the court and raining down the type of destruction I'm sure you're capable of, you're a masochist, aren't you?" Richard asked.

Derek rolled his eyes. "I have been accused of having identity issues, if that's what you mean."

The lawyer turned back to Nicole. "The spell will find Holly, if she's alive, and any other Cathers."

Nicole straightened up. "You mean, that's all we would have had to do to find other relatives? Holly didn't have to go off with Alex? We could have just worked this spell?"

"No, this spell is the exclusive property of the law firm I represent. It's one of the specialized services we offer. No one else can use our spell, and we don't run a detective agency and so are not in the habit of using it just to find missing persons."

"So, what, you've got a patent on the spell?" Richard asked, letting his cynicism show.

Derek smiled faintly. "Something like that."

"So, then, just use the family locater spell," Nicole said.

"Do you want to consider, as many witches do, putting the Mother Coven into your will as beneficiaries or possible caretakers for Owen?"

"No!" Richard and Nicole chorused together.

"Glad we've got that settled," Derek said, raising an eyebrow.

"Can we be done now?" Nicole asked.

"I think I have enough here. I'll have my assistant draw these up, and I'll be back out Friday so you can sign them," he said, gathering his stacks of paper.

Richard rose, ready to accompany the younger man to the door. They moved toward the side door of the kitchen, which led to a garden outside. The front entrance had been almost completely destroyed by the dragon, and Richard and Tommy hadn't been able to finish clearing away all the debris.

"Do you want me to have the house repaired?" Derek asked, pausing for one last look around.

"We're fine," Richard said. The last thing he needed was more people in the house, where they could hide any number of traps and curses. "You sure that dragon wasn't in the will?"

Derek shook his head. "I'm afraid not, which means they weren't keeping it as a pet."

"No kidding."

Frankincense

It was the day before Thanksgiving, but Amanda felt anything but thankful as she made breakfast. Every day the darkness at the corners of her mind seemed to encroach a little more, swallow up the light. The worst part was, with the exception of the still mysterious dragon, there was nothing she could point out to her family. No, the danger seemed to be all in her mind, though she refused to believe she was imagining it.

Since the engagement, Tommy had been trying to coax her to stay in his room, but more than ever she didn't want prying eyes upon her when she slept. She knew that she had nightmares, and more than once had woken up to find that she had been sleepwalking. Still, even though she recorded all her memories, it wasn't enough. It didn't tell her why every third night she woke up staring at a portrait of Sir William in what had to have been his study. She had been working on a spell, though, that, while it would not capture her dreams, would at least allow her in the morning to watch herself having them. It was a third night, and she was determined to watch herself in the moments before she woke up in front of the portrait.

She stared down at her notebook with her latest collection of dreams. There was the usual collection of people, Holly being predominant this time. There was also a series of images including a great phoenix with a key in his talons.

"I knew I shouldn't have watched that Harry Potter movie on television last night," she joked to herself, thinking about the phoenix the school's headmaster kept as a pet.

She closed her eyes and tried to conjure the image to mind, fairly certain that the movie and not the house had been to blame for that one. *What do I know about that phoenix?* Suddenly she could hear a scream in her head followed by a woman sobbing and the crackle of flames. She gasped and opened her eyes. Around her the entire kitchen was engulfed in flames and her very skin was on fire.

She woke up screaming. Her bedroom door flew open and her father raced in, eyes wild and gun in hand. She stared at him wondering how on earth he had come to be there, or even how she had come to be in her room instead of downstairs in the kitchen.

"Amanda!"

She shook her head and stuttered, "Wh-what? Where am I?"

Seemingly convinced that there were no dragons in the room, he settled down on the edge of her bed and grabbed her hand. "You're in your room. It's three in the morning."

"It is?" she asked, her eyes seeking out the clock on her nightstand.

Sure enough, it was. She watched as the digital numbers changed to read 3:01. Why couldn't she remember anything after breakfast? she thought in a panic.

"I'm looking forward to a turkey dinner tomorrow," her dad said, suppressing a yawn.

She blinked at him. It was three a.m., which meant that she had been dreaming about being in the kitchen and fixing breakfast and thinking about the phoenix.

"Me too," she managed to say back, despite the sudden fear that gripped her. The dream had felt absolutely real. Was she losing it? If she could no longer tell the difference between her waking life and her sleeping life, what did that mean? She shivered.

"You want me to get an extra blanket?" her father said, noticing and misinterpreting the action.

She shook her head slowly. "No, thank you. I'll be fine. I'll see you in the morning," she said, desperate to be alone so she could try to sort things out.

Her dad, however, seemed to have other ideas. "You know, I've noticed something strange since we moved here."

She perked up, actually daring to hope that she wasn't alone, that she wasn't crazy. "What?"

"I haven't had any dreams."

Disappointment flooded through her. She wished she could say the same. "Maybe you just don't remember them."

He shook his head. "I don't think that's it. Ever since the war, I've had nightmares. Everything that's happened lately has made them worse, or at least more frequent. We came here, though, and not a single one. I talked with Tommy and Nicole yesterday. Neither of them is dreaming either."

Amanda sat up straighter. Now, that was strange. As kids, Nicole had been a lot more prone to dreams and nightmares than she had. "And I'm having nightmares every night," she admitted.

He nodded. "Yes. I don't know what it means, but one thing I've learned in life is there are no coincidences, just plans you don't know about. I'm starting to think we should get out of this house."

"No!" Amanda burst out, surprising even herself. "If there is something going on here, I need to find out what it is. I feel like there's something I'm supposed to do or find."

He nodded slowly. "Anything I can do to help with that?"

"I don't think so. If there is, though, you'll be the first to know."

She sat there staring her father in the eyes, praying to the Goddess that he understood.

"Okay, but if things get too intense, we go when I say, no arguments."

She actually laughed. "Given the fact that we're still here after the dragon, I'd hate to see what you think too intense is."

He laughed for a moment, but it didn't reach his eyes. "No, you really wouldn't want to."

He kissed her forehead and stood up, and moved toward the door. She glanced at it, still somewhat surprised that Nicole and Tommy hadn't also come to check up on her.

"One other thing, sweetheart."

"Yes, Father?"

"I saw you tonight in the hallway when you cast the sleeping spells over Nicole and Tommy. Just don't ever do that to me. Are we clear?"

All she could manage was a nod as terror closed around her throat like a giant fist. She had no memory of casting those spells.

Outside Mumbai:
Armand, Pablo, Holly, Alex, and the Temple of the Air

Armand woke covered in sweat. As he lay still trying to slow his heartbeat and regulate his breathing, he tried not to dwell on the nightmarish faces that still swam behind his closed eyes. The hair on the back of his neck prickled, and he threw himself to the side and opened his eyes just in time to see a black, scaly demon slice through his pillow with a sickle.

Without a word Armand raised his hand and sent a blast of fire toward the demon. It hit him full in the chest and only burned a moment before snuffing out. The distraction was all that Armand needed. His lips moved in prayer, and a moment later the demon exploded, showering him and his sleeping covenates with gore.

"Not again, Armand," Pablo said sleepily.

"I just washed my hair," Holly groaned, sitting up and looking at him crossly.

A few weeks before, they would have thanked him. He knew it was confirmation that they shared his fears. Ever since he had exorcised Holly, something had changed. If there was a demon anywhere around, it seemed to sense him, to find him.

"Demon magnet," Alex muttered before going back to sleep.

Two of Alex's followers—Armand still didn't know their names—rose and set to work repairing the wards that the demon had somehow managed to break through. It had become standard procedure to ward any place they were going to be at for more than an hour. Any longer than that, and the demons started coming.

Armand lay back down, but he knew he would get no more sleep that night. Something had to give.

Frankincense

The demons who were being drawn to him were all different, and every time they came, he flashed back to exorcising Holly and the sheer number of different rituals he had needed to perform.

His path had never been an easy one. He had studied to be a priest and at the last moment had turned aside to study the ways of the Goddess. He had managed to blend the two religions and had found others with similar beliefs and needs. Sometimes he wondered what would have happened if he hadn't quit. Would he have had his own parish by now? Would he have advanced through the ranks? Would he have ministered to the lost and suffering? Or would he have become an exorcist? For so long the church had stopped teaching the sacred rite. Almost too late they had seen their mistake. Now they were scrambling with only a handful of trained exorcists still alive, who were dying as old men without passing on their wisdom.

"Tell me what to do," he breathed to whichever deity would answer.

A sudden thought came to his mind with such startling clarity that he knew it *was* an answer. He remembered when he was just a boy back in Paris, he had met a great man, a prophet who could see the future and read a person's soul. He had come to speak to the congregation at Armand's church.

His name was Jacob.

And he had told them that he lived in India.

On the outskirts of Bombay . . . now known as Mumbai.

How could I have forgotten that? he thought. But Armand had been only three years old then. How could he have remembered?

His heart began to pound. His mind tried to tell him that he didn't even know if this Jacob was still alive.

Seek and ye shall find.

He rose silently, then froze. What if it were a trick, designed to lure him away from Holly and the others? What if, by leaving, he abandoned them to demonic attack and worse—possession?

And yet . . . Jacob had been a holy man. He had told Armand that he would become an orphan. His parents had laughed . . . and then crossed themselves.

They had died within the year, both of them. To a strange malady.

Perhaps Jacob had given them the disease.

I don't know what to do, he thought. So he sank to his knees and prayed.

Venga, said a voice. *Come.*

Warmth spread through him, taking the edge off his terrible fear. Resolved, he touched Pablo on the shoulder and moved away from the others. Pablo was beside him in a moment.

Frankincense

I must find a man, a prophet named Jacob who lives somewhere near here.

Pablo closed his eyes in concentration. Finally he nodded and opened his eyes. *He's waiting for you. He lives a few miles away to the east. I'll guide you, in your mind.*

I will be back as soon as I can, Armand thought, laying a hand on Pablo's skinny shoulder. *I will not leave you here. It might be better if you keep the reason that I've gone to yourself.*

I know. I agree.

Armand turned, made a hole for himself through the wards surrounding the camp, and slipped into the night. Once out of earshot, he abandoned caution and began to run. The farther he got from the camp, the greater the sense of urgency.

When he came to a small village, his feet guided him around it and to a house well past it, secluded and private. *Gracias, Pablo.*

He stopped, out of breath, and stood for a moment. Then he walked slowly up to the front door of the house, only mildly surprised to see that it stood open. Inside he could see into a back room where an old man sat at a table laden with two cups filled with steaming liquid, and a single candle for illumination. He was gaunt, with a long beard, and was wearing a weathered sweatshirt and a pair of tan trousers. His feet were bare.

"I've been waiting for you, young man," he said in French.

"Jacob," Armand whispered, walking inside and closing the door behind him. "How did you know?"

The old man chuckled. "Prophet, remember? Or have you forgotten that as well?"

"As well?" Armand asked as he seated himself at the table.

"You were just a boy when we met, but I promised you we would see each other again. One might say we have unfinished business. Have some tea."

As Armand sipped his tea, he marveled at how with a few simple words Jacob had seemed to transport them back through time. Once again Armand was the wide-eyed child, eager to learn, to ask questions and to be told his future.

"Why did you choose to follow both the Hebrew God and the Goddess?" the old man asked, staring intently at him.

"I felt like there had to be something more out there. I wanted to know everything I could."

"Then why didn't you become Buddhist as well?"

Armand felt himself flush. "I guess I found what made sense to me, and . . ."

"And you didn't feel the need to keep going with your quest."

"I guess not," Armand admitted.

"You like the mystical, the supernatural."

It was a statement, not a question. Armand just dropped his eyes to his cup, wondering if he was about to be scolded.

"You had the misfortune to come up in the church at a time when these things were frowned upon, discouraged."

"Yes," Armand admitted.

"You would have done well as an exorcist, or a healer. In this technologically driven world of ours, though, there is very little place for faith, let alone the miraculous."

"I have often thought that," Armand said.

"Of course you have, and so you went looking for something more exciting." He smiled, his lined eyelids crinkling like venetian blinds.

Armand opened his mouth to protest, but Jacob waved him off. "You did not see how you could be yourself inside the church, so you left. It happens to many."

"I don't see what you're getting at," Armand said. "What I need to know right now is—"

Jacob took a sip of tea, peering through his lashes at Armand. "You have demon problems, yes?"

"*Oui.*"

"They are getting worse since you have set yourself up as one who can banish them, correct?"

Armand nodded.

"Then you should know they will only get worse. Soon the Dark One is coming to destroy the earth. The demons also sense this, and it makes them both bolder and more afraid."

"You mean, Satan is coming?" As Armand spoke the name, the tea in his cup froze to ice.

Jacob stared at him long and hard before giving him a tiny smile. "You're not asking me to explain; you're asking me what to believe. That, as always, is your choice. But, no, the Dark One is not Satan. He goes by many names, but that is not one."

Jacob touched Armand's cup, and the ice changed back into steaming tea.

"I'm not sure that makes me feel any better," Armand murmured.

"It shouldn't. Terrible things are coming, and what you have seen is only the beginning."

"What must I do?"

"You must fight." Jacob leaned forward and took both of Armand's hands in his. His grip was strong. His frail appearance was deceiving. Appearances so often were.

"You have been assigned a role in this since before your birth. The powers beyond us always have plans for us. However, you can only fulfill your destiny if your heart is undivided."

"What do you mean?" Armand asked, even though he was afraid he knew the answer.

Jacob gripped harder, as if trying to press answers into Armand's flesh. "You must choose. You must follow either the Hebrew God or the Goddess. If you try to serve both, you will not have the focus you need and you will be one of the first to die."

Armand trembled, and Jacob released him. "Which must I choose?"

"That is up to you, but you must do so quickly and without doubt." He drank another sip of tea.

"How do I do that?" Armand was baffled.

Jacob closed his eyes, and the expression on his face reminded Armand of the look Pablo had when concentrating especially hard on a distant voice he alone could hear.

"The time is coming when a choice will be presented. Then you must make it, and swiftly." He picked up both their cups and scooted out his chair. "But now you must go so that you are not missed."

Armand had so many other questions, but the prophet raised his hand as though to stave them off. Reluctantly Armand stood and bowed.

Jacob bowed back. "I salute you, pilgrim," he said.

"Would you come with me?" Armand asked him.

"If I could, I would. But I have a battle of my own," Jacob replied. "Now go."

Armand left the small house and with a heavy heart turned his steps back to the camp.

He knew something was wrong when he was still about a mile away. He felt as if he heard the whisper of shouts on the air. *Pablo, can you hear me?* he thought.

There was no answer.

He began to run.

Seattle, Five Years Ago: Nicole and Eli

It was the first day of high school for Nicole Anderson and her twin sister Amanda. Nicole was jazzed! Of course, Amanda was her usual quiet self. It was too hard to tell what went on half the time in her sister's head.

No big. Life was for living, not worrying. Still, when lunchtime came, she dutifully found Amanda in the cafeteria and sat with her, just like she had promised her mom she would. It was only the first day, and besides, wherever Nicole sat, her best friends, Kat and Steph, would follow.

"So, how's it going?" Nicole asked Amanda. "Any hot guys in your classes?"

Amanda sighed. "So far, just lots of homework. But I think I'm going to love my math class."

"Gag me," Nicole said, grimacing as she slurped her diet soda. "I'd rather take six periods of PE than—"

Whoa.

Across the room the hottest guy she had ever seen was staring *right at her*. Dark bedroom eyes, long dark hair. Amazing. She let her lips curve into a smile around the straw, realized that was kind of, um, sexual, and made herself look away. She knew how to play the game. She'd been playing it for years.

"Who's that?" she asked, lowering her voice.

Everyone at the table turned to look, then turned back.

"That's Eli, Jeraud Deveraux's older brother," Kat breathed. "A senior."

"He's trouble," Steph said. "My brother says his family's into some really weird stuff. Like devil-worshipping or something. But his dad is totally hot, for an older guy."

Trouble. Nicole smiled. She liked the sound of that.

Across the room Eli Deveraux was still staring at her, and he started smiling too. Even though he was all the way across the noisy cafeteria, she was sure she could see right into his eyes and lose herself in them. . . .

"Nicole! Nicole!"

She jumped and turned to Amanda. "What?" she snapped, irritated.

"What are you saying?" Amanda demanded.

"What do you mean?" Nicole grabbed a french

fry off Amanda's plate, swabbed it in her ketchup, and ate it.

Amanda batted her hand away. "Just now you were staring at Eli and you were saying . . . something. I couldn't understand you."

"It sounded French," Kat said, stealing a french fry from Amanda too.

"I don't speak French," Nicole said, annoyed with all of them now.

"Are you on drugs?" Amanda cried. "I am so telling Mom—"

"I am not on drugs," Nicole said.

"And if you're so hungry, why don't you eat your own lunch?" Amanda continued.

Nicole glanced down at the table and realized she hadn't eaten a thing. *How did that happen?* she wondered briefly. She crammed a bite of turkey sandwich into her mouth and washed it down with the rest of her soda.

Then the bell rang. As everyone scrambled, she looked over toward Eli.

He was gone.

When they got home, she was big-time going to lecture Amanda about distracting her when she was in flirt mode.

Finding her a boyfriend would do wonders for my love life, she realized. A second later she dismissed it. They had only one class in common, and after today they didn't even have to eat lunch together. *I so should have been an only child. I'd be great at it.*

Nicole fidgeted through the rest of her classes. She couldn't stop thinking about Eli. There was something so powerful about him. She closed her eyes and envisioned his broad shoulders. She imagined what it would be like to run her fingers through his dark hair and kiss him.

Her algebra teacher droned on and on, and Nicole started checking out. It was her last class of the day and she was hoping that she'd be able to catch a glimpse of Eli before he left campus.

Eli.

So gorgeous.

Eli.

So dangerous.

Eli.

That name didn't seem to suit him, though. There was another.

She was standing in the back of a different class, his class. She could see him staring out the window. Was he thinking of her?

Can you see me?

Suddenly he turned around and looked right at her, right through her. Her skin felt as though it were on fire. It was all so . . . familiar.

The bell rang and she snapped awake. For a moment she was disoriented until she stared down at her piece of paper. There she had written "$2x + y = Eli.$"

She blushed and scratched it out quickly before stuffing her notebook into her bag. She was going to have to move fast if she hoped to see him before he left school. Everyone else had filed out by the time she made it to the door. She ran so hard right into a broad chest that she had the wind knocked out of her. She looked up and melted into Eli's eyes.

"It's you," she whispered.

He looked a little puzzled, but he nodded anyway.

His eyes were more intense than she had even imagined them. *So very Deveraux.*

She brushed the thought away. Of course, he was the first Deveraux she had actually met. She had seen his younger brother, Jer, but only from a distance. Amanda had made Mom drive by his house when they were twelve.

Oh, my God, was Amanda crushing on Jer?

"You want to go somewhere?" Eli asked.

"Anywhere," Nicole said.

They started walking toward the student parking lot, and Nicole found she couldn't take her eyes off him.

"Nicole, I've been looking for you," Amanda snapped, running up and grabbing her arm.

Frankincense

"Not now," Nicole said through her teeth, shaking her off. "Tell Mom I'll be home late."

Amanda was pissed, but Nicole didn't really care. Amanda was always pissed.

A minute later Nicole was seated in Eli's low-slung black Corvette, and all thoughts of her sister vanished.

He drove her to the park by the library. Pine trees swayed in the autumn wind. They got out and walked a short way on the gravel path, looping past the statue of Chief Seattle, not speaking. He stared at her the entire way. She stared back.

Finally they stopped and Eli wrapped his arms around her. When his lips met hers, her body jolted as though shot through with electricity. He must have felt it, too, because he pulled away and again gave her that strange look she couldn't quite fathom. Everything about him seemed so right, so familiar.

"Do you believe in reincarnation?" she asked.

He shook his head.

"I don't either, but I feel like I've known you for a very long time and l—"

She stopped short as she realized she was just about to save "love you." She shook her head to clear it. No way was she saying that before he did, and especially not the first time they hung out.

He was staring at her in a way that made her feel dizzy, off-kilter. He had mad flirting skills.

"And what do you know about me?" he asked.

His eyes seemed to trap her. Her heart pounded. She knew she wouldn't want to deny him anything. He leaned closer to her and squeezed her tightly.

"You're trouble," she said. "That's what I heard."

He laughed, and kissed her long and hard. He used his *tongue*. She had never done that before, and she thought her legs were going to collapse out from under her.

He was a *senior*.

"What else?"

"Your family is into weird stuff," she gasped as his lips trailed down her throat.

"And?"

She shook her head, not sure what he was looking for.

"Your friends didn't tell you anything else about me?"

"No."

He pressed his lips to her ear. "They didn't tell you I was a warlock?"

"No," she whispered.

"They should have," he said, the fingers of his left hand caressing her throat.

Okay, that *was* weird. Weird that he should believe it, or say it, she didn't know which, but weirder that *she* should believe it. Then and there, she knew it was true.

Frankincense

The wind kicked up, pitching bits of gravel against her shins. She should leave, she should run as far away as she could, as fast as she could. She didn't want to, though. And somewhere deep inside a voice urged her to stay, that it was okay, that she knew him.

"Eli?" she whispered, although the name still didn't seem right to her.

"Yes?"

"Are you bad?"

"Baby, I'm the worst," he purred.

And even though she knew she should run away, Nicole found herself tearing off his clothes instead.

A week later, "I made you something," Eli said as Nicole slid into the 'vette.

Nicole eagerly took the box from him. She hadn't seen him at school since he had dropped her off at home that first night, and she'd begun to panic, wondering if he had dumped her. He had called fifteen minutes ago, and she had had barely enough time to throw on the sexiest outfit in her closet.

She turned the box over for a moment and stared at it before she opened it up. Inside was a silver bracelet with a symbol burned into it. It looked like a star with a twisty circle in the middle. "You made this for me?" she asked in amazement.

"Yes."

She looked at the symbol more closely. "It looks like the tattoo you have on your chest," she exclaimed, blushing. Twisty circle, star.

He nodded slightly.

"What does it mean?"

He cleared his throat. "It's for protection. Put it on."

She did, and it fit snugly around her wrist. "It's beautiful. Thank you so much."

"You're welcome," he said.

She kept staring at the bracelet. "I—I was beginning to think you didn't want to see me again."

He laughed, deep in his chest. "No, I'd like to see a lot more of you. Like, all of you. Again."

She blushed again. Every time she tried to recall that afternoon in detail, it was fuzzy, as though she were seeing it through someone else's eyes.

"So, protection from what?" she asked, quickly changing the subject. And that made her think about what they'd done. . . .

What did we do? Did we do it? She couldn't exactly remember.

It was his turn to look uncomfortable. "Oh, a lot of things."

"Like what?" she pressed.

"Mostly it is supposed to protect the wearer from possession. But, you know, I just think it's a cool symbol. If you don't like it, no big, I can get you something else."

"Possession?" she asked. "Like, being possessive?"

He stared at her. Her lower belly tingled. Her cheeks burned. "You know exactly what I mean."

She started to shake her head, but he caught her chin and held it.

"You're the one who asked about reincarnation. That's basically a myth. But possession . . . it can happen. It *does* happen. So . . . wear it."

"Um, I—"

"*Wear* it. Or don't," he said suddenly. "If you don't like it. Or me."

He grabbed at the bracelet, but she was quicker, snatching her hand away. "No. I love it, really. Thank you," she said.

"I'm just messing with you." He laughed, all seriousness gone. "If you don't like it, I'll get you something else."

"No, I do love it." *And I love you. Oh, Eli, I shouldn't, not yet, but I do. . . .*

He nodded and started the car. She didn't know why but she couldn't shake the feeling that he really did take it all very seriously. She closed her eyes and leaned her head back. Her body was blazing. She was sure he knew it.

"Tell me about being a warlock," she said.

"Maybe I will. If you're good," he replied.

He was exciting, dangerous, and passionate. Over the next several months she pushed him to tell her more about magic, and she had the feeling that he humored her. He showed her his ritual knife and he lit a candle with his finger.

She tried to do that on her own. Tried to make shadows glow in a darkened room. She thought she made a needle swing on a piece of thread, but she wasn't sure.

Then, one night in his basement, while they were making out, she felt the room grow warmer.

"Did you do that?" she asked him, and he kissed the tip of her nose.

"Don't tell anyone," he made her swear. "Not your friends, or your sister. No one."

And she didn't.

Mumbai: Philippe and Anne-Louise

The whole city felt wrong to Philippe. He paced the small hotel room and waited for Anne-Louise to return. Ever since the swami's disappearance, and likely death, everything had felt . . . off balance.

Suddenly the door opened and Anne-Louise rushed inside. Her face was chalk white, and she started grabbing up her things.

"*Allons-y,*" she said in French. Let's go.

"What's wrong?" he asked her.

"There's a Deveraux in the city."

His blood turned to ice. "Why? Which one?"

"All I know is that it wasn't Jer," she said in clipped tones.

"Eli, after Nicole? Who else is left? Their father is dead."

"Philippe, *je ne sais pas.*" I don't know.

"We could fight."

She kept packing. Ten minutes later they were downstairs and mingling with the Bombay crowd. Car horns blared; the crush of people was nearly stifling in the humid, pungent air.

Magical energy pressed in around him—dark and powerful, with a distinct feel of Deveraux to it. He let Anne-Louise lead the way while he concentrated on deflecting it, camouflaging them from its attention.

But the magic got stronger, and darker. It lay like a wet snake along his skin. Anne-Louise looked at him over her shoulder, and he nodded, once. She felt it too.

At the next busy intersection, she stopped.

"We can't outrun him," she said.

"Then let's confront him out in the open," Philippe said, still unsure which Deveraux it was. If it was Jer, he might be a friend . . . but that one was so changeable, it was difficult to know.

"Sanjay Gandhi National Park is a few blocks away,"

she said. "It's the largest urban park in the world."

"*Bien*," he said. "Let's lure him there, and see what we can do."

She turned and crossed the street.

Scarborough: Amanda

Her spell had worked.

Amanda sat huddled in the kitchen at four in the morning watching images of herself shimmering in the air. She watched herself as she dreamed, tossing and turning through nightmares. Finally she saw herself get up off the bed and walk through the house until she reached the study of the former occupant. She pulled some books off the shelf and then put them on completely different shelves scattered around the room.

It made no sense to her, but she continued to watch, fascinated, as her sleeping self left the study, climbed down the back stairs, and came to a stop before the same blank stretch of wall that she had woken up in front of before. She watched closely and was stunned to see herself reach out, push hard against a section of the wall almost above her head, and then step through an opening that magically appeared. Once through, the hole sealed itself and the vision ended.

Amanda stood, sweating and trembling as she

thought about what she had just seen. There was a secret passage in House Moore and her dreaming self had discovered it. When she woke up to see that same wall, was it before or after she had gone inside? She knew that she should tell the others. They had a right to know what dangers lurked in their current home.

She glanced at the clock on the microwave. It would be at least a couple of hours before anyone else was up. She grabbed a flashlight and headed for the wall. Once there, she slid her hand up and pressed, hoping that she was hitting the right spot. She wondered if there was any spell she was supposed to say and wished that she had thought to include audio on her little video spell.

She felt around for a moment, but the wall appeared to be completely smooth. After a moment, though, she must have hit the right spot because the hole opened before her.

I shouldn't go in there, she thought, even as she was stepping across the threshold. *I really should get the others.* The portal closed behind her and her flashlight was the only thing to illuminate the darkness.

"Come on, feet. You've been here before; lead the way," she said through gritted teeth.

She stepped forward hesitantly and then, as the footing seemed to be sound, more boldly. The floor began to slope and then to turn and twist like a snake. After a minute she couldn't tell where she was in relation to the rest of the house or even if she was still within its walls. At last the tunnel emptied out into a large chamber, surrounded on three sides by doors. One door was charred and hanging off its hinges. The room beyond looked like some sort of giant cage.

Is this where the dragon came from?

She stepped away.

In the center of the room was a table containing a candelabra and several ancient-looking manuscripts. A chair was pushed out from the table as though its last occupant—probably *her*, she realized—had left in a hurry. One manuscript lay open on top of the rest. It was giant, at least a foot tall and about five inches thick. By the feel, it was made of some sort of animal skin. She marked the place with a finger and flipped back to the beginning.

"Ye Prophecies of ye Magus Merlin."

She shuddered. The island that Nicole had been trapped on was supposed to have been Avalon, and the spirit of the dark wizard Merlin was said to still haunt it.

She turned back to the page she had marked, and tried to read. It was in an ancient language that she couldn't decipher. She put the book down, closed her eyes, and then touched each of them with her fingertips. "Goddess bless what I see, bless my eyes and let them read," she said.

She opened her eyes and looked at the manuscript, and was a little surprised to see that it had actually worked. It looked like it was in English now. She wrinkled her nose. Old English. At least that was better than whatever it really was.

"And ye Ciety naymed Seattle shal be layid to Ruinne when ye Monsterums of Ye Eryth & Sea are freeyd by Ye Dark Wyzarde."

Amanda blinked and reread it three times. "But that's happened; that was us, or Michael. It's true!"

She continued to read. *"Ye Moste Powerfyl Witch of Hr Tyme shal be tormenteyd by Daemons from Evry Realym & a Wyzard Priest shal free Her."*

"Holly and Armand!" she gasped.

She flipped back a page and could clearly identify other prophecies that had come true before their eyes. She found prophecies dating back centuries, dealing with wars and scientific breakthroughs and everything of importance that she could think of: the discovery of penicillin, the general theory of relativity, even the stock market crash of 1929.

She was about to check to see if there was anything about Isabeau and Jean, the Cahors and Deveraux ancestors who had started the whole curse, but she wanted to know more about the future than the past.

About Owen.

She skipped forward again, but before her eyes the letters changed, rearranged. Her seeing spell must have worn off. She frowned, about to recast it, but the shadows around her seemed to have crept closer, pushing in against the circle of light cast by her flashlight. With a shiver she decided that maybe the better course would be to leave and take the book with her.

She tucked the book under her arm and started back the way she had come. She shook the flashlight as the light started to become weaker. She had put fresh batteries in not that long ago, but that didn't seem to matter.

She made it back to the entrance and then stood for a moment, beginning to panic as she realized she had no idea how to exit the tunnel. She slid her hand up the wall, trying to approximate where it would be on the opposite side to trigger the portal to open.

Nothing happened. The flashlight winked off and then on.

Oh, no, I am not getting trapped in here.

Somewhere behind her she heard a low rumble. A growl? A cave-in? She was more certain than ever that she didn't want to know what other creatures Sir William had chained up down there. She moved her hands all around the rock wall, searching for some trigger to make it open.

The growl— it was definitely a growl—grew louder. Amanda glanced down the corridor but could see nothing in the failing light. Her flashlight flickered once, twice, and then went out.

Tommy! Her rational brain knew that he was too far away to hear her through the stone walls, even if he had been awake.

Call to him.

She wasn't sure if the voice was inside her head or outside. It seemed to echo for a moment before fading away in a high-pitched trill. *He won't hear me,* she thought.

Call your thrallmate.

Okay, that definitely wasn't her subconscious whispering to her. "Thrallmate" was a word she had never heard, let alone used.

Now!

Tommy! she thought in a panic. *Come to me, Tommy, find me.*

And then she pushed with her mind, really pushed. It was as though she were free outside the tunnel, ascending to the upper floor and touching Tommy on the cheek where he slept in his bed. He rose, still asleep, and followed her as she took him by the hand and led him down, down. Then they were standing on the other side of the wall. She lifted his hand to the place that would open the portal, and . . .

The wall slid open, and she nearly fell over Tommy as she staggered out. Clutching the book to her chest, she stared at him as the wall slid closed behind her. His eyes were closed, his face slack. She took his hand and he followed readily back to his room. She watched as he climbed into the bed, grabbed a blanket, and flipped onto his side.

She stood for a long time watching him. How had she done what she had done? The bond she had with him was strong, special, but how had she used it to manifest herself and manipulate his sleeping mind and body?

Somehow it scared her more than the creature that had been growling in the dark. She slipped quietly out of the room. She had to hide the book before he woke.

Why? she thought. *Why do I have to hide it?*

You do. You do, you do, you do, said a whispery voice, eager and insistent.

I . . . I do, she thought, as veils of secrecy came down over her mind. *And I will.*

SIX

SAGE

☾

Our hearts are black from all our deeds
Upon our souls the maggot feeds
The dead will walk and the dead will rise
Make us answer now for our lies

Old ones, young ones, hear our cry
Dust we are and all must die
That doesn't mean we shall not fight
For right is wrong but blood makes might

Seattle: Kari, Hecate, and Osiris

Nigel was asleep. Kari had made sure of that.

She didn't know if the vast assortment of sleeping aids he kept in the medicine cabinet of his downstairs laboratory were meant for her, or for himself. Maybe trying to make the dead live again gave him insomnia. Despite what he thought, her former graduate advisor had not made the dead live again. He had only made the dead walk again.

As for her, she did all she could to stay awake. Her nightmares were unbearable.

She revolted herself. She had unwound the bandages and screamed when she'd seen the hideous snakes of stitches and stapled incisions winding around her chest and over her breasts. The puckered mass of dead white and purple served as proof that she had sustained killing wounds. She shouldn't be there. She should be lying in her grave.

I'll never make love again. I'll never be able to undress in the light.

And her thoughts went to Jer, who was also horribly scarred. The Black Fire had melted his craggy, handsome face into hideous pulp, incised with rivulets, as if acid had run down his forehead and cheeks. Or lava.

Maybe now we can be together, she thought. But she knew he didn't love her anymore.

Standing in Nigel's living room, waiting for the cab, she tried to stop scratching her itchy flesh beneath the black turtleneck Nigel had bought for her. Her black wool pants sagged on her. None of her own belongings had survived the terrible floods and fires that had overrun Seattle. Everything was gone, except for her laptop. It was an old model she had used as a backup, and with it she had withdrawn all her money from her online bank accounts to buy a ticket to England.

The sky was a silvery white downpour of sleet, the storm ripping the midnight blue with cat-scratch lightning. A night not fit for man nor beast.

And yet.

Hecate sat in the bay window and growled low in her throat. Black with a silver blaze down his forehead, Osiris was pacing behind Kari, back and forth, his claws ticking on the hardwood floors. He knew he was being left behind.

Both cats knew things, told her things, and Hecate promised that she could lead Kari to Nicole Anderson-Moore, who was Hecate's mistress. Maybe the witch could help them both—make them truly live again. She wasn't certain what Hecate would do to Holly. Holly had sacrificed Hecate to gain magical power—had heartlessly drowned the poor cat in a bathtub. How could Jer love someone like that?

Hecate yowled; she wanted Osiris to come too. Maybe Nigel could drag something else back from the afterlife to keep the poor thing company.

All this Kari thought in a sensible, cohesive manner. But when she tried to speak, it was a struggle to string more than three or four words together. She could barely write.

She remembered the name of a condition caused by brain damage—aphasia. When she had been doing her folklore research, she had come across dozens of

fairy tales in which the heroine was unable to speak—
the Little Mermaid, the girl threatened with death if
she didn't defend herself in "The Six Swans." She had
written a paper suggesting that it was a means by which
simpler folk explained the presence of aphasia, saying
the silence was brought about by magic, or a curse.
Maybe magic could lift the curse.

Maybe death had struck her dumb.

"Okay, Hecate, crate," Kari murmured as she
glanced at the time readout on Nigel's cable box. It
was almost one a.m. The cab should have been there
at twelve forty-five. The crate sat beside Nigel's wide-
screen TV; it was a plastic box with a see-through
metal door. Labels reading LIVE ANIMAL were plastered
all over it. She had found several such crates in Nigel's
basement—for lab animals, she guessed. How many
failures had he had, before successfully revivifying
Osiris? And her?

Hecate stared straight ahead, growling. Kari
reached for the cat; Hecate leaped off the bay window
and trotted over to Osiris. The two animals turned as
one and stared at Kari, and then meowed in unison.
They sounded insistent, grief-stricken.

She shook her head. "One cat." It was strict airline
policy. She had checked and double-checked.

An image poured into her mind: Osiris in a shipping crate, in the belly of the plane with the cargo.

Just pack him in, stow him away. But they would x-ray the box to see what was inside it. She would be caught, maybe even thrown off the plane for cruelty to animals.

He cannot die, came the thought. And then, a clear image of all Nigel's many sleeping pills filled her mind. As understanding dawned, she recoiled in horror. The cats wanted her to give Osiris an overdose.

He cannot die, the thought repeated.

She took a deep breath. "The cab . . ."

When you are done, the cab will come. Hecate stared hard at her with her yellow eyes, which seemed to glow in the lightning flashes. Kari knew the thoughts were Hecate's thoughts. She knew she was communicating with a dead cat—that, apparently, had magical powers.

"All right," she said.

Cold dread filled her as she went down into the basement and collected the bottles of pills from Nigel's medicine cabinet. As she placed them into an empty yellow plastic bin she'd located beside her hospital bed, she couldn't help but wonder if he had planned to sleep with her once he'd brought her back. She'd known he was in love with her. But she'd only had eyes for Jer Deveraux. Nigel had been too much of a gentleman to push.

She stared at the vast array in the bin. It would be tempting to take them all, just go unconscious, but she knew it wouldn't end there. She wondered if she would have to go back to hell. Maybe what Nigel had done was actually rescue her from another hellish version of the Dreamtime, as Richard had rescued Jer?

She carried the bin back up to the living room. The two cats were waiting for her. Hecate was licking Osiris's head. To comfort him, maybe.

Another image filled her mind: Osiris, limp, his heart stopped. And then his eyes opening. His heart starting again.

He could not be killed.

Because he isn't alive, she thought as she opened a small amber plastic bottle. It was Ambien. She knew that was a prescription sleeping aid, very strong. She saw herself emptying all the capsules and mixing them with the cat food. *If we're dead, why do we eat?*

Then she saw herself taking a couch cushion and smothering him. With a cry she dropped the bottle back into the bin.

She couldn't, wouldn't, do such a thing. But how was it different from an overdose? The degree of violence? That it was so direct?

Get it done, Hecate urged her.

And in that moment she felt a twinge of sympathy for Holly, who had killed Hecate in the first place. Just a twinge.

Sage

When she finished getting the poison ready—that was exactly what it was—she found Osiris inside a heavy cardboard box filled with clothes. He was snuggled inside a large, old-fashioned lead-lined pouch, used back in the day for storing camera film when suitcases passed through X-rays. She had no idea where the cats had found it, nor why Nigel had it, but it twisted her stomach to see him placidly curled up inside it. It reminded her of a body bag.

Her hands shook badly as she held out the food. He gazed up at her and licked the tip of her finger, then gobbled down the food.

Twenty minutes later the taxi arrived.

Scarborough: Amanda, Nicole, Tommy, Richard, Owen

The childe of magicks is made in a minute, borned of womane in a moment. His fatheyr be unknowne, even unto ye Motheyr. And ife theys childe be growne until a manne, The Wordl be forfeiyt, yea, the very Erth and Skye Runneth as Dragonne's Bloode . . .

"No," Amanda said aloud as she shut Merlin's book and leaped away from it. She shuddered as if someone had thrown a bucket of ice water over her head—or desecrated her grave. She rubbed her arms and shook her head. She must have read it wrong.

She had been reading in bed, and it was three in the morning. In magical terms, it was the dark night of the soul, when Black Magic was strongest. Maybe an evil spell lingering in the house had jumbled the words. Or maybe she'd fallen asleep and dreamed it.

Gingerly she murmured a spell of protection and opened the book again. The words were still there. A child whose father is a mystery, "made in a minute." If such a child grew up, the world would end.

Her stomach clutched. *It can't mean Owen. Not our little baby.*

She read on:

Three signes there be: ye childe will possesse a Marke, behind his Ear Sinister; Ye childe will sing, and Ye Monsters will comme; Ye childe will kill a creatuyr most innocente. An ye babe shews these sigyns, better thou grab it bye its ankles and dash its head upon the chimneye, than you suffar him to live. If he liveth, all else dies.

She actually laughed out loud. "Sinister" meant "left." Owen didn't have any kind of mark behind his left ear—or his right, for that matter. And as for the other two—

Not gonna happen.

She closed the book and set it on her nightstand, then wiped her palms on her pajamas. That wasn't enough; she wanted to wash her hands. She grabbed her flashlight and went into the hall. As always, she paused before Tommy's door. They were engaged now. It would be okay for her to climb into bed with him, find some comfort there.

Not with Daddy in the house, she told herself.

She walked down the hall toward the bathroom, passing the door that led to Nicole's, Owen's, and Richard's rooms. She heard soft snoring, and smiled to herself.

And then she heard . . . singing—sweet, high-pitched, and breathy.

She stopped dead, listening. Five notes, over and over again. *La, la, la, la-la.* Maybe it was a toy. You could record your voice, to be played back when a child squeezed his toy around the middle or tugged on its nose.

Five notes. *La, la, la, la-la.*

Owen.

Her face went numb. He was too little to sing. She wasn't really hearing it. Someone was making her think she was. It was this house, this terrible, evil house.

But remember what happened that day, when Nicole said he spoke and he transformed before her eyes? She shivered.

"We're going to move out of here," she said aloud. And suddenly she meant it. She would do whatever was necessary to get Nicole to leave. The house, or castle, or whatever it was, belonged to a dynasty of murderous, barbaric warlocks. Not the right kind of place to raise a child.

But the book . . . It had foretold about Seattle, Holly's possession, everything.

"I'll tell them about the book," she said.

No. It is for you. The book is for you. Do not tell.

"I . . . ," she murmured, suddenly confused. What had she been thinking about?

La, la, la, la-la. Chills went down her spine; she opened the door and poked in her head.

"Nicole?" she whispered. She walked past Richard's door and opened the door leading to the bedroom Nicole shared with Owen. She hesitated, afraid to open it—afraid of what she would see. What it might mean.

No one is going to kill Owen.

La, la, la, la-la.

She kept her flashlight lowered, afraid to announce her presence, but more afraid to move through the dark without it.

She heard squeaking.

Footsteps. Rapid, and small, across the room.

Chills washed over her. She tried to call Nicole's name, but her throat was bone-dry. The arm holding the flashlight seemed to weigh a thousand pounds. She couldn't move.

The footsteps changed direction. They were headed for her.

Her mouth worked; her thumb played over the flashlight switch. She couldn't make it go on, couldn't make it work . . .

. . . and then a tiny hand slipped into her free hand, and gave her a little squeeze.

He's not walking yet.

"Nicole!" she screamed.

At once the room flowed with light from Nicole's bedside. Nicole was leaping out of bed. At the same time, Owen started wailing—from his cradle.

"Amanda, what's wrong?" Nicole cried as she grabbed up Owen and ran to Amanda.

There was no one standing beside Amanda. No one had squeezed her hand. No one visible, anyway.

"Oh, Nicole," she said, bursting into tears. Owen began to wail.

"Amanda," Nicole said, rushing to embrace her.

At the same time, Richard appeared in the doorway, in a white T-shirt and black sweatpants. He flicked on more lights.

"What's wrong?" he shouted, gazing around the room as he ran to them.

Don't tell him. It was a voice deep inside her, maybe the same one that had sung the eerie little tune and squeezed her hand. Maybe the one that had urged her to call for

Tommy when she'd been trapped in the secret tunnel. She didn't know what to do. Her father was protecting them, but he wasn't a member of their magical circle.

"Amanda?" That was Tommy, thundering into the room. Nicole was still hugging her. Owen was crying.

She should tell him. She was in thrall with him. But he wasn't a Cathers witch.

"I—I had a bad dream," she said, holding tightly to Nicole. Tommy took her hand—the same one a ghostly hand had squeezed—and pulled her against his chest. As she loosened her grip on her twin, she thought she heard the eerie singing . . . coming from Owen, who was still crying.

Am I losing my mind?

Mumbai: Philippe, Anne-Louise, and Eli

Eli had tracked the magic emanations to a huge park. Now he stared in disbelief at the two witches. He had no idea who the woman was, but the man was the European witch Nicole was in thrall to.

The bastard.

"No freakin' way," he grunted.

They were twenty feet apart, plenty close enough that Eli could kill him with magic, not close enough to kill him with his bare hands. He growled low in his throat, clenching and unclenching his fists. From the look on the witch's face, Eli was pretty sure he was thinking something similar.

The woman stepped forward, and with a flick of his wrist Eli sent her flying. She landed in a heap on a pile of rocks close to the lake.

"You are Eli Deveraux," the witch said.

"In the flesh."

"I am Philippe. Nicole is in thrall to me."

"I guessed that much. Tell me where she is."

"I wish I knew."

"Tell me, damn you!" Eli threw a fireball at his head.

Philippe reached up and plucked it out of the air, extinguishing it with his fingers. So. The jerk had some magic skills.

"Why are you looking for her?" Philippe asked.

As an answer Eli threw another fireball. "Just tell me."

This time Philippe not only blocked it, but sent it back to Eli.

Oh, yeah, this is going to be a long fight, Eli thought.

He dropped to the ground and sent a hailstorm of fire Philippe's way. The witch deflected the wall of flame to his right, where it set a tree on fire.

"If you kill me, you'll never find her," Philippe yelled, sending bolts of electricity flying at Eli's head.

"You can't keep me from her . . . or my kid," Eli

shouted, spinning out of the way as he tore a crack in the ground beneath Philippe's feet.

Philippe tottered wide-legged for a moment before jumping away, dropping to his knees, and throwing a small cyclone into Eli's chest.

Eli grunted as the force made impact; he heard ribs cracking and rattled off an incantation to dull the pain.

"You didn't honestly think it was *your* baby," Eli taunted.

The French witch swore in French, probably damning Eli to hell. *Not yet,* he thought.

He could taste blood on his lips. Not good. Had he punctured a lung? He twisted the cyclone up tighter and sent it back to Philippe, who deflected it back to the burning tree. The wind spread the fire, and suddenly not one but a dozen trees burst into flame.

"The child might not be mine, but neither is he yours," Philippe said.

It was the truth that Eli was afraid of, and he could tell it cost the other man to say it out loud. And suddenly Eli wanted very, very much to break every bone in the witch's body.

With a roar he crossed the distance between them. He slammed into Philippe and they both went down in a tangle of arms and legs. Philippe regained his footing first and staggered away, trying to put space between them. Eli made it back to his feet and closed the distance again. He grabbed Philippe around the throat and started squeezing.

Philippe exploded a fireball in Eli's eyes; he went blind, but he held on, knowing it would pass. Philippe staggered backward, and Eli went with him. As they grappled, Philippe's hands found Eli's throat and he could feel the breath being squeezed out of him.

"The water," he heard Philippe wheeze. Eli's vision cleared just enough to show him that they were on a ledge above a vast lake covered with water lilies. And then he heard Philippe in his mind.

Those who are loved by a Cahors witch are cursed to die by drowning.

Eli grinned wickedly at Philippe, remembering the bad old days when suspected witches were tied to stools and dunked to determine their innocence. Witches and water had a long, unhappy history. And to lay a curse of water on top of that . . .

The odds were decidedly in a warlock's favor.

So, which one of us does she love? I guess there's only one way to find out, Eli thought.

Anne-Louise sat up with a groan. Whatever Eli had thrown at her had sliced through her personal wards as if they were tissue paper. She struggled to her feet; pain shot through her left arm, and she guessed that it was broken.

Trees were blazing. Sharp winds cut through the smoke, and as she staggered forward, she saw neither Philippe nor Eli.

"Philippe?" she called, breathing a prayer to the Goddess for his safety.

There was no answer, but a moment later she heard an angry shout. She spun around and saw Eli and Philippe, their hands locked around each other's throats, teetering on the rock ledge above one of the lakes.

"No!" she screamed, and ran toward them.

Philippe turned, gave her a ghost of a smile, and then the two of them went over the side and tumbled into the waters below. Anne-Louise ran to the edge and tried to conjure a spell that would lift them out of the water.

Nothing happened. She strained her eyes but could see nothing beneath the surface. She considered jumping in after them, but that seemed like folly. She stood for several minutes, eyes probing the surface of the lake.

Nothing.

They were both gone.

France, Thirteenth Century: Sasha

Sasha had been trapped in the past for nearly a year. She had been forced to watch, helpless, as history repeated itself. Jean and Isabeau married. The Cahors attacked the Deveraux and the lovers died. All she could do was watch and try to stay alive.

She had studied the origin of the blood feud between the two families ever since she had left her husband, Michael Deveraux, and found sanctuary in the Mother Coven. Living through the storied events, though, she had come to discover something very important.

The deaths of Jean and Isabeau did not herald the start of the blood feud. Indeed, Cahors and Deveraux history went back much, much further. At one point they had been very closely allied. Then something, she still didn't know what, had happened that had driven the families apart forever.

The other thing that she had learned was that Jean's lover, Karienne, had been pregnant with his child when she was sent away. Sasha had no idea if the child was male or female or whether there were more offspring that carried Deveraux blood without the Deveraux name.

One other thing she had discovered was fascinating. There were two types of magic practitioners—"natural born" and "borrowers." Natural born witches and warlocks inherited their power from their parents. It ran in the blood. Those who were borrowers had no natural talent, and only came to the practice later in life through close contact with a practitioner. She was still trying to figure out how it all worked, but as near as she could tell, the borrower's magic came not from within but from the one they were close to. Which meant that she, Sasha, was a borrower. She had known nothing of witchcraft when she'd met Michael Deveraux, and in all her study since then she had never found a single witch or warlock in her family tree. So, whatever power she had was courtesy of Michael.

She desperately wanted to return to her own time. She spent many sleepless nights wondering how her sons were and whether their father was dead. She began to think that there might be a way for her to use her borrowed magic against Michael. Maybe she could set up some sort of feedback loop that would destroy him, or at the very least render him powerless.

More pressing than that question, though, was the one regarding how she could make it home. Time travel was not a skill possessed by ordinary witches and warlocks, although she had heard vague rumors that a handful had mastered it. A piece of a manuscript she had found in a monastery had led her to think that a combination of magic and science could get her home. She had even discovered a man who might be able to help her. Unfortunately, he was dead.

So she had traveled to India looking for something that the Persian scientist and scholar Abū Rayhān Bīrūnī might have left there almost two hundred years earlier. The trip was dangerous, but not half so much as staying in the Deveraux-Cahors war zone.

The area she was searching was under Hindu rule and in her own time was known as Bombay, or the more contemporary Mumbai. The fragment of text she had found had said that just as the phases of the moon could be charted, so could they be changed. Since it was unlikely that the scientist had believed man capable of affecting the moon in such a way, she thought it could mean that man could affect time.

She had about convinced herself she was crazy, when another line of the text had stated that by so doing a man could walk with his ancestors and see beyond his years.

Now, as she stood in a large field outside of the village, she wondered if she was crazy or if Abū Rayhān Bīrūnī had been, or both. She had known his name before finding it on the piece of parchment. She had studied him in college, and later as a witch had been fascinated by his illustration for the different phases of the moon.

The text had led her to the field near the village, but it had given no more specific insight for finding the object that he had said he'd buried.

"From unseen to seen from earth to sky, give me the eyes to seek what he did hide."

A small patch of earth off to her right suddenly zoomed into focus. She dropped to her knees and began to dig, and an hour later she struck something metal. The object glinted dully as she brushed the earth from it and gently pulled it free from its resting place.

It was a crude circle around which the moon appeared in its various phases. She touched one with her finger and they all began spinning slowly counterclockwise. She felt a crackle of magic along her skin . . . and then . . . it was morning.

She blinked, not entirely sure what had happened. For a moment she wondered if she had fallen asleep, but then she glanced around her and realized that the earth looked exactly as it had earlier that day *before* she had dug the object up.

She stepped to the side and then spun the moons counterclockwise with more force. Around her the world seemed to change. There were flashes of light and dark that were almost like a strobe light. Each time the light appeared, she saw something different. The place where she had recovered the device was overgrown with flowers. Around her, trees were shrinking in size and number.

And then something prompted her to reach out and stop the spinning of the miniature moons. Everything slowed for a moment, and then sitting beside her was a man.

Sasha jumped, startled, but he looked at her with kindly eyes that sparkled with humor. "I have been waiting for you," he said in Latin.

"Are you Abū Rayhān Bīrūnī?" she asked.

He inclined his head. "I am."

She showed him the device. "Did you create this?"

"No. It was given to me by a very old and wise man. I was told to hold it and keep it safe for a great lady."

"Who?" she asked, still trying to get her bearings.

"I can only assume he meant you."

"How does it work?" she asked.

"I have spent many years studying it, and I do not know. However, I do know that if you hold your purpose in your mind, it will help you know when to stop the moons from spinning."

"That must be how I found you," she said. "But what if I want to go forward in time?"

"Then you must spin the moons the other way. The science or magic or whatever it is that controls it is beyond my comprehension. Fortunately, it is not so much of a mystery as to how to make it work."

"Who is the man who gave it to you?" Sasha asked.

"He refused to tell me his name. I know only that he was a religious man, a follower of Zoroaster. He also told me that even though you can change your moons, you must act quickly if you are to save them."

"Save who?" Sasha asked, heart in her throat.

"Again, he did not say. He was a man of very few words."

"Thank you."

"You are welcome." He stood. "Now that I have fulfilled my promise to him, I will return home. I believe you will wish to do the same. Go with Allah."

She rose and bowed to him. She watched him walk away, and then turned her attention back to the object she held. She was ready to go home. She took a deep breath and spun the planets clockwise.

Around her the world changed, and a city replaced the village. Then, suddenly, she was underwater, but whatever magic or science was working the object kept her safe and dry in a protective bubble.

With a gasp she stopped the moons. There in the water above her was her son, Eli, and the witch, Philippe. They were struggling together but a moment later separated. Each tried to swim toward the surface, but it was as though they could not. They were drowning.

London: Kari, Hecate, and Osiris

Somehow, everyone treated her more nicely if they thought she was deaf. Or maybe Hecate was working her magic. Kari got upgraded to first class on her flight from Seattle to Heathrow Airport in London.

At Heathrow she was reunited with her "parcel," and was amazed to discover that the baggage handlers hadn't bothered to open it. After trundling it on a baggage trolley to a dark corner with Hecate riding in her carrying case, Kari found Osiris calm and awake. She wondered what dead cats dreamed of.

It was a simple thing to rent her car, which was a white Vauxhall Corsa, and put her meager overnight bag, carrying toiletries and her two other changes of clothes, into the trunk—the boot—and let the two cats roam inside the car as they pleased. Both of them settled on the seat beside her. Hecate stared hard at her as they pulled out of the rental lot.

I will guide you. It will take at least six hours.

"Tired," Kari protested.

Inner Ring East.

Kari sighed and started on her way, just as the skies opened up and rain began to pour down in buckets. She felt a frisson—would floods and fires follow her too?

I want out of all of it. Out, Kari thought.

Berlin: Jer and Eve

Jer groaned in his sleep, waking Eve. She flipped onto her side to look at him. They were in a small bed-and-breakfast in Berlin that they had found just before nightfall. She wondered what he dreamed about. She also wondered how much longer she could keep up the charade. A dozen times already she had nearly told him the truth.

They needed to find Eli. The Supreme Coven was willing to welcome the Deveraux with open arms. When the day came that Eli and Jer returned and took their place at the head of the organization, everything would change.

She had served a very long time as Sir William's attack dog. She didn't mind killing, but even she was growing tired of the constant battle for survival. She had always known that sooner or later Sir William would turn on her, just as he did with all his other pets. Now that he was gone, though, there was a chance for change. That was, of course, if he was really gone.

She had her doubts about that. The body might be dead, but she was certain Sir William had found a way to cheat death. Where was he, though? Why was he silent and waiting, especially with Michael Deveraux and his own son, James, dead? Plots within plots within plots. Warlock politics were harder to follow than that of the mundane world.

It was entirely possible that the offer to give the Skull Throne to Jer was just another one of those plots, but if it was, she couldn't see the puppet master at work behind the scenes.

"Holly," Jer murmured.

Eve rolled her eyes. He was dreaming about the Cathers witch. *Romeo and Juliet had nothing on them as far as star-crossed lovers go,* she thought. She got up and slipped outside, reveling in the brisk night air. The Goddess might rule the nighttime, but Eve was one warlock who didn't fear either night or day.

"Is there a reason you keep following me?" Jer complained, staring moodily at Eve.

"Sorry. Not so much following as traveling with you," she said, in clipped tones.

"Why?"

"Because, in theory at least, you're searching for your brother. I figure the best way to find him is to stay close to you."

"So you can what, offer him the Skull Throne instead of me? Supreme Coven doesn't care who leads as long as it's a Deveraux?"

She averted her eyes from his. "That's not entirely true," she said.

He watched her carefully. She was powerful, sexy, everything you would want in a warlock. The attraction was there, he couldn't deny it, but there was something else, some sort of connection that went beyond physical. He wondered what it would be like to work magic with her. His instinct told him it would be wild, uncontrolled magic. And there was enough of the warlock in him still to be tempted.

He sighed and turned away. In a strange way Eve had been helping him. Since she cared nothing about his scars, he had been slowly forgetting—at least when it was just the two of them—how deformed he was. If only it could have been that way with Holly.

Not that she cared about the scars.

Perhaps the most devastating lesson of his life was one that he was becoming more painfully aware of every day. He had made a mistake. He never should have left Holly. She loved him and had been willing to be in thrall to him. His own pride and fear and selfishness had gotten in the way. It might have been their one chance at salvation. Now he feared it was too late for him. He was almost certain that if she was still alive it was too late for her.

He had left England to get away from the temptation that the Skull Throne provided. He was arrogant enough to believe that if he was in charge he could actually make a difference. He was realist enough to realize that the throne would change him and not the other way around. He had fled to Germany not so much to look for Eli as to put more distance between him and London.

They had been in the city two days, and he was making the rounds of the tourist sites. *Nothing better to do. Not like Jer Deveraux ever saved anyone.*

He stood now where the Berlin Wall had once stood, dividing West and East. Good and evil. Witch and warlock. Unfortunately, nothing was ever quite that simple. How many years had he spent trying to straddle that fence?

"One day you're going to have to choose, you know," Eve said quietly.

"Choose what?" he asked, feigning ignorance.

"Who you are, who you really want to be."

"My destiny was chosen for me. Deveraux by name, scarred by fire, cursed by all the gods."

Eve slapped him so hard across the face that it spun him partly around. The hood of his sweatshirt fell back, exposing his face to the light. He waited for the gasps of people around as they saw his ruined flesh, but none came. Suddenly, though, a little girl was standing in front of him. She held out her teddy bear to him. Bewildered, he took it from her.

"The bad men hurt my daddy real bad too," she said. Her wide blue eyes were trusting, loving. She patted his hand and then turned and walked away, leaving her teddy bear with him. He stared down into the lifeless black eyes and realized that he had never felt so lost.

"You want to know what I see?" Eve said. "I see a coward. I see a good man with great power and unlimited potential who has always enjoyed playing helpless.

You've shirked all your responsibilities to yourself and others, whined about how bad your life is, and failed in every task you've ever set for yourself, not because you weren't up to the challenge but because you can't stop pitying yourself for five seconds."

"What are you saying?" he asked.

"I'm saying get over yourself. A lot of people have had tougher lives than you'll ever know. So you had a father you didn't like. So you were terribly scarred in battle. So you lost the love of your life because you were too damn selfish to let anyone in. Boo frickin' hoo. You want to make the world a better place? Hell, you want to make your own wretched life better? Tell you what, when you decide to man up, you know where to find me."

She turned and stalked away, and once again Jer was alone . . .

. . . on the fence . . .

. . . holding a teddy bear.

Outside Mumbai:
Holly, Alex, Pablo, Armand, and the Temple of the Air

Holly smiled appreciatively as Alex said *"Incendio"* and a fire blazed into being. She and he had created a beautiful bower inside a cave, conjuring silken pillows and mosaic lamps, and low carved tables inlaid with abalone. Alex had located a small outpost of Supreme

Covenates about three miles to their west, and they would attack before dawn. For now they needed to eat, rest, and thaw out.

"I never thought I'd wind up hunting warlocks in India," Alex said, rippling his socked feet close to the bright orange flames.

"Life is full of surprises," Holly replied faintly.

"Amen," Armand said, crossing himself. He seemed troubled, and Pablo, too. Yet each time she'd asked him if something was wrong, he'd hesitated and said no.

Doesn't he trust me? she wondered.

"Let's eat," Alex said, unpacking the cheeses, bread, and other delicacies they had loaded up on in the last village. "I think this is some kind of local moonshine or something." He pulled out a leather bag and pulled off the stopper with his teeth. "What shall we drink to? Death to the enemy?"

"To life," Armand said. This time Pablo crossed himself as well.

"All right." Alex placed the bag against his lips and tipped it back. He grimaced as he swallowed. "That is *sour.*"

He handed the bag to Holly, and his grimace faded as he gazed at her. The light played over his craggy features. "To life," he said softly.

Holly took a taste. It was actually very sweet.

"The powers of darkness are marshaling their

forces," Armand said darkly as he stared into the heart of the fire.

He was right. They all knew it, and Holly had caught herself looking over her shoulder almost constantly. She had the feeling that something big was happening, that there was a larger picture and somehow she had only been given a few small jigsaw pieces.

How am I supposed to know what to do with them? she fretted. The Goddess had been silent lately, and Holly wasn't sure if that denoted approval, disapproval, or indifference. Given the sacrifices the Goddess had already asked of her, indifference might not be so bad. At least Holly knew where she stood with herself. And even though they did not discuss things with one another openly, she was pretty sure she knew where she stood with Armand and Pablo, too.

Alex stretched out lazily beside her, like a cat sunning himself. She frowned. She knew where she stood with him. The time was coming when his patience would run out and he would push for them to be in thrall to each other.

The thought terrified Holly. The last time she had been in thrall, it had been while she was possessed and her archenemy Michael Deveraux had taken advantage. To the best of her knowledge it had been a spiritual union only. With Alex it would not be that way. He would demand a complete union, body and soul.

Sage

Holly had hoped for so long that when she finally gave herself to a man, it would be to Jer. He had shut that door, though, not her. She closed her eyes and remembered the feel of his lips on hers. Even as the memories stirred, she could feel another's thoughts, her long dead ancestress Isabeau who burned for her husband, Jean, also moving in her thoughts.

"Où? Où est-tu?"

Where are you?

Mon âme?

My soul?

SEVEN

ANISE

🌙

Deveraux hearts are always cold
Despite whatever lies we've told
But something's changing deep inside
Even our wickedness can't hide

Trapped we are by all our years
While fire burns and fire sears
At the end, sacrifice is all we know
But it only makes the darkness grow

Scarborough: Nicole, Amanda, Richard, Tommy, and Owen

"No," Nicole said brokenly, as she rose from Amanda's bed and began to pace. She went to the window and gazed out at her little son, wrapped in a soft blanket cradled against his grandfather's powerful chest. Tommy walked beside Richard, and the two were talking earnestly. They kept glancing back at House Moore, almost as if they knew she and Amanda spoke of matters regarding life and death.

Owen's death. Her child, her baby . . . Her heart

wouldn't stop racing. She wasn't sure her feet were touching the floor.

"It's a book of prophecies," Amanda said gently but firmly, gesturing to the ancient manuscript. "Merlin's prophecies. And many of them have come true."

She had fought the voice, and won. It was a secret no longer, despite the pain it was causing. They had to face it.

Had to deal with it.

Had to decide what to do.

Tears streamed down Nicole's face. "No, you're wrong. Merlin is a mythical person. It's a trick. It's not real."

"Niki, I'm so sorry," Amanda said. "But . . ." She trailed off, as if she couldn't bear to continue.

"But, Amanda, it's *Owen*." Her face crumpled and she began to let go, to give in to her fear. If she broke down, Amanda would have to pull her together, and maybe it would distract her twin long enough for her to . . . to what?

No. She had to keep her wits about her. Owen was counting on her.

"It's Owen," she managed. Everything inside her was clenched and terrified—bones, blood, soul.

"I know." Amanda hung her head and began to cry.

"You said yourself the house is evil. That's an evil

book." Nicole could barely get the words out. The knot in her throat was choking her. She wanted to take the book and throw it out the window, burn it in the fireplace.

"It's the Book of Merlin, one of the greatest wizards who ever lived," Amanda replied. She got to her feet and walked to Nicole. "That night, I heard singing. It was Owen, Niki. It *was*."

"You said someone grabbed your hand. And Owen was fast asleep." Nicole seized on the argument like a woman with a noose around her neck pleading for her life. "He was asleep. You can't deny that."

"I don't know what happened. But—"

Nicole whirled around. Amanda's face was blotched with crying. The sight terrified Nicole; it was as if Amanda had given up all hope.

"And what about the rest of it?" Nicole added quickly. Her voice rose. "He doesn't have a mark behind his ear. He hasn't killed anything innocent or otherwise. He hasn't, Amanda. Admit it!"

Amanda hesitated, and she felt Niki's desperate surge of hope.

"Maybe the book *is* wrong," she ventured, even though her heart was breaking. Because she didn't think the book *was* wrong.

Kill Owen? Her sweet little nephew? A *baby*?

She couldn't imagine doing such a thing. She

couldn't even see herself doing it; who could? Her father, who was Owen's grandfather? Tommy? They'd sooner die. Maybe even sacrifice the whole world, rather than harm their baby—for he was theirs now, all of theirs. Maybe they didn't know who his father was, but Owen was child of their blood.

We can't do it.

Only one witch she knew would be capable of killing a baby, to keep the coven safe.

"Where is Holly?" she wailed aloud.

"No," Nicole breathed. She went completely white. "Don't even speak her name. Please, Amanda."

"Niki," Amanda said. "If it must be done, then—"

Suddenly there was shouting. Amanda ran to the window. Niki trailed after, crying.

Below them, in the courtyard, a white Corsa slowed to a stop. The driver's side door opened, and Amanda caught her breath. If it was Holly—

—but it wasn't.

Kari Hardwicke stepped out. *Kari.*

"But she's dead," Amanda said.

Nicole gasped. A black cat hopped out of the car, followed by a second. As Nicole flattened her hands on the glass, the cat stopped and looked up at her. Amanda ticked her glance at her twin. Nicole and the cat were staring at each other.

"Amanda," she ground out. "That's . . ."

Nicole couldn't say Hecate's name. She had to be wrong. It couldn't be her wonderful cat, the one Holly had murdered. It couldn't be, and yet, the delicate head, the way she flicked her tail . . . it had to be.

"Oh, my God."

Amanda put her arm around her shoulders. The room felt icy. Nicole couldn't think. All she could do was stare at the apparition, a flesh-and-blood twin of her dead familiar, Hecate.

"Maybe she had kittens before she . . . died," Amanda ventured.

Nicole didn't answer. She wasn't sure her heart was still beating as she turned from the window and flew out of the bedroom. She didn't know if Amanda was following her. All her energy was focused on the little black cat.

She took the servants' stairs—the circular staircase had been destroyed—and raced from the back section of House Moore into the castle that had been revealed by the fire. She and the others had swept the floor clean of layers of ash and dust. If the great entry hall had been furnished, the fire had erased all trace. All that was left was stonework, including a long table like an altar, and a stone with a deep cleft in it.

She pushed open the stone front door and ran down the stone steps outside, skipping the last two and pushing past Kari, who was wearing all black, including a large pair of dark-rimmed sunglasses. Nicole scooped up the smaller of the two black cats and nuzzled her.

Energy surged between them—faint, but present.

"It's you, it's you," Nicole sang, kissing the top of Hecate's head, her cheeks, and her front paws. "Oh, Hecate, how?"

The cat didn't respond. Nicole kissed her over and over, loving her, crying tears of joy now. "Oh, my kitty, my Hecate." She cried a little more, and then she looked up at Kari.

Kari, who should be dead. Nicole had seen her cut nearly in two. A lake of blood had gushed out of Kari's chest. And they had left her there. Kari who was standing inside the gate without having been invited in.

"Someone saved you," Amanda cried. "Oh, thank the Goddess!"

"No one," Kari said flatly.

Nicole settled Hecate under her chin. Kari was heavily made up, with lots of blush and colored lip gloss. Slowly she took off her sunglasses, and Nicole jerked. Her eyes looked inhuman.

Dead.

"I died," Kari said.

Amanda, Richard, and Tommy gathered around. In Richard's arms Owen cooed. Nicole cast an agonized glance at him. Amanda was wrong. She had to be. Had to be.

Had to be. Kari and Hecate must have been sent by the Goddess Herself, to stop them. . . .

"Died?" Tommy said. The other cat approached Nicole and sat down. It tilted back its head and gazed at Hecate. The two meowed.

"Tired," Kari murmured. She turned and headed up the stairs of the castle. Nicole took Owen out of his grandfather's arms and held him and Hecate both, trailing behind as Amanda walked with Kari up the stairs. It seemed natural for Amanda to take over the hostessing duties. Back home Amanda had been the sweet one, the thoughtful one. Nicole had been too busy starring in school plays and getting what she wanted with magic spells to think of anyone else.

Kari stood statue-still while Amanda opened the heavy stone door leading into the castle. Tommy bounded up the stairs to help her. Without any reaction at all, Kari walked inside.

Amanda looked over her shoulder at Nicole, raised her brows and grimaced, and followed Kari in. Tommy went next. Richard put his hand on Nicole's shoulder, sliding it down to cup Hecate's chin. The cat allowed him to study her face.

"Is it really your cat?" he asked his daughter, making as if to take Hecate. "She ran away, right?"

Hecate hissed and dug her claws into Nicole's Irish wool sweater. Richard grunted and tried again.

The cat retracted her claws just long enough to free her front left paw; then she took a swipe at Richard.

"I don't think you should hold her with Owen in your arms. She might scratch him."

"No," Nicole said quickly, but she immediately relented. Her father didn't know that Holly had killed Hecate. He'd been in a drunken depression then, brought on by the death of Marie-Claire, his wife—Nicole and Amanda's mother. They knew now that Michael Deveraux had killed her.

"Go to Daddy, Hecate," Nicole told the cat.

But Hecate wasn't listening to her. She was staring at Owen, and the baby was just as transfixed. Nicole waited for a sign.

Owen began to cry without breaking his gaze.

Don't look at him anymore. Don't, Nicole ordered the cat. Then Hecate growled in protest as Richard scooped her up with a soft pat on her head.

"I wonder how Kari got two cats onto a commercial flight," he mused.

"I don't think Kari did," Amanda said slowly, as she came up beside her father and her sister. "I don't think Kari's here."

Seattle: Dr. Temar

Dr. Nigel Temar awoke with a start and sat up, but instantly regretted it. His head felt like it was going to explode, and his mouth was so dry that his lips were stuck to his teeth. A quick glance at his atomic wall clock sent him flying back up again.

Two days! How could he have been asleep for two days? He ran into the other room to check on Kari. Her bed was empty.

And his head began to pound as the room tilted.

Comprehension dawned. She had drugged him, and then she had left.

"Oh, no," he whispered. "No."

He thought of Kari alone in the world, practically a zombie. He pictured her frightened, desperate . . . and if he was honest . . . very honest, he imagined someone taking an interest in her, and studying her . . . and finding out what he, Nigel Temar, had done. Reverse-engineering her. Learning his methods and protocols . . . his secrets.

And hurt.

"Kari," he groaned, slamming his fist against the doorjamb.

Time was not his friend, but technology was. He knew he would find her, and this time it would be a lot easier than the last time. Before he had revived her he had stitched up her chest, *after* putting a GPS tracker inside it. Ghoulish, perhaps, but now he was glad that he'd done it.

"I'll find you," he whispered.

Anise

He rushed to the tracking monitor, nestled among the many machines he had employed while raising her from the dead, and flicked it on.

There was no signal.

Scarborough:
Nicole, Owen, Amanda, Tommy, Richard, Kari, and the cats

Richard had seen many dead bodies in his time. Some of them were men—and women, and demons—he'd killed himself after joining the battle against Michael Deveraux and his allies. Others were from Nam.

But he had never seen the dead walk.

Kari Hardwick was unnatural. He didn't like looking at her, let alone having her in the house. The others seemed to have forgotten that Kari had abandoned them and fled to their enemy, Michael Deveraux. It was true that she had been killed in the battle at the Supreme Coven, but that didn't mean she was any less a traitor. She had turned on them once, and she could do it again, even if she was dead.

Maybe she's here to show them where we are. Or she's been programmed to kill us. Michael Deveraux forced Holly into a state of demonic possession and she tried to kill us. If Armand hadn't exorcised her, she might have succeeded. Maybe a warlock promised Kari that he would make her whole again if she betrayed us a second time.

Or if she smothered my grandchild in his sleep.

213

At Richard's insistence Nicole put Owen down in his heavily warded crib for a nap. The baby lay upstairs, safe from Kari, before Richard sat down to interrogate her.

"Do you drink?" he asked her bluntly as he passed around cups of tea. He would have preferred straight bourbon, but those days were behind him. He had sunk into a terrible depression during the last days of his marriage, and then Marie's death. He wondered now if Michael Deveraux had engineered it, to keep him passive and weak. But the warrior in Richard was awake now. Nothing would cross his lips that could diminish his power.

"Thirst," Kari said, taking a cup from him with bluish-white hands. Her cold, dead fingers brushed his, and it took all his self-control not to jerk away.

He took his seat with his own cup of tea and stared at his daughters. Nicole was pale and shaky. Amanda was staring at Kari as though Kari were a lost puppy in need of help. Tommy sat protectively next to Amanda, but all his attention was focused on the two cats, who paced the room as though looking for something. Richard had realized there was something wrong with them as well.

"What happened to you?" Richard demanded. Amanda blanched; his little girl had always been so careful of other people's feelings. But he wasn't about to sit around chitchatting with a dead woman when he had a family to protect.

"Killed. Dr. Temar. Laboratory," she said. She shifted, and he saw intelligence in her dead eyes, if nothing else. She was speaking in halting sentences, but it had to be an act.

"He . . . reanimated you?" Richard pressed. His two daughters shifted uncomfortably. Nicole glanced upward, as if she could see Owen through the ceiling. Maybe she could. Richard knew he didn't fully understand all the things his daughters could do.

"Frankenstein." She didn't smile. Was she mocking them?

"How could he?" Richard asked. "Is it possible to do that with magic?"

Kari shrugged. Through the steam of her cup, she gazed down at Hecate.

The cat hissed. Richard stared for a moment until he could look into the cat's eyes. *Damn, she's dead too.*

"Dr. Temar is a witch?" Tommy asked uncertainly.

"No," Kari said. "Hecate. Technology. Experiments." She pointed at Osiris. "Then me."

Tears streamed down Nicole's face. Amanda reached out and took her hand. Richard felt the temperature in the chilly room raise by a few degrees.

"That's dangerous technology," Richard said. He

couldn't help but think about what a nightmare it would be if that knowledge fell into the wrong hands. For the briefest of moments he considered returning to Seattle to find the doctor and destroy his work for the good of humanity. But that would mean leaving Owen and the girls unprotected, and that was unacceptable.

"Dangerous," Kari repeated, studying her own hands.

"How did you find us?" Nicole asked.

"Hecate," she said. "Escaped."

Escaped. Richard shook his head. How many of them had been trapped like lab rats thanks to this endless war of good versus evil? After the emergence of the dragon, their retreat appeared to have been honored. It had been tempting to believe that they were really safe, that their part was over. In his bones, though, he believed it had just begun. If nothing else, Kari's appearance and her state reinforced that for him.

"What was it like?" Amanda asked.

Kari swiveled her dead gaze to her. "Hell." She stuck her finger into her boiling hot tea, and didn't flinch.

"Fire, everywhere."

"Black fire?" Nicole asked. "Did Michael Deveraux send you there before he died?"

"White fire. Worse," Kari said. "Worse." She kept her finger in the cup. Richard was half-afraid it would burn off. "Burning, always. Suffering. Remembering. Torment. Penance."

"It really *was* hell," Nicole breathed.

Amanda began to cry. Nicole trembled too hard to hold her cup. Tommy just continued to stare at the two cats, but Richard didn't think he was actually seeing them.

"There must be something we can do, magic, to make you better," Amanda said at last.

"Magic brought Hecate," Kari said.

"Whose?" Richard asked quietly.

"Michael Deveraux's," Kari replied.

Richard clenched his fists. Even dead, Michael Deveraux was still a thorn in his side, the snake in the grass.

Acid burned in Amanda's stomach. Watching Kari, hearing her talk about hell, how could there be a place so terrible? Why would the Goddess allow Kari to suffer so? And now, knowing what Amanda knew, how could she send Owen there?

But he's a baby. How can a baby go to hell?

The tears streaming down her cheeks were for the innocent baby upstairs and not for the wretched Kari. If there was something she could do for Kari, she would, but she had a feeling Kari was beyond hope and beyond saving. The same couldn't be true of Owen, could it?

Goddess, what am I supposed to do? she prayed, clutching

Nicole's hand. Then Tommy took her other hand and squeezed tightly. He didn't know.

Where is Holly? She would cut through her own feelings like a laser. She's good at making tough decisions.

As Amanda stared at Hecate, though, she shivered. Holly might be good at making hard decisions, but that didn't mean she always chose the right thing to do.

And Amanda thought then and there to reveal what had been happening to her. These people who loved her most deserved to know—

—to know—

What was I just thinking about? she thought with a start. The last minutes were blank. She thought back, frowning, trying to piece the conversation together, and add in her private thoughts.

It was as if a veil had fallen—

"Amanda?" her father said.

She stirred herself. "Sorry," she said. "What?"

She had the strangest feeling—

"One way or another this has to all stop," Tommy declared. "We can't keep living like this." He glanced at Kari. Or dying like this.

Outside of Mumbai:
Holly, Alex, Pablo, Armand, and the Temple of the Air

Holly jerked awake with a start.

She sat up and looked around the cave at the others.

Alex and Armand were gone. Pablo was sitting up, his head cocked to the side as though listening for something.

Holly tried to stretch out her own mind, to see and feel what she could not see. She pushed and strained at the edges of her consciousness but to no avail.

You need to empty yourself before you can see and hear beyond what your eyes and ears can perceive, Pablo said inside her head.

More and more Pablo had taken to communicating this way. She knew it was because he didn't entirely trust Alex.

That's okay. Neither do I, she replied.

She tried to do as Pablo instructed, empty herself of thoughts, fears, dreams, everything. She inhaled deeply and then expelled her breath, imagining all those things being carried out on the air escaping her lips. She did it twice more until she felt . . . nothing.

And then she heard . . . everything.

The burst of sound and voices inside her head paralyzed her as for one terrible moment she thought she'd become possessed again. Panic set in; she began to choke on her fear. Then Pablo's voice, in her ear, outside of her head, cut through the chatter and the static.

"Be still. Listen for the sound that does not belong," he instructed, his hand on her face. "Listen for disorder. And imbalance."

They breathed together, and she listened.

Slowly she could start to cycle through the different sounds. Maeve and Stanislaus were awake and making love. Holly squirmed, wishing she could purge those sounds from her brain. In another part of the cave, Janet was praying to the Goddess for strength, but to do what, Holly didn't know. Somewhere a long way off a dog was howling.

"You are close," Pablo whispered. "I sense it too."

Finally she heard it, and she knew instantly that she had found the sound that didn't belong: Somewhere in the darkness a man was praying to the Horned God.

The Temple of the Air did not pray to Him. He was their enemy.

Holly shot to her feet with a cry. Pablo leaped up beside her, and together they raced toward the sound.

"Danger! Traitor!" Holly yelled. "A warlock!"

An unseen wave of pure evil smacked against her, throwing her to the ground. Next to her, Pablo gasped and fell as well.

"Where, Holly?" Alex shouted, as men and women clambered to their feet, grabbing weapons, intoning spells. Alex's hair was tousled as if from sleep. He grabbed her hand and helped her up.

Pablo looked at her, and she looked around the cave as the coven prepared for battle.

"Where's Armand?" she asked. "Armand handles

the demons. If a warlock was praying, demons will answer." She stared into the darkness, conjured a fireball. "Where's Armand?"

"Where's the warlock?" Alex demanded, almost shaking her. To the others he cried, "Fan out!"

"Demons," she whispered, as the group moved into attack formation. She was losing it.

All these months traveling with Alex. Every coven they had attacked had been weak and had fallen with hardly a cry. Every demon they had faced had focused its energies on Armand, and she had come to believe in some strange way that they were his area of expertise, his responsibility.

Be honest, Holly. You're still afraid of them after what they did to you.

She winced, trying to shut up her inner voice. She focused instead on the memory of the whispered prayer. The one that had whispered it was a flesh-and-blood warlock, and she feared no warlock. She raised her hands and prepared to fight.

"Bring it on," she said to Alex.

He grinned at her. "Let's go."

London: Anne-Louise and Rose

Anne-Louise had never liked Rose, a witch who ran a Mother Coven safe house in London. The woman had ulterior motives for most things that she did. Rose was, however, well-connected and could be counted upon to be paranoid. That was why Anne-Louise headed straight for her house after leaving Heathrow.

The Mother Coven itself was in a state of upheaval following the destruction of the London headquarters of the Supreme Coven. Anne-Louise was not surprised. She had come to suspect that Luna, the high priestess, had her own reasons for not taking down the Supreme Coven herself. It made no sense. If the Supreme Coven stood for everything that the Mother Coven was against, why did they seem to coexist with obvious but ultimately meaningless hostility?

There was something greater at work, and Anne-Louise was determined to know what it was. She wasn't sure if she was kept in the dark because of her age or her skill or her rank, or if all of her witchly brothers and sisters were being purposefully lied to.

After the battle in the park she had stayed in Mumbai for two more days, searching for signs of Philippe or Eli. Or their bodies. She grieved for Philippe. Eli was a Deveraux, and she hoped he was dead.

But she had found nothing, and ultimately had made the choice to leave and continue searching for the girls.

"Blessed be," Rose breathed as Anne-Louise entered her house.

"Blessed be," Anne-Louise murmured.

Anise

A few minutes later the two women settled on a sofa with cups of tea in hand. Anne-Louise sipped the hot liquid gratefully. There was an art to good tea, and the British had spent centuries perfecting it.

"Not that I don't appreciate visitors, but why have you come?" Rose asked at last.

Anne-Louise raised a brow. "Can't you guess?"

The other woman paled, and an alarm went off in Anne-Louise's mind. Rose had done something, something that she didn't want the Mother Coven to find out about.

Anne-Louise was none too happy with the Mother Coven herself, but she couldn't let it go. At the very least, if she had something on Rose, it would be easier to obtain her help. She had played Mother Coven judge and jury on more than one occasion, just as she had when she had first been sent to meet with Holly.

She let her smile go cold and stared hard at the other woman. "So, why don't you tell me your side of it," she said.

It was a good opening. It would allow Rose to decide for herself just how much Anne-Louise knew, which would be likely to be a great deal.

"I was just trying to find Sasha, I swear," Rose blurted out.

Anne-Louise blinked, silently ordering Rose to go on. She'd no idea that Sasha was missing. No one had told her. Maybe no one else had realized it.

It's as if everyone who is connected to Holly has just . . . vanished.

"Dr. Frankenstein was looking for Kari, and we ran into each other online."

"What's his real name?" Anne-Louise asked.

"I don't know. I just know he's a professor at a university in Seattle."

"Go on," Anne-Louise ordered.

"He was quite cagey at the first, but he knew all about witches, knew what Kari had gotten herself into. I told him she was dead, and he informed me that that wasn't a problem." She took a breath, as if steeling herself to go on.

Anne-Louise remained silent, and Rose stumbled on.

"I . . . got some help, and we retrieved her body, preserved it, and shipped it to him." Her confessions then curled up, as though she were expecting Anne-Louise to lash out. "He was going to bring her back to life."

Anne-Louise was shocked. She knew of no magic that would do such a thing.

"How?" Anne-Louise asked. If he was calling himself Dr. Frankenstein, then she was willing to bet it wasn't through magic.

"I don't know. He was supposed to tell, if he was successful. But I haven't heard a thing." She swallowed hard. "I suppose that was naïve of me."

Anne-Louise sat for a moment studying Rose. She sipped her tea before addressing Rose again.

"You *suppose*?" she asked harshly. "You realize what you've done?"

"Yes. I've not only revealed our existence to an outsider, but I've also used magic selfishly and recklessly, in violation of my oath." Her voice shrank. "Because . . . because I wanted something more than this."

Anne-Louise looked around the safe house. It was actually owned by the Mother Coven, and Rose was allowed to live there and run it without cost to her. If the coven knew what she had done, she would doubtless lose her position.

"Wh-what's going to happen to me?" Rose asked.

"In light of recent losses and the upheaval here in the city. we will allow you to remain here, for now," Anne-Louise said.

Rose closed her eyes tightly. "Thank you."

"Don't thank me. You must know that the evil will come back to you threefold. That will likely be punishment enough."

Rose bowed her head in acceptance.

"However, what you have done must be undone. I will need from you the hairs you collected from Kari and her covenates—all of them."

"Of course," Rose said, scurrying into another

room. She returned with several bundles, neatly wrapped and labeled. Rose was nothing if not thorough. As a matter of course, she collected hairs from any who stayed in her home. A witch could use a person's hair to find them. An extremely powerful witch could use that same hair to summon. It was for this reason that Anne-Louise had come in the first place. Wherever Holly, Nicole, and Amanda were, they were well shielded, and she would need the hair to find them and warn them of what she knew.

Anne-Louise took the packets and tucked them away inside her coat. She took one last sip of her tea and stood, heading for the door. She touched her head, making sure she had left none of her own hair behind.

"Anne-Louise," Rose said, trailing after her.

"We'll be in touch," she said briskly, and stepped onto the busy London street, where none of the passersby had any idea that a witch walked among them.

Whisper the cat joined her. The familiar, who had suddenly appeared to her while she was recuperating from battle, trotted beside her, acquiescing when Anne-Louise picked her up.

"No warlocks. All is well," Whisper murmured into her ear.

The wind blew, and she hurried to the hotel where she planned to spend the night. A few months before, it would have been unthinkable for a member of the Mother Coven to flaunt their presence in the city. However, with the fall of the Supreme Coven headquarters, much had changed. The city was still the purview of warlocks, but they now lacked the centralized power and the guts to strike openly.

Later in her room, she ate a light supper. Whisper ate tinned cat food. Then Anne-Louise purified herself for Ritual, and drew a circle on the carpet with the hand lotion provided by the hotel. She placed candles at the four corners and sat down inside. Whisper paced the circle on velvet paws. Anne-Louise centered herself and began.

"Blessed be, a boon grant me; I seek Holly of Cahors witchery," she informed the unseen world. "Here is her hair; I ask 'where.'"

A wind blew through the room. The candles flickered.

And Whisper said, "Mumbai."

"You have got to be kidding me," Anne-Louise groaned, frustration rushing through her. "We must have been there at the same time."

She pushed the angry buzzing thoughts out of her head. They were unproductive and distracting.

Next she took Kari's hair. She was going to have to do something about her, although she had no idea what. She expected to discover that Kari was in Seattle.

Therefore, she was shocked when she had her answer.

"Scarborough," Whisper said.

Why would Kari be in Scarborough? What could she possibly be looking for there?

"Not what. Who," Whisper said.

"Who?" Anne-Louise asked.

The cat, however, just stared at her, tail flicking back and forth. On a hunch Anne-Louise tried Amanda's hair.

Scarborough.

She could get there by midday tomorrow, she realized, with dawning relief. She grabbed up the lock of Nicole's hair, but hesitated. Philippe had said that Nicole and Amanda had been together when he'd last seen them. Better to save Nicole's hair in case she should have need of finding one of the Cathers witches again.

She finished her ritual, closed the circle, and got ready for bed. All the time she kept wondering why it was that the twins were in Scarborough and why Kari had gone there too.

Whisper had no answers. The familiar curled up beside her on the mattress, cleaned her fur, and went to sleep.

Berlin: Jer

Jer wandered the streets of Berlin as a blind man. He didn't see any of the stores, or the people walking past, or the cars that nearly ran him over. All he saw was his life, glimpsed through Eve's eyes. And so he walked, and thought, the teddy bear tucked into the oversize pocket of his trench coat.

He was a Deveraux, and he had spent a long time trying to fight that, trying to somehow make it not true. He realized now that had been a mistake. All his friends, Eddie, Kialish, Dan, Kari, they had all died for his vanity. How many lives could he have saved if he had just killed his father one night while he was sleeping? Instead he had tried to play the white knight even though he knew very well that he wasn't and never could be. And then because of his own selfishness, his own obsession with what he couldn't be, he had pushed away Holly.

Time to stop feeling sorry for myself. Time to stop making excuses. Time to man up.

He pulled the teddy bear out of his pocket and stared at it long and hard. His childhood had been anything but normal. At some point, though, he had to take responsibility for himself, for his own actions and reactions.

His wandering footsteps led him back to the site of the Berlin Wall. He stared at the monument long and hard. So much in life was beyond a person's control, just like the Black Fire that his family mistakenly believed they could harness. They might be able to create it, but they couldn't control it.

Other things, though, were in the individual's hands. One could choose to be miserable. One could also choose to stop.

Jer took a deep breath . . . and chose.

Scarborough:
Nicole, Amanda, Tommy, Richard, Owen, Kari, and the cats

"Are you going to Scarborough Fair? Parsley, sage, rosemary and thyme."

Nicole sighed as she took a piece of each herb and threw it into the soup she was attempting to make. She consulted the cookbook once more and then wrinkled up her nose as she got a good whiff. *More like I'm cooking up a witch's brew.*

"Remember me to one who lives there."

Her thoughts flew to Philippe, and she sent up another prayer that the Goddess would protect him and guide him safely back to her. She missed him so much; and she needed his steadying presence and his wisdom. He was her anchor, as Amanda once had been.

But now she avoided Amanda, afraid she would bring up the prophecy again. Demand they kill Owen. The arrival of Kari had given everyone pause.

A reprieve.

"Then she'll be a true love of mine."

"Song?" Kari said, intruding on her thoughts as she

trudged into the kitchen and stared down at Nicole's soup pot.

"Song? The song? What do you mean?" Nicole asked, puzzled.

"Constant. Tommy, Amanda, you," Kari said.

A chill danced up Nicole's spine. She tried to keep her tone light. "Well, we live in Scarborough. I guess that just kind of gets in your head, and *voilà!* Song."

Kari shook her head. "Spell," she said.

Nicole took a breath. "No, it's not a spell," she said uncertainly. She looked at the dead girl's eyes. "Do you *know* that it's a spell?"

Kari made no answer.

Nicole felt cold. And frightened. "How about a Christmas carol, then? Do you have a favorite?"

Kari shook her head.

Can the dead have a favorite anything? Nicole wondered. And could a soul that had gone to hell have a favorite Christmas carol?

"We three kings of Orient are," Nicole began to sing.

"Bearing gifts we travel so far," Tommy chimed in as he walked into the kitchen.

"You're both in a good mood," Richard noted as he joined them.

Nicole shrugged and smiled at her father. It was a fake smile, but she'd charmed her father with it for years.

"Where's Owen?" she asked.

"Amanda has him," Tommy said.

"No," she blurted.

"Dungeon," Kari said.

Tommy shook his head. "We looked, Kari. There's no dungeon."

Kari shook her head. Nicole came over to her and put her hands on her shoulders.

"Kari, are you saying that Amanda—"

"I hear my name," Amanda said, entering the kitchen with a sleepy-eyed Owen. "He insisted on getting up," she explained.

"Give him to me," Nicole almost shouted.

"Is there something wrong?" Richard asked.

Suddenly the house shook. The liquid in Nicole's pot sloshed over the sides, and she cried out and clutched Owen hard. He began to cry.

"Oh, man, not again!" Tommy blurted out as he grabbed hold of the counter to steady himself.

Richard was already in motion, throwing open the refrigerator and rummaging behind a carton of milk and a block of cheese. He pulled out two Micro Uzis and handed one to Tommy.

"I hope it's not another dragon," Tommy said, looping the strap around his neck.

Owen wailed. Amanda reached over and turned off the stove.

"I hope it is. At least I know how to kill those," Richard growled. "Girls, time to get out."

Nicole grabbed Amanda's arm and tugged her toward the door. Before they could take two steps, the wall exploded, showering them with bits of stone. A dozen tiny flecks cut into Nicole's scalp and arms as she curled herself around her baby.

Then a giant figure more than seven feet tall strode through the debris. It looked vaguely human, but it was covered in dark matted fur that reeked of death and decay. As Nicole scrabbled backward, it threw back its head and made a screeching sound.

Every nerve ending in Nicole's body convulsed in pain; she screamed and covered Owen's ears. She would have fallen if her legs hadn't locked along with the rest of her muscles. Beside her, Amanda whimpered.

But Owen began laughing and waving his chubby arms in the air.

Tommy found his voice first. "Goddess let my legs unroot and make this creature become mute."

As spells went, it was one of the most ridiculous things Nicole had ever heard. A moment later, though, the creature threw its head back again, but no sound came out.

She regained the use of her muscles just in time for Tommy to push her, Amanda, and Owen down and cover them with his own body. Richard sent a hail of bullets at the creature, but it only grunted and swatted at them as if at flies.

"What is that thing?" Amanda screeched.

"Yowie," Kari said, seated on a stool, her face and voice passive.

Nicole grabbed Kari by the ankle, and wished she hadn't. She shuddered as she felt the unnatural cold of Kari's flesh. "What is a yowie?"

"Australian aboriginal myth. Bigfoot. Cannibal," Kari reported.

"How do we kill it?" Richard asked.

"I don't know," Kari said.

"We need to do magic. These bullets aren't doing it," Tommy shouted.

The yowie looked around at all of them before setting eyes on Owen. With a roar he lunged toward him.

"No!" Nicole screamed, raising up on her knees. With her free hand she sent a fireball into the creature's chest, but all it did was singe the fur a little bit.

The creature reached down and grabbed Owen out of her arms. Nicole screamed; Amanda shouted something that Nicole couldn't understand, as Tommy and Richard halted fire.

"Owen!" Nicole shrieked.

Amanda shouted again. Owen slid from the monster's grasp, and Richard dove forward, grabbing the baby as he fell.

Amanda shouted a third time.

And then the yowie exploded, in a shower of organs and tissue and fur and blood, coating them all.

There was complete silence for a moment. Then Tommy fell to his knees, gagging. Nicole grabbed Owen. Both of them were covered in blood and intestines. Kari still had not moved.

"What did you do?" Nicole asked Amanda.

Amanda shook her head.

"What was it you said?"

"I don't know," Amanda admitted, her voice barely a whisper. "I just knew I couldn't let him get Owen. Then everything went a little . . . fuzzy . . . for a second, and then boom."

"Is everyone okay?" Richard asked.

Nicole looked around. With everyone drenched in blood and gore it was hard to tell what injuries they had sustained. She knew she had cuts from the exploding rock, and she guessed the others must as well.

Richard opened the drawer containing dish towels, wet down several, and tossed them to people. Nicole wiped as much of the muck off her baby as she could. He smiled at her as if nothing had happened.

A minute later they were able to assess their injuries. Only she, Amanda, and Tommy had been hit by the flying shrapnel. Richard and Kari had both been far enough to one side that they hadn't gotten hit.

Nicole continued to clean the gore off Owen. She would have to bathe him.

In water.

She spied Hecate, slinking through the wreckage. The cat Holly had drowned. Panicking, she clutched Owen against her chest.

"Hold up a second," Richard said, bending down next to them. He carefully turned Owen's head, took the dish towel from Nicole, and wiped the boy's head. "Looks like he did get one pretty nasty cut. That's going to leave a scar, but it should be mostly hidden by his hair."

Nicole couldn't bring herself to look. Instead she locked eyes with Amanda and saw her fear mirrored in her twin's gaze. "Where?"

"Here, behind his left ear," Richard said.

The mark behind the sinister ear. The world tilted, and for a moment she thought she was going to faint. Amanda bent over double and began to vomit.

"Grab only what you have to have. We're getting out of here," Richard said.

Nicole couldn't have agreed more.

EIGHT

CINNAMON

☾

Deveraux reign in numbers strong
We know no right, only wrong
And as we play with God's own fire
We'll burn the witches on a pyre

Old moon, full moon in our sight
We dance and weep in Goddess light
The year turns as we spin about
All is change and we must not doubt

Outside Mumbai:
Holly, Pablo, Armand, Alex, and the Temple of the Air

Holly hadn't felt such fear in a long time. *What's wrong with you? You've led thousands of warriors, alive and dead, into battle. You are the most powerful Cahors witch alive, perhaps ever. You can do this.*

Somewhere in her mind she heard a shadowy laugh that seemed to echo, getting louder with each moment.

Beside her, Pablo breathed in great, ragged gasps. She could smell fear rolling off him. Pablo, who rarely showed any emotion; Pablo, who was usually so fear-less.

Something was terribly wrong. Fear and confusion battled for control of her mind. Her entire body began to shake, and she felt a creeping numbness in her hands and feet. She opened her mouth to cast a spell, and only a tinny squeak came out.

She turned to Pablo and saw the terror in his eyes. He opened and closed his mouth as though trying to say something.

Wrong . . . wrong.

It was Pablo's voice inside her head, but it was as though he were speaking slowly, slurring his words.

Have we been drugged? she wondered wildly.

Out of the dark, monsters came—gray and leath-ery demons with reptilian eyes, winged batlike shapes with glistening fangs and talons in their cheeks. Half a dozen cloaked and hooded warlocks appeared behind them, lobbing magical bolts of energy at the Temple of the Air.

"Go, go, go!" Alex bellowed, giving better than he got. He stood in front of his people, legs wide apart, a fierce warrior.

Holly forced her hands up and tried to conjure a fireball. It flickered for a moment on her fingertips before winking out of existence.

A horned demon with red skin picked her up in

his giant fist. *I'm going to be killed by Hellboy,* she thought as she struggled to free herself from his iron grip. The demon laughed, his sulfurous breath making her eyes tear painfully.

With his free hand he swiped with taloned fingers at Pablo and the boy went down with a gaping wound in his stomach.

No! Holly kicked and clawed and prayed for the ability to perform a single spell. There was no surge of power, no appearance of a black veiled woman, be it the Goddess or her own evil ancestress Catherine.

The demon squeezed harder, and her ribs cracked, making her grunt. She bit him, and thick black blood oozed into her mouth. As she gagged, the demon laughed harder and spoke in a voice that shook the ground.

"You would drink my blood, little witch? Do you think you are a Cursed One? You are nothing, just a child, and a very foolish one at that. You will die, and when you do, there isn't anything that will make it out of this human shell."

That voice . . .

"Yes, you know me," the demon said as he clapped his free hand over his wound. It had already stopped bleeding. "You know me, Holly Cathers. You saw me die."

And she had, back in the headquarters of the

Supreme Coven, in London. He had crumpled to the floor, and then this . . . this monster had pushed out of him.

"Sir William," she gasped. It was over, then. He was going to kill her.

He smirked. "In the spirit, so to speak. And don't worry. I've been keeping an eye on your cousins, and they will die next."

She was dying; she could feel it. Her heart was pounding too fast and too hard. It was going to explode. The rest of her body tingled with shock. A cold numbness poured through her veins; it was just as well—she didn't want it to hurt anymore.

Utterly defeated, she closed her eyes. And thought of Jer.

Then someone was shouting her name, but she didn't know who it was. Was it Jer? Was the Goddess kind after all, uniting them in death?

"Holly, for the love of the Goddess!"

She opened her eyes again. Armand was standing behind the demon, hitting it with everything he had. She remained defeated, then.

If Armand can't kill it, no one can.

Suddenly Sir William bellowed. With a roar of fury he dropped her. She hit the ground hard, her limbs flopping.

"You bastard. Die!"

Cinnamon

Alex charged Sir William, his hands lifted, magic shooting like thunderbolts at their sworn enemy. He scored direct hits against Sir William's huge horned head. A talon ripped from its nail bed. Alex hit his chest. Behind him Armand showered his back with fireballs.

She smelled burning flesh.

Then Sir William threw back one arm and swiped at Alex. He was going to hit him.

No!

She tried to call to him, warn him.

But she was out of the fight, as everything went black.

Berlin: Jer and Eve

Eve had been right: Jer found her easily. When he knocked on her door at two in the morning, he was only slightly surprised to find her dressed and packed.

"I'm here," he said, because in the end that was all that needed to be said.

She nodded. "I just found out where your girl-friend is. We'll have to move fast, because she's in a lot of trouble."

Scarborough:
Nicole, Owen, Amanda, Tommy, Richard, Kari, and the cats

Prisoners.

Nicole smelled gingerbread and pine as she watched the snow tumble down into haystack-size drifts in the yard. The topiary animals were frosted white. Anger and fear churned in her stomach as the clock ticked the countdown to Yule. She wanted to be anywhere but there, with the zombielike Kari, Osiris, and her lost, beloved Hecate.

With her father in the lead, they had fled, but as they drove past the gate that marked the property, Owen became sick and pale. She, Amanda, and Tommy murmured incantations over him, but nothing worked. Richard was about to drive him to the hospital when Kari said dully, "Turn back. Baby . . . dies."

Back they went, like prisoners, and as soon as they were past the gate again, Owen regained his pink glow and waved his chubby little hands in the air. They were stuck.

So they decided to concentrate on making sure they were safe inside the house. No more surprise visits from yowies. The sisters strengthened all their wards, summoned Lawyer Derek. He arrived with a Yule gift—a plum pudding—and they made him inspect their magical work and check the warlock magic that had been installed as well.

"I'm surprised something got through all the wards," he told them.

"Who do I sue?" Nicole asked hotly.

He also showed them how to put magic spells on

their ammunition, so that when shots were fired, a spell as well as a bullet would hit their target. Actually, he used the word "enemy" in place of "target."

He said aloud what Nicole silently feared. Dragon and yowie aside, they were safer in House Moore than anywhere else in England—or the world, for that matter. The Cahors witches had a lot of enemies.

"So you don't think it was the Deveraux," he said, dressed for the season in a black suit, holly and mistletoe pinned to his lapel. Red and green were the Deveraux colors, from perhaps milder days when they'd honored the Horned God in his incarnation as the Green Man. Cahors colors were black and silver, and Nicole wore silver whenever she could. Real silver was said to ward off werewolves and other creatures of evil; she hoped it kept her and her loved ones safe.

"No," Nicole said, as she and the others drank spiced wine with him. They were seated in the castle section, watching a log blaze in the hearth. She and Amanda had agreed not to tell Derek about Merlin's Book or the prophecy. Why should they? He was affiliated with the Supreme Coven.

He stretched out his long legs. "And you haven't heard from them."

His voice was casual, but Nicole heard the tension in it, the eagerness. She wondered if there was a bounty on the heads of the two brothers.

Stay away, Eli, she thought, rocking Owen in her arms. *I think these people want to hurt you.*

But part of her wanted Eli to show up at her door. They'd been a wild pair, the extreme couple people would talk about all over Seattle—Eli Deveraux and his wild-child underage girlfriend, Niki Anderson. Drinking too much, driving too fast, making out while somewhere in their house Eli's father, Michael Deveraux, did bad things. Unimaginable things. And boinked Nicole and Amanda's mother. . . .

Michael and Mom are both dead now, she thought. She wished with all her heart that her mother could see Richard now—their own Special Forces guy, their warrior, their protector. He had spent years trying to forget that he'd been a fighting man; Nicole was glad down to her soul that he hadn't succeeded.

"No," she said. "Nothing."

After Derek left, Richard, Amanda, and Tommy started decorating the Christmas tree. It was a weak attempt at normalcy, but there could be power in the act. Christmas trees were part of the Wicca celebration of Yule, as well as traditional Christmas. The first tree Richard had brought into House Moore three days before had been a healthy, living tree, complete with a root ball, and he'd hoped to plant it in the garden after the holiday season was over. But it had shriveled up as soon as he'd brought it inside—the needles had turned brown and fallen off. It had died inside House Moore.

Was it because it was a living thing, and we didn't invite it? Nicole thought anxiously. They hadn't formally invited Kari, or either of the cats.

They're not living things.

She started shaking. The urge to bail was almost overwhelming. When Holly had still led their coven, Nicole had split for Europe, trying to leave it all behind. But Michael Deveraux's minions had trailed after her, sometimes as crows, other times as menacing shadows that had slid down the walls of buildings as she'd passed them. She still remembered sitting in the chilled dimness of Cologne Cathedral in Cologne, Germany. The bones of the Three Wise Men were buried there, in an incredible golden box studded with stones. Light glinted off the faces of the saints as she sat on the hard pew, inhaling incense and age, trying to pray but dozing off. A priest had confronted her, assuming she was homeless, and telling her she would have to leave. So much for sanctuary in the house of the Lord.

Outside, the shadows had waited for her. Through the stone, stained glass, and raised voices of the choir, she heard hundreds of crows, minions of Michael Deveraux. She felt their evil mushrooming over the cathedral like a poisonous fog. She'd cut herself off from Amanda and Holly to escape their magical heritage, but instead she had made herself vulnerable.

She had left the cathedral heavier with fear than when she had entered it. And the shadows had found her at last on the island of Avalon, where James Moore had kept her prisoner. Then Eli snuck in, and rescued her.

He loves me. He does. It's more than lust and possessiveness.

Her throat tightened at the confusion she felt. She was in thrall with Philippe, and he was a good man, a better man than Eli ever could be. Unless the bones of the Three Wise Men could perform miracles, as many claimed. . . .

"Nicole, what do you think, more tinsel?" Tommy asked, breaking her from her reverie.

She smiled faintly. He was a good man too. Amanda was lucky to have found her one true love. They were trying to decide how to get married—if they should invite a vicar to House Moore, which might raise questions or go terribly awry (especially if the man met Kari or tried to pet one of the cats), or go into Scarborough to have a civil ceremony. However they did it, she envied them; she certainly didn't see a traditional white wedding in her future. And her forced marriage ceremony with James had been a nightmare.

"It's on the side you can't see," he said.

Cinnamon

As she rose, Owen leaned toward Tommy, cooing. Tommy held out his arms for the baby. It was still very difficult for her to let anyone else take him, but Tommy was Owen's uncle in all but name. So she gave him her child, kissing Owen's little head as she did so, and approached the tree.

Brilliant silver ornaments glittered and gleamed. Dressed in jeans and a dark blue cabled sweater, her father was perched on a ladder, straining to put a silver five-pointed star on top of the tree. Some said the pentagram and the Star of Bethlehem were one and the same—that each Wiccan rite was in truth a salute to the Christian God. There was so much they didn't know. And Nicole didn't know whom to ask.

Amanda was looping silver garland over the branches. Kari sat in a chair with a steaming mug of cider on a small octagonal table to her left. Osiris and Hecate lay at Kari's feet; Hecate looked up as Nicole brushed past, and glided toward her.

"Hi, kitty," Nicole said warmly, but secretly Hecate frightened her. She wanted to be glad that her cat was back from the dead, but she could hardly stand to touch her.

Her father smiled at her, but she could tell old memories were pressing heavily on him. He came down the ladder as she walked to him, and he put his arms around her. She wanted to sink against him and cry. She wasn't even nineteen yet, but she was a mother and a widow. She'd thought that at nineteen she'd be in college majoring in drama, or maybe even in L.A. breaking into the business.

Her attention ticked toward Kari, who stood up like a robot. Kari said, "Someone is coming."

Sure enough, invisible bells clanged, signaling that one of their wards had been set off. Richard let go of Nicole and stepped in front of her, reaching for a machine gun. Nicole had protested about the spells on their ammunition—what if one of them was accidentally shot? But as she stood behind her father now, she was glad no one had listened to her.

Tommy handed Owen to Amanda and picked up another weapon. Amanda frowned slightly but hung back, sidling over to Nicole.

"We're two of the most powerful witches in the world," Amanda drawled, "but our menfolk are protecting us."

"What if it's someone . . ." Nicole swallowed hard as she took Owen from her sister. His little baby head smelled so sweet. His hair was like silk. "What if it's Owen's father?" She felt faint.

"Then we'll know who he is." Amanda kissed Owen's head. "We'll protect you, baby." She smiled sweetly at Nicole and added, "And you, Niki. We'll protect you both."

Cinnamon

Nicole felt a rush of shame. Amanda had probably never realized just how much she, Nicole, depended on her. She'd been so caught up in the drama of her own life that she'd needed Amanda to balance her out. Back in high school she'd thought Amanda was boring and uncool, and she had excluded her whenever possible.

"I just had a really bad thought," Amanda murmured. She nodded in Kari's direction. "Maybe we should send her out, see if anything happens to her."

"Oh, my God, that's . . . practical," Nicole replied, bouncing Owen in her arms. "If anything ever happens to me . . ." She trailed off as Owen made little gurgling sounds and stared at the door. If anything ever happened to her, she'd come back from hell itself to watch over her child. Come back, or live in it. That was, if her child wasn't there with her. If she hadn't had to send him there herself. She tried not to glance at the scar he now had behind his left ear, but like a magnet it drew her eyes. There were three signs. He had only two. It was going to be okay.

More wards chimed, signaling an unrecognized presence. Richard handed Amanda a scrying stone. He couldn't see the image of their visitor in the piece of crystal, but she could.

She gasped. "It's Anne-Louise Montrachet," she announced. "With a familiar."

249

"Anne-Louise," Nicole said happily. "I can't believe it."

Anne-Louise had been their liaison with the Mother Coven, and a dear and loyal friend to them. She had been wounded defending them from Michael Deveraux, and they hadn't seen her since.

Amanda hurried toward the door, but Richard and Tommy blocked her way. "It might be a trap," Richard said, as he cautiously opened it.

Amanda peered around him. It was Anne-Louise at the gate. She was dressed for winter travel in a long white coat and matching white boots, and in her arms she held a slinky gray feline with large golden-yellow eyes.

"Oh, thank Goddess," Anne-Louise called.

"Wait!" Amanda warned her. "Nicole has to invite you in."

"I invite you, Anne-Louise," Nicole cried. "And your familiar, too."

"His name is Whisper," Anne-Louise said as she ran up to the house and practically leaped over the threshold. Her eyes misted at the sight of the twin sisters and their loved ones, and her face softened when Owen cooed at her.

"Precious child," she said, raising her hand in benediction over him. She paused, as if she wanted to say more—maybe to ask who his father was—but

let it go as she glanced around the castle in amazement, and then turned to a waiting car. "I have a small
suitcase."

"I'll get that," Richard said, trotting out into the
cold as he shut the heavy door behind himself.

"Why are you here?" Amanda asked. "Not that
we're not happy to see you, but . . ."

"I couldn't risk a phone call or an e-mail," Anne-
Louise replied, lowering her voice. She hesitated. "Is
this place well warded?"

"Yes," Nicole assured her. "With our magic, and
warlock magic too."

Anne-Louise paled slightly. Then she nodded. "As
a Moore and a Cathers witch, you're afforded excel-
lent protection. But I have terrible news. I performed
a series of rituals in search of other members of your
family, and I had a vision. Alex Carruthers isn't related
to you. He's an imposter. And he has gone into the
past, and changed it."

Amanda glanced at Nicole, then back at Anne-
Louise. Nicole was silently shaking her head, as if she
didn't want to hear any more.

Anne-Louise came forward and took Amanda's
hand, and then Nicole's, whose hand was icy. Nicole
swallowed hard. Cradled against Anne-Louise's chest,
Whisper stared at the two Cathers witches.

Gone into the past?" Amanda asked.

"Who is he?" Nicole demanded.

"I don't know, but I have my suspicions. Whisper and I have sensed great evil, terrible power . . . and I think Alex Carruthers may actually be the Duc Laurent de Deveraux, come back from the dead."

Nicole felt the floor give way. Anne-Louise's hand around hers was firm, strong. Warmth radiated from it to Nicole, and she stood firm.

"Back from the dead. Like her?" Amanda asked, glancing at Kari.

"Oh, child," Anne-Louise said to Kari as Kari turned toward her. "Powerful magics are at work. I think he plans to reunite the Deveraux family and wage war."

"On the Mother Coven?" Amanda asked. Nicole was chilled to the bone.

Anne-Louise shook her head. "On the world." She gazed around at the castle walls, then at the girls. "On anyone who stands against him. He wants to marshal all the forces of darkness and pit them against us, and humanity."

"Holly," Nicole breathed.

"We've been searching for her," Anne-Louise said. So far, we've been unsuccessful."

"Oh, God," Nicole breathed. "What if he's killed her?"

"I don't think he has. Yet," she said. "Michael Deveraux drove your cousin out of her mind. She became possessed by demons, and he used her against you, until the exorcism. But a warlock as powerful as Laurent de Deveraux would be fully capable of doing it again—on a much more intense level."

"Is that what you meant about changing the past?" Amanda asked.

"I'm not sure what I mean," Anne-Louise said. "But things are not as they should be. Whisper appeared to tell me. We're living in a world that has been altered."

They looked at one another in horror. Just then Richard came back into the castle carrying a small white suitcase.

"What did I miss?" he asked.

"Oh, Daddy," Nicole cried, "it's . . . it's wrong. Something's wrong." Tears slid down Nicole's face. It never ended. They would never be safe. What kind of world had she brought her baby into?

"What do you mean?" Richard asked. He turned to Anne-Louise. "What's going on?"

"As you know, Philippe left you because he received a psychic plea for help from Pablo. Our paths crossed in Mumbai."

"Philippe. Is he coming too?" Nicole asked, wishing with all her being.

"India?" Richard asked. "What on earth—"

"A swami warned me that some kind of balance had been damaged. He mentioned the Temple of the

Sun. I thought he was speaking of Machu Picchu, in Peru. But we pointed out that it's called the Pyramid of the Sun. The Temple of the Sun is a term used in Zoroastrian magics."

"Zoro-what?" Tommy asked, putting his arms around Amanda. She laid her head on his shoulder. As if sensing that Nicole needed comfort too, Richard put his arm around her shoulder.

"Zoroastrianism is a faith, a magical system," Anne-Louise explained. "Many believe that the Three Wise Men in the biblical story of the Christ's nativity were Zoroastrian sorcerers. Wizards. And they were astrologers, which is why they were aware of the star in the east."

"Cologne," Nicole said softly. As the others looked at her, she said, "Their bones are kept in a big gold box in the cathedral there."

"All three of them? It must be a big box," Tommy said.

"We of the Mother Coven believe there may have been more than three sorcerers who went to visit the Christ," Anne-Louise continued. She looked tired and frightened. "It is traditional to assume there were only three, as there were only three gifts mentioned in the story—gold, frankincense, and myrrh. But there could easily have been more, and more gifts as well. Magical offerings are occult. Hidden."

Tommy grimaced. "I wonder where Duc Laurent's bones are hidden. Maybe if we destroy them, or put a hex on them . . ."

Then Whisper spoke. "It's too late. The past has been altered, and unless he is stopped, he will win."

Everyone stared at the cat. Nicole said, "Who are you?"

"I am a messenger of the Goddess," Whisper announced. "I, too, seek Holly Cathers, who sacrificed the familiar Hecate." Whisper looked at Nicole's zombie-cat. "Alas, handmaiden."

Hecate growled low in her throat, and silence fell over the room.

"You won't hurt Holly," Amanda said to Whisper. "We won't let you."

"She and I will deal with each other on another occasion," Whisper replied. "I seek her power. Time has been altered. She must help me set it to rights."

"She's with Duc Laurent. Two others are with her too," Amanda continued, quaking.

"The Christian witches Pablo and Armand," Whisper said, dipping her head. "I know."

"We have to save them," Amanda insisted.

"Or stop them," Richard added, "if he's bewitched them."

Everyone fell silent. It was too terrible to contemplate.

"What about Jer and Eli?" Tommy asked. "Have you seen them?"

"Not Jer, but I have seen Eli."

At that Anne-Louise stopped talking and averted her eyes.

There's more bad news, Nicole thought, feeling her stomach clench.

"Have a seat and I'll get you some hot tea," Richard said in the silence.

Anne-Louise took off her coat and chose a seat. The others sat down too and there was a stillness, a heaviness in the air that had nothing to do with what Anne-Louise had said and everything to do with what she hadn't said.

Richard handed her some tea, and she sipped it for a moment before putting it aside and clearing her throat. "In Mumbai, Philippe and I ran into Eli. There was a fight. Both of them fell into a lake . . . and they didn't come out."

Nicole stared at Anne-Louise. "What do you mean, they didn't come out?"

Amanda burst into tears. Tommy and Richard looked stricken.

"What do you mean?" Nicole shouted.

Owen wailed.

"I think they both drowned," Anne-Louise said with pity in her eyes.

"That stupid curse," Tommy said.

Those beloved of a Cahors died by drowning. Nicole shuddered, and when Richard grabbed Owen out of her arms, she didn't object. Philippe and Eli. Dead. James. Dead. And still she felt deep inside of her that Owen's father was coming for him.

"Help me," she whispered, going boneless, falling, as everything dissolved into a scream.

A few minutes later she awoke on the couch. Anxious faces slid into her view.

Owen, I want you out of this, Nicole thought, despairing. *I don't want you to have anything to do with this. I'll take you away.* But she knew she couldn't.

Philippe and Eli dead. She wanted to cry, to scream, to blame someone, anyone, and lock herself in her room. But she knew she couldn't do that, either.

She knew exactly what she had to do. She sat up slowly and cleared her throat. "We need to talk about the prophecy," she said, looking at Amanda. "We have to tell Anne-Louise about Owen."

Amanda heaved a sigh. "I've been waiting for you to say that, Niki. I didn't think it was my place."

"What about Owen?" Richard planted himself between his grandson and Anne-Louise.

"Save the world," Kari murmured. "Save."

Amanda moved from the protective circle of Tommy's arms and held up her and Nicole's scarred palms. The two thirds of the lily they formed with Holly's palm glowed very slightly.

"Yes," Nicole choked out. She was in agony. Every fiber of her being shouted at her to protect her child at all costs.

All costs.

But she couldn't.

"We have to tell you this so we can save the world." She swallowed hard. "My son was brought into this world to destroy it."

Then she told them everything—or at least, everything she knew.

Because, as Anne-Louise had said, the ways of the occult were hidden.

Mumbai: Eli and Philippe

I'm alive, Eli thought. *But I drowned. . . .*

And then he remembered: beneath the water, losing consciousness, and there had been a flash of light, and a woman with long flowing hair had reached out and touched his hand. A woman who had risen from the depths of the lake and saved him.

He sat up with a groan and opened his eyes. There were white sheets pulled around a hospital bed . . . and Philippe was sitting nearby on a rickety wooden chair, watching him closely.

Eli gritted his teeth. "There was a lady in the

lake . . ." He thought about what he was saying. It sounded like something out of a fairy tale.

Philippe nodded slowly. "I think it was your mother, Sasha Deveraux."

Eli blinked. "My mother is trapped back in the Dark Ages—in the time of Isabeau and Jean."

"She seems to have found a way back." Philippe shrugged like the Frenchman he was.

"Where is she?" Eli demanded.

Philippe shook his head. "I don't know. I saw her grab you before I lost consciousness. Then I woke up here a while ago, and made them bring me to you."

A while ago. Philippe could have killed him while he was sleeping. The thought put Eli into an even darker mood. A part of him wanted to strike now, when the witch wasn't expecting it and would be less able to protect himself.

He shook his head. As much as he wanted Philippe dead, things had changed.

"Where are we?"

"It's a hospital."

They exchanged looks. Philippe seemed to be waiting for something.

"I'm betting witch and warlock conjuring magic together can be awesome," Eli said.

"Or an abomination," Philippe replied steadily.

"To find Nicole, and my mother."

"Oui." Philippe held out his hand.

Eli frowned. And then he took it. "Let's agree to kill each other once this is all over."

"Agreed." Philippe's eyes flashed; so male witches weren't so different from warlocks after all.

"Good. Now let's get to work," Eli said.

Outside Mumbai:
Holly, Alex, Pablo, Armand, and the Temple of the Air

Night was falling, shielding the Temple of the Air from the harsh glare of the sun. Those who worshipped the Goddess performed their rites and rituals by moonlight, especially the most solemn and binding.

Standing on the banks of a lake, sandalwood scenting the darkening air, Armand and Pablo kept vigil over Holly as she prepared herself to be put in thrall with her distant cousin Alex Carruthers. Evil was gathering around them like a storm. They had all felt it, seen it—demonic figures in the darkness skulking around them, planning, plotting, waiting. The minions of Sir William.

Alex had managed to send Sir William running, but the battle had been brutal. Four of the Temple of the Air had been killed in the attack. Pablo had been gravely wounded, and although they had done what they could for him, he still moved carefully, so as not to tear open the stomach wound again.

Holly herself was a little faster to mend, but her cracked ribs were still sore and caused her pain with every movement. She hadn't been able to sleep for more than fifteen minutes without reliving the terror of what had happened.

It couldn't happen again. They had to be ready, prepared, stronger than they were now if they hoped to kill Sir William in his demonic form. And he was only the harbinger, the messenger that the darkest of days were upon them.

She and Alex had tossed the runes; they had all seen the signs; and they knew something worse was coming—something terrible, and overwhelming. Something that could end the world as they knew it.

When Alex had first asked Holly to join forces with him back in London, she'd known this day would come. Enthrallment was their only option.

And yet . . .

Nothing. I have always made the hardest choices. I've done whatever I could to protect my people. I can't do any less to protect my world.

She wore all white, like a bride, and her black curly hair cascaded over her shoulders. A crown of laurel circled her head, and as she faced the dying sun, she wept silently for her hopeless love, for Jeraud Deveraux, who had rejected her.

Jer, her renegade warlock, who had insisted that

he was too tainted by darkness to be joined with her, but she knew he had fought against that darkness all his life. And won. It wasn't Jer the warlock who had turned away from her, but Jer the hideously scarred man.

When he looked in a mirror, he saw a monster. He couldn't believe that when she looked at him, she saw love made flesh—a thing of indescribable beauty. His shame hid the shining mirror of her soul from his eyes. She understood now that love could heal anything, but it was a gift that had to be accepted. If Jer let her love him enough, he would see how handsome he really was.

But he couldn't. Maybe life with Michael and Eli had broken him beyond repair.

I don't believe that. There is no one on this earth who can't be saved by love—

No, I don't believe that, *either. I've done terrible things, sacrificed loved ones. . . . I bargained with the Goddess, and with Catherine, to give me enough power to save other loved ones. I can't be forgiven. I knew what I was doing, and I did it willingly.*

"Holly," Alex said softly, coming up behind her. "It's almost time." She heard the eagerness in his voice. Kneeling on the ground on either side of her with swords planted in the ground, Armand and Pablo shifted.

She turned her back on the sun, wishing that moonrise would never come. No, that wasn't so; she was eager too. They could weave stronger magic if they worked together, bound themselves each to the other. . . .

He was handsome, and he was good. Dressed all in white like her—a white tunic over leggings, very medieval, like her white shift. Warmth radiated from him as he protected himself against the bitter cold. He, too, wore a crown of laurel, magically conjured, like their clothes.

"I know," he said gently, cupping her cheek. His hand was warm satin. He smelled of cleansing cinnamon. "About Jer. And your love for him."

"I'm sorry," she said. "It'll fade. In time."

"No, don't let it fade," he said. "Love is powerful. We'll need all the power we can muster, for the coming days."

It was as if he had read her mind. Perhaps he had.

"But we'll be in thrall," she said as shadows lengthened and trickled around her feet, spreading over the glassy surface of the lake, and reminding her of the pools of blood they had seen in their attacks on the strongholds of the Supreme Coven. Once they were bound, there would be more blood, and more carnage. They would bring death. When would it end?

"You'll know that I'm thinking of him, not you."

"Holly, we follow *Notre Dame,* the Lady Mother, who loves all Her children equally," he reminded her. "I can rise above my petty jealousies."

But you hated him, she thought. *I saw how much. And I know he hates you.*

He didn't respond. Maybe he couldn't read her thoughts after all.

The sun winked out, disappearing behind the craggy mountaintops. Armand and Pablo got to their feet and faced the couple. The four stood quietly, waiting for the moon to rise, and the enthrallment to begin. Somewhere in the gathering darkness were Alex's followers, keeping watch against the things that would try to stop this bonding.

"Give me your sword," Alex ordered Armand.

The Spanish witch hesitated. He looked at Holly for a long time, as if to ask, *Are you certain?*

Sometime: Sasha

Sasha screamed in frustration as she rained her fists on solid walls of colored crystal. She had pulled Eli and Philippe from the lake and had just made it to shore when she had suddenly disappeared. She must have hit the magical time device against something, because it had started spinning so fast that she couldn't even tell in which direction. Her fingers were bleeding where they had finally caught and stopped the moons.

Cinnamon

Now she lay inside what appeared to be a cave made out of crystal. Was this the distant past or the far future? She had no way of telling, and if she spun the moons, she risked choosing wrong and sending herself even farther in the wrong direction.

There was a sudden flash and a man appeared before her, wearing long dark robes spangled with comets, moons, and suns brushing the prismatic surface beneath her elbows. His face was angular and powerful, though lined, and his hair and long beard were white.

He bent down, and she thought he meant to help her up. But before she could stop him, he pried the device from her hand.

"Thank you, my dear." He spoke in a British accent as he clutched the moon-spinner against his chest.

"For what?" But she knew. She looked at the time machine in his arms.

"Returning that which is rightfully mine." He ran his long forefinger over the moons. "My brothers stole it from me so very long ago."

"Your brothers."

"Yes." He didn't elaborate.

"When am I?" she asked.

He smiled. "Strictly speaking, we're outside of time. Trapped. Frozen."

"Who are you?" she asked.

265

"That is the first question you should have asked me," he said with a bow. "I am Gushnasaph."

She blinked. The name meant nothing to her, and yet obviously he expected that it would. She shook her head.

He raised himself up proudly. "The fourth Magi, the one who gave the Christ child silver."

"There were only three wise men," she said.

He muttered something under his breath that sounded like a curse, and his eyes flashed darkly. "Perhaps, then, you know me by the name those barbarian Britons called me. Myrddin."

That name she did know. Shuddering, she stared up into the eyes of the dark wizard Merlin and knew with dawning horror that she was about to die.

NINE

HAWTHORNE

☾

Now the time has come to pass
All our lies come home at last
We circle round our wounded prey
Who will not live to see the day

Treachery and deceit have taken hold
Destroyed all, both young and old
And now we cry out because we must
Teach us now who to trust

The Twelfth Century, Scarborough Fair: Pandion

There was a hanged man in a gibbet; he was not mentioned in the song. There was treachery, duplicity; there was a change. Time was forced, as if by a device. The scales were altered.

Flying high above the fair, Pandion, spirit familiar of the Cahors, squeed in dismay and knew that once upon a time she'd had a mate, most beloved. And with that falcon lord, she had created life.

Gone, all to dust.

Robbed.

Destroyed.

She would avenge.

Near Mumbai: Jer and Eve

"No," Jer groaned, sliding and stumbling on the massive roots of a banyan tree hugging the churning river. "We have to stop them."

Eve turned around and frowned uneasily at him. "Jer, what's happening? What do you see?"

"I see," he began, and then he slid again, backward, backward, backward in time:

Moonlight and firelight gleamed across the courtyard of Castle Deveraux. The great stone gargoyles that had haunted Jean's childhood nights stared down at the assembly, fire pouring from their snouts. Torch flames whipped in the warm air, and great bonfires flared from the tunnels leading down to the dreaded dungeons, infamous throughout France as bastions of unspeakable cruelty. *Woe betide him who crosses a Deveraux,* went the saying, and it was true. The Cahors had been wise to entangle their fate with the Deveraux, now that they knew the Deveraux had achieved the creation of Black Fire. They would be loath to have it used against them.

As was the custom of the day, Isabeau joined Jean

in front of the closed chapel doors. Men and women married before church doors; thus it was no insult to the bishop that they did not go inside the church. On this night of the Blood Moon, the two stood facing each other before banks of lilies and twining ivy. Lilies were the flower of the Cahors, and ivy, of the Deveraux. The magical birds Fantasme and Pandion, greenwood familiars of Deveraux and Cahors respectively, were present, each preening on a beautifully decorated perch. Loose them, and they would kill each other.

Isabeau was like a fantastic she-dragon, dressed as the mighty lady she was, and would become, in ebony shot with silver thread. But she trembled like a shy virgin, and by the light of the full moon he saw how pale she was beneath her black and silver veil.

How long will you be my lady? he wondered silently. *How long before our Houses feud once more, and I poison or behead you, or burn you at the stake?*

At this she looked up at him, her eyes flinty. She didn't blink, didn't waver as he returned her gaze. Her eyes glowed a soft blue. The air between them thrummed with tension. He was delighted; this lady had a spine, by the God! He'd best look to his own person, or *she* would be the one to do *him* in.

He chuckled low in his throat, then turned his attention to his father.

As the two houses chanted in Latin and languages even more ancient, Laurent held his athame at the ready, preparing to cut open the wrists of the marrying couple. The hood of his dark crimson robe concealed his face, and he towered like a dark statue before the altar. Isabeau's mother, Catherine, also wore black and silver.

It was a glorious sight for those assembled, and power and passion flared and rose between the young couple as they were joined, soul to soul, until the end of days. Their wrists were cut, and blood mingled together in flesh and into flesh as Laurent and Catherine bound their children's left arms together with cords soaked in herbals and unguents designed to ensure fertility. Both Houses were strong and boasted many young ones, but those of the Coventry were scattered throughout the land, and there could never be enough witches and warlocks in France to please either family.

And then Jean was touched by the devil witch herself, Catherine. The woman who would massacre his family, and forge the vendetta that would chase Isabeau and him through time and space.

I have the means to prevent it, he thought, feeling the dagger that, suddenly, hung from a chain around his neck. Wild magic had put it there; and it was hidden by the rich fabric of his doublet, the blade so sharp it sliced the hairs on his chest. *I can plunge this into her heart, and end it before it begins.*

He saw himself tearing open his doublet and grabbing the dagger, running Isabeau through—

No, not Isabeau, he protested. *It is Catherine I mean to slay.*

Then he blinked, realizing something was amiss with him. He was Jean, and yet not Jean. He looked to his father, Duc Laurent, and spotted a figure standing a great distance away, a woman he knew, a woman who was crying. Her name was . . . What was her name?

Sasha?

Attends, *wait,* he thought, suddenly confused. *My mother . . . My mother is dead.*

"*Ma mère?*" he whispered, to himself, not to her.

The assembly stirred. Jean de Deveraux's mother and stepmothers were dead. Everyone knew the duke had killed them when he'd tired of them.

The Duc himself stared at Jean, and Jean felt the hair rise on the back of his neck. Something was very wrong . . . and he thought his father knew what it was.

Thunder boomed, lightning flashed, and the torches flared like comets. Isabeau's hand tightened around his, and through her veils he saw a death's head.

He heard his father laughing. Heard him whispering in his ear, "I will outlive you, whelp. You and my other prince and all my bastards. I have tilted the scales, once and for all, I and my minions. There is no balance, and never will be again. Chaos is my nation, and I am her lord and master."

Jean swayed. He felt as if he were dissolving into ether. What mischief was this?

"My lord?" Isabeau whispered anxiously, her white face hidden by veils of darkness and shadow. "How is it with you?"

Je m'appelle Jeraud, he thought. My name is Jeraud.

He turned and looked over at the crying woman. *We don't belong here,* he thought.

Then he felt other eyes on him, from above: He gazed up at the steeple of the church to see *her* there, Karienne, his mistress of long standing. How defeated she looked, even haggard. He'd offered her to a nobleman, to make certain her way was easy. She was to leave tonight. Her things were packed, and they'd bade one another *adieu.* In bed.

She was magnificent.

She's Kari. A grad student. By the God, I killed her. I slit her throat! And that woman is my mother, Sasha Deveraux.

His knees buckled, and the spectators gasped.

"Jer?" Eve said as she peered at him, standing stock-still.

"He's changed time," Jer told her, trembling. "He's cheating." He skirted around the slippery slope he'd failed to climb and spotted a rockier path toward the summit. "Come on. We have to hurry. We have to stop him."

"Him who? What?" She hesitated for a second, then followed after him. "Eli?"

"Come on." Thunder rumbled, and lightning sliced the night as Jer scrabbled over the rocks like a madman. He had to stop Holly. Had to save her.

"Jer?" Eve was struggling to keep up with him.

"Damn you. *Vite!*" he screamed at her.

Outside Mumbai:
Holly, Alex, Pablo, Armand, and the Temple of the Air

Did Jer's voice echo off the black mountains?

"It is done, my love," Alex said to Holly. Alex, who was the lord to her lady, her thrallmate, closer to her than anyone in the world. Closer—

And then she knew, as the evil poured out of him and rushed into her soul. As his contamination ruined her.

As she was damned.

"No," she whispered, trying to step away from him. But his gaze held her in place. "Please."

But she was in thrall to him—the great enemy of the Cahors, warlock, mage son of the Lost Son of Light: demon, devil. Brilliance blazed around him; he stood in the center of a sphere of light so white that it was blue; and then the colors shifted and changed like the northern lights. He was magnificent, and terrible.

Duc Laurent, of House Deveraux, dead these many centuries.

His face changed; shadows and angles and sharp features cracked the softness, and his smile was a filthy leer. He reached out a hand and cupped Holly's chin, grinning down at her body. Paralyzed, she was forced to endure his touch, and then his kiss.

Pablo, Armand, she pleaded.

Shadows flew across the moon, and the cawing of a thousand crows, a million, screeched in her ears. The ground shook, and she would have fallen to her knees if Alex—Laurent—hadn't moved his hand, and kept her upright through magic alone.

Then through the screaming of the crows she heard Jer shouting her name.

"You are in thrall with me, the lady to the lord," Laurent said to her. "You know the curse: Those who love the Cahors witches die by drowning. He loves you."

No, she thought. *No.*

"He loves you and he always has. It is the curse of my bloodkin to fall in love with you witchwomen. Jean first and now this idiot. He could have ruled a kingdom, a *world,* but instead . . . he fell in love with *you.*"

Jer, run, she called to him.

"He is cursed to die by drowning." He smiled at her. "You do it, Holly. Drown him. Take Jer Deveraux under the water and send his warlock soul straight to hell."

I refuse.

He murmured under his breath, and hot whispers skittered through her bloodstream, heating her veins. Her muscles jerked; she tried to shake her head, refuse him. But as he stepped back, she spun around and charged at Jer, who was running toward her. Eve, the warlock, was with him.

She flew at him. If he smiled, his face was such a ruin that she couldn't tell. Superhuman strength propelled her into his arms; then she shoved him backward, hard, and they both shot into the lake. Down she pushed him, down, harder. Crows covered the moon. Eve was screaming. Pablo and Armand splashed into the water after her.

Kill him. Drown him. Yes, she wanted to. He deserved it. For all the misery he had brought her, hunting her through the centuries. No rest. Forever feeling his wrath, hateful and relentless.

Yes, yes, Duc Laurent urged her.

She couldn't see him in the black water. She didn't need to breathe. But he would. He did. She grabbed his arms and held them against his body; then she covered his mouth with hers, and sucked all the air out of his body.

Die, Jean, she thought. *Die, as you should have when*

my family attacked your family's castle. When I crept out of our marriage bed to leave you to the flames, and then told you to run. Instead you hunted me down, tried to kill me when I'd risked all for you. Die. Damn you to hell and back.

He went limp. She smiled. She had fulfilled her lord's will. Laurent, her love . . .

No! He was not her love. He was *not.* Jer . . . She was killing *Jer.*

She grabbed him and forced the air back into his lungs. Nothing happened. He dangled limply in the water.

No, help me, no, she begged, kicking her legs as she fought back to the surface. The face of the Goddess gazed down on her, demanding another bargain, a sacrifice, in return for the power to save Jer's life.

"No," Holly said, gasping, as she broke the surface. "I'm done with you. Done."

Weak moonlight revealed Jer, lying facedown in the water. Crying out, she flipped him onto his back and headed toward shore. The crows were attacking Pablo, Armand, and Eve. The three had created a magical barrier, but she could see that the crows were pecking at it. Laurent stood apart, laughing.

"You are my lady," he said in a booming voice. "And you've killed him."

No, she thought. *No.* But Jer trailed behind her in the water, limp and unresponsive.

Somehow she dragged him to shore. Her dress hung in tatters around her legs as she straddled him, putting her ear to his mouth. He wasn't breathing. There was no pulse.

He was dead.

Our God can raise him up from the dead, Pablo thought to her as he, Armand, and Eve focused their magical power on the invisible barrier between Laurent Deveraux's crows and them. *Let Him in, and He will do it.*

Pablo watched as Holly began CPR, lamenting that she would cast her magical powers away at such a crucial moment. Armand glanced at him; they were thinking the same thing.

Then Eve shouted, "Damn it, Holly, bring him back!"

And suddenly light poured from Holly's body and covered Jer like a shroud. Or maybe a warming blanket. She lost sight of him. Searching wildly, her fingers touched soft, smooth skin, and the familiar angles and hollows of his features—all the scars gone, whole and healed.

Oh, I love you, I love you. I could never kill you, she thought. But she had. He was dead.

I take it back. Take back time, or take my soul; take whatever you want, only save him.

She saw Catherine, mother of Isabeau, in her black and silver gown, heavily veiled. She was standing in a dungeon, with a dagger in her hand. She held it out, and in her mind Holly reached out her palm. Catherine sliced open Holly's hand.

I will come to you, and demand my price then. And you will pay it.

Holly watched her blood well along the wound in her palm. *Yes, yes, I will,* she swore. *Only save him.*

The blood flared into fire. It ran along her hand like ignited gunpowder. Instantly unbearable pain shot through her; she smelled her own flesh burning. Smelled her hair. Her *teeth*. Her bones.

It was unbelievable agony.

It was what he had felt. *Jean. Jer.*

It can go away, Catherine told her. *Say the word. He will die, now, but you will no longer suffer.*

"No," she screamed. "Jer!"

The pain intensified. It burned the air around her, every space she had ever touched. It burned time.

Holly screamed.

And screamed.

Jer woke. Holly had tried to drown him. Now she was on fire, and all the demons of hell were diving after them.

Jer grabbed Holly and flung her over his back as Armand, Pablo, and Eve hurled fireballs at scaly creatures and monsters with talons, and hulking giants and winged nightmares. And his ancestor, the terrifying Duc Laurent, rode a skeleton warhorse that breathed fire and galloped above the rocks, crushing them with his hooves. Hellhounds bayed and clacked their teeth.

"Faster!" Jer shouted at the others.

And Holly's burning body sizzled into his scarred and suffering flesh.

"Fire in the hole!" Eve shouted.

Jer jerked his head around just in time to see the landscape behind him explode in a shower of rocks and debris. He ducked his head to avoid getting hit, and kept running.

"Holly, work with me!" he shouted.

She groaned in agony, and his heart broke for her. And suddenly, in the distance, he saw two figures appear, running toward them. More of Duc Laurent's men? Behind him Jer heard people dying, and he realized in a second that the Duc was killing his own coven. So much for the Temple of the Air. It sounded like at least a couple of them were fighting back; Jer just prayed that would give them enough time.

Eve ran up beside him. "Jer, there's something I haven't told you." She was panting heavily.

"Please let it be that you know a way to stop this guy."

She swallowed big gulps of air. "I might."

He glanced over at her without slowing. "What?"

"I think we can conjure the Black Fire."

He almost tripped. "That's impossible. Only Deveraux can do it. Even if we could find Eli, we would still need three of us."

"We'll have three of us."

"What are you talking about?" A fireball whizzed past Jer's ear.

She stared at him for a full beat as they ran. And then she said, "Jer, I'm a Deveraux."

Scarborough: Nicole, Amanda, Tommy, Richard, Owen, Kari, Anne-Louise, and the cats

In the kitchen of House Moore, Kari watched Nicole pacing, anxiously whipping out her cell phone to check for messages, cuddling the baby against her chest. Owen was swathed in a silver shawl covered with amulets and sachets Anne-Louise had brought as baby gifts.

The kitchen was redolent of cinnamon and cloves, and a tiny flicker of longing for lost Christmases tugged at the recesses of Kari's ashen memory.

A vein pulsed at Nicole's temple, and she kept pacing and chewing her lower lip. Her nervous energy made it all the more obvious to Kari that she herself was dead inside. Kari knew she should also be upset, and frightened, but she was neither. She was flat. Empty.

Standing at the granite-topped kitchen island,

Anne-Louise, in white and silver, peered at a scrying stone, one of thirteen she had set up in a circle on the counter sprinkled with salt and crushed hazelnuts. White candles burned at the four corners of the counter, and in the center stood a statue of the Goddess in her incarnation as the Virgin Mary. A low-burning flame in an arched alcove beside the refrigerator was dedicated to Hestia, Greek goddess of the hearth, and a lock of Holly's hair was burning in it.

Kari moved so that she could see over Anne-Louise's shoulder. She saw Holly, writhing in agony, her skin turning black as though from fire. She was in trouble. So were those with her, including . . . Jer!

Kari remembered pain and death. She remembered Jer's knife at her throat as she lay dying on the floor of the Supreme Coven's headquarters in London. The loving words in ancient French they had exchanged before he'd slit her throat. She had begged him to; it had been Wind Moon, and whoever killed her would acquire her magical strength. Rather than allow it to flow to Michael Deveraux who had wounded her, she willed it to Jer, the man she had lost in this century, and in France, long ago.

In another century, in medieval France, they had been lovers—Karienne and Jean. She was his beloved mistress, his exquisite French lily, and they lived in a perpetual state of decadent pleasure. When his arranged marriage to Isabeau was successfully negotiated, he had set Karienne aside, and she had accepted that, for she knew the ways of politics; and, as one allied with the House of Deveraux, she agreed that he must marry the enemy witch to keep their noble family safe. But Kari knew that Jean loved *her*. She had his heart, and that would comfort her in the long years ahead.

Count Alois, her new patron, had informed her he would come for her after the wedding ceremony. Her things were packed, and they would live in Paris. She had one precious hour before she must fasten her admiring gaze on a man who was not Jean. He would become her legal husband. And so, she stole into the church, to watch from the steeple, for seeing him given to another in name only was preferable to not seeing him at all.

Wind and firelight cast shadows over the glittering assembly. Silver and black, for Cahors; red and green, for the doublets and gowns of the Deveraux. Gems, gold, and silver. The blood of sacrifices hung in the air. The wailing of the serfs over those who had died.

He is mine, she thought as she gazed down on her handsome, lost Jean. She dug her fingers into her palms, and prayed that she might be pregnant with his babe. She wasn't certain, but she had her suspicions.

As droplets of blood welled and slid down the lifeline in her right hand, Jean's father, Duc Laurent, opened Jean's vein with a ceremonial dagger, and Isabeau's mother did the same to her. Their wrists were bound together.

Lightning flashed. Thunder rumbled, and the torches flared. Who was that woman, standing off to one side, weeping?

Clouds rushed the moon. Overhead, lightning sizzled like falling stars. And then, a dagger of grief cleaved Karienne's heart: As his blood mingled with Isabeau's, his face changed. From standing stiff and guarded, half-glowering at the bitch, now he leaned toward her, gazing at her like a starving man at table. He glowed with rapture, and adoration. *He loved Isabeau, his bride.*

"*Non,*" she protested, gripping the wood railing. It was to be a political match; no one dreamed the two would harbor anything but sheer hatred for each other . . . and yet, as Jean looked upon Isabeau, his hard face softened as it never had for her, for Karienne.

Karienne, alors, viens ici, a voice murmured to her. *Viens. Je t'espére.*

Come here. I am waiting for you.

"*Qui?*" she murmured. Who? Was it Jean, at last, calling to her? Had he seen how wrong he was to love that murdering witch?

Karienne, viens ici. Maintenant.

And the voice urged her again, to come . . . now . . . to leave the room at House Moore, to quietly get a coat, and take a lot of money from Anne-Louise's purse . . . to walk down to the gate, and to the lane, where the bus would come, and to take the bus, and then go to Dover, and from there to take the ferry . . .

. . . to France.

By the time they realized she had left . . .

. . . she was gone.

Mumbai: Jer, Holly, Eve, Pablo, and Armand

"You're a Deveraux!" Jer shouted in disbelief. "When did that happen?"

She had the decency to look ashamed. "My family has hidden their true name for a long, long time. I—I didn't know when to tell you. I wasn't sure . . ." She trailed off.

It made sense. Deveraux had not exactly been popular with the Supreme Coven for quite a while. It also explained the weird sort of kinship he had felt with her. It explained a lot of things.

"We're still only two," he said finally. "We still need Eli to make Black Fire."

That is not going to be a problem, he heard Pablo say in his head.

Why?

Look carefully at the people in front of us.

Jer looked again. Running toward them as fast as they could were Eli and Philippe.

This must be a miracle, Jer thought. *Magic didn't do this. No magic that I have, anyway.*

Yes, perhaps, Pablo replied.

"Philippe!" Jer bellowed. "How did you find us?"

"Eli cast a finder's spell. He saw you. In fact, he insisted there were several Deveraux with you. I didn't really want to come."

Jer smiled crookedly. "I'm glad you did. Take Holly," he said to Armand, holding her out to him. "Be careful."

Armand slung her over his own back. Jer grabbed Eve's hand and ran for everything that he was worth. His scarred legs screamed in agony, but he ignored the pain and instead fixated on his brother, and his . . . What was she, a cousin?

A moment later the three of them collided. Jer reached out and grabbed Eli's hand. "Black Fire! Conjure it. I know you know how!"

For once there was no sarcastic retort from his brother. Instead Eli began chanting in a deep, ringing voice. Jer and Eve listened intently, and when the chant began to repeat, they joined in.

"Incendio, Agni . . . Dando . . ."

Armand, with Holly in his arms, and Pablo beside him, passed the three and began casting magic with

Philippe. Jer turned and faced the oncoming Duc. He imagined him on fire. He imagined him burning as he had, and as Jean had, and as Isabeau. He imagined him dead.

And, ten feet away, the Black Fire sprang into life.

Scarborough: Amanda, Tommy, Nicole, Richard, Owen, Anne-Louise, and the cats

Anne-Louise listened to everything Nicole and Amanda told her. She paced, and then she whirled around and said, "Nicole, Amanda, where did you find this book?"

"I'll show you," Amanda said, as she rose and led them through the house. She led them into the study, below the portrait, and headed for a wall. She took a deep breath and waved it open, and the others moved back.

"I—I should go with you," Nicole said. But it was clear she was conflicted.

"I'll protect Owen," Richard promised.

"If you hear me knocking, move your hand over the wall like I did," Amanda told him.

Reluctantly, Nicole handed her child over, and then followed Amanda into the darkness. She smelled evil. The shadows whispered warnings.

She wanted to turn back.

"What is this place?" Tommy asked when they'd reached the inner sanctum.

"It's the heart of House Moore," Anne-Louise said. "There are dark magics working here."

"We shouldn't be here," Nicole murmured.

"No," Anne-Louise countered. "It's the very best place we can be."

Mumbai: Holly, Jer, Philippe, Pablo, Armand, Eve, and Eli

The battle raged around Philippe, and the air before him shimmered with fresh magic.

What now? he thought, bracing himself.

The shimmering grew blinding, popped like a firework. And to his utter astonishment, Amanda and Tommy tumbled out.

Eve spun toward them, hands raised, and Philippe stopped her with a shout. She took a closer look at the newcomers.

"What the hell?" Eve cried.

"Holly!" Amanda cried, reaching for her cousin, who was half-clinging to the back of Armand.

"Look out!" Armand shouted, and Amanda turned in time to see a winged demon flying over a huge, billowing wall of ebony flames. Black Fire. Her heart stuttered. She had seen Black Fire once before, seen what it could do.

Holly moaned. Fire seemed to dance along her skin. Amanda reached out and grabbed her hand, touched their palms together. She could feel the mark of the lily burning.

"Fire within and fire without, cease your burning here about."

A moment later Holly opened her eyes. They widened, and filled with tears.

"Amanda," she rasped. "Oh, Amanda, I thought I would never see you again."

"We're here. Tommy and I. We were in the study and we *saw* . . ." Amanda knew she should save her explanation for later.

Holly squeezed her hand. "Armand, put me down."

He set her on her feet and she spun around with a shout, and electricity shot from her eyes and hands and destroyed the demon in midflight. Amanda started to cheer, but a sudden pulse of white-hot light blinded her, and when her vision returned, Holly was gone.

Scarborough: Nicole, Richard, Owen, and Anne-Louise

"Okay, bring them back right now," Richard ordered.

"I . . . can't," Anne-Louise confessed. "That portal opened, and before I could stop them, they went through."

"And my little girl is in *India*?" Richard shouted. "In another goddamn battle?"

"I'm sorry," Anne-Louise replied.

Nicole sat in her room and rocked Owen, trying to

sing him to sleep. She tried to sing over the shouting. "Parsley, sage, rosemary and thyme."

She tried not to think about her loved ones in India fighting for their lives.

"Then she'll be a true love of mine."

She tried not to think about the curse that had been put on her family.

"Tell her to wash it in yonder dry well."

She tried not to think about her Owen destroying the world.

"Parsley, sage, rosemary and thyme."

She didn't want to know where Kari had gone off to.

"Which never sprung water nor rain ever fell."

She tried not to think too hard about the lyrics of "Scarborough Fair."

"Then she'll be a true love of mine."

Even if they were nonsense and set forth a series of impossible tasks. It was just a song.

And she was just a girl.

And magic was impossible.

Scarborough, 1268: Nicolette and Elijah

"What shall I tell your love, your Nicolette?" the servant asked Elijah of the House Deveraux.

Elijah thought for a moment. "Tell her she must perform a task for me."

"What manner of task?"

"One that is impossible for a mere mortal, one only a follower of the Horned God could perform. Tell the fair maiden of the Cahors that she must make me a cambric shirt." He held up a finger for emphasis. "Without seam or needlework."

The servant bowed low. "And if she can produce such an impossible garment?"

Elijah laughed. "Then she'll be a true love of mine."

The servant bowed out of his presence, and Elijah threw himself down onto his bed. Tomorrow was the first day of the fair, and if Nicolette was half the woman or the warlock he believed she was, he would marry her by fair's end.

They had met the year before at the fair, her first. Beautiful, bewitching, her family had kept her closely guarded. This year would be different; she was old enough to be courted, old enough to marry. He changed for dinner and went downstairs to join his family in dining with their gracious hosts, the family Moore.

Nicolette regarded the servant with wide eyes. "He wants me to make him what?"

The servant repeated the request. "Will my lady make such a garment?" he asked at last.

"Yes, but tell your lord that I expect him to do something for me."

"What do you ask of my lord?"

"Tell him . . . Tell him to find me an acre of land between the salt water and the seastrand."

"But, what my lady asks is impossible!"

"No more so than what he is asking of me."

The servant bowed. "Anything else?"

"Yes, tell him that then he'll be a true love of mine."

The servant bowed again and left, and Nicolette sank into a chair and laughed. "Elijah thinks he is clever, but I'll show him."

Her younger sister, Catherine, looked up at her with wide eyes. "Will you make him the shirt?"

"Of course I will," Nicolette said.

"But how?" Catherine asked.

"Why, with magic, of course."

The servant had been in the employ of the Deveraux family since birth. It was long enough to know them well and long enough to know that no matter how loyal he was, he was never safe from their wrath. So he trembled slightly as he entered Elijah's presence again with the news from Nicolette.

"Did you tell her to make me the shirt?" Elijah asked.

"Yes, and she asked a favor of you in return."

Elijah slapped his leg when he heard what it was. "Well chosen."

Elijah's youngest brother looked at him with solemn eyes. "That is impossible."

"Not for a warlock, Laurent," Elijah assured him.

In the morning Nicolette awoke early, eager to see Elijah Deveraux. She took pains with her clothes and arranged her hair in perfect braids, with flowers laced throughout, and herbs. Parsley, sage, rosemary, and thyme. All powerful herbs with their own magic use and significance. Used together they made a love charm.

She made her way to the fair and began winding her way through, looking at all the things people had to sell or show. As she walked, she could feel eyes upon her, and she knew that they were Elijah's. Her heart beat faster as she pretended she could not feel his presence.

He stalked her as the hunter did a fox, and she knew she would have to be very clever not to be caught. At least, too soon. She wound her way past performers and merchants. She avoided people she knew so that she could keep moving.

She paused for a moment and tried to feel him. He was near, so near it was as though he filled her senses. She turned to the left, hoping to hide for a moment behind a gypsy cart. As she moved behind it, a pair of strong arms wrapped around her and lifted her clear off the ground.

It was her Elijah. As their lips met, fire exploded in her veins and she clung to him. At last her senses took over. "We must not let them catch us."

"Why, does this go beyond the bounds of acceptable courtship?" he asked, his lips trailing down her throat.

"Yes, and you know it," she said, pushing against his chest.

He released her and she struggled to regain her composure. There was a game to be played, and when he was standing so near, it was hard to remember her part.

"Have you found me my land?" she breathed.

"Yes. And my shirt?"

"Finished."

It was true, she had conjured it into being before she had gone to bed, though she dared not tell him she had then used it as her pillow. "So, when do I see my land?" she asked.

He raised a finger and placed it against her lips, and she could feel his heartbeat through it, pounding as hers did.

"First I want you to wash my shirt, in a dry well into which neither water has sprung nor rain has fell."

She smiled at him. "Then you must plow my acre with . . . a lamb's horn."

"And?"

"Sow it all over with a single peppercorn."

"Nicolette!"

She turned at the sound. "My sister calls. I must go."

He caught her by the wrist. "Then will I be a true love of yours?"

She let her smile speak for her, then she tugged her wrist free and fled.

"Are you going to marry Nicolette of the Cahors?" Roland of the House of Moore asked Elijah several days later.

"It is my plan," the warlock admitted. "In fact, she has only one task left to perform."

"What impossible thing did you ask of her this time?"

"I told her to dry the shirt on a thorn."

Roland shook his head. "The two of you really should be more careful, you know. Your exploits are getting noticed."

"You're not worried what the peasants think, surely!"

"No, more worried about what the priests think," Roland said pointedly.

Elijah waved a hand dismissively. "The priests are paid not to notice these things, especially during the fair."

"That may be true, but there are limits even for us."

"For you maybe, Roland, but not for me. And not for my sweet, wicked Nicolette."

★ ★ ★

House Moore was powerful, but it always lived in the shadow of Houses Deveraux and Cahors. A closer alliance between those two houses would essentially create a king and queen of Coventry. That couldn't be allowed to happen. Roland's father was old and ill and could do nothing to save his house.

Roland sacrificed every manner of animal and human to the Horned God and was at last given his answer. He watched and he waited for his time to strike.

"Where are you going?" Catherine asked Nicolette. It was late, and their parents were asleep. Nicolette had woken Catherine up.

Even in the light of the single candle Catherine could see her sister blushing. "I'm going to see Elijah," she whispered.

Catherine crossed her arms. "I don't think Father would like that very much."

"That's why you're not going to tell him," Nicolette said, her voice hardening.

Catherine wanted to stop her and she couldn't. As she watched Nicolette's dark figure slip into the night, she felt helpless. Something bad was going to happen and she couldn't stop it.

When the morning came and Roland Moore arrived

to tell them that Nicolette had been murdered by Elijah, who had escaped, her fears were realized. She should have stopped her sister from going to see the Deveraux man. She wished she had more power, and she vowed she would find it no matter the cost and no matter who she had to sacrifice to.

Roland Moore wept openly as he returned home and delivered the news that Nicolette Cahors had murdered Elijah and then escaped capture. The Moores and the Deveraux grieved together and began to plot their revenge against the treacherous Cahors.

Laurent seethed with rage. His brother, the only one of his family he had ever cared for, had been taken from him. He would never let something like that happen again, no matter that he had to move heaven and hell or change time itself to do it.

Part Three
Gaspar

☾

And when the dark one is loosed none will be safe. Children will die, beasts will weep and the world will burn with terrible fire.

—Second Revelation of John 3:25

TEN

MYRRH

☾

We live by all the lies we've told
Some are worth their weight in gold
But none can know the truth we hide
The Deveraux keep the pain inside

Cahors witches, take to sky
Lift your head to moon and cry
All alone, lost and bereft
Sacrifice is all that's left

The Frozen Wasteland: Holly

"Jer," Holly whispered as she jerked awake. She was lying in snow, and the sky above her danced with colored lights. She was no longer in the thick of battle. She sprawled on a barren plain of snow—no trees, no rocks, nothing but the snow and the lights.

"Jer?" she called, but his name seemed to freeze in her mouth. Shivering, she pushed up onto her elbows. Prisms of color—green, red, bluish-white—threw shifting patterns on the vast fields of white. Was she still in India?

299

Her teeth chattered and her head began to ache. She jerked like a windup toy as she stared in wonder and confusion at the lights. What magic had flung her here? Had Jer done it to save her? Or had Alex—*make that Duc Laurent*—pitched her through space to murder her? Was this Hindi magic, or warlock mischief—or both?

She trembled violently as cold seeped through her and seized her with bone-cracking numbness. After a few moments she couldn't tell where she stopped and the snow began. Her heartbeat slowed; her blood congealed.

I'm . . . dying, she thought. She tried to move. *Jer, please, help me.*

Where are you? a voice answered, but it wasn't Jer. It was Duc Laurent, with whom she was in thrall. *My lady?*

"No," she said, gasping. "I—I—I'm n-n-not—"

Then she remembered that she was not a helpless girl; she was a powerful witch, and she had magical gifts. In a low guttural whisper she croaked, "Ice and fire, fear and desire, comfort I claim, in the . . . in my own name." She knew she had made terrible bargains in the past, losing bits of her soul to the Goddess, and to Catherine of the House of Cahors. She wouldn't indebt herself further, if she could help it.

She closed her eyes, waiting for the spell to take effect. Suddenly she felt as if she were whirling inside a spinning sphere of white, and her frozen lips pulled up in a tiny smile. Warmth poured through her, and her smile grew.

"Ice and fire, fear and desire, sanctuary I claim, in my own name."

More warmth coursed through her veins. She could almost imagine that her heart was glowing inside her chest, and she was certain she had either transported herself to shelter or created one around herself.

She opened her eyes. The beautiful lights were gone, and a fat golden moon hung overhead. The same snowfield stretched in all directions. There was no cottage, hovel, no cave, not even a single tree or boulder. A slicing wind whipped up, slamming her backward. She fell, hard, and her ears rang.

"Help," she managed, as dots of grayish yellow popped behind her eyelids.

"Ah, there you are. Do not fear. I will come for you, Holly," Duc Laurent whispered inside her mind.

"No," she demanded. *I am free of you. I don't know how. Who sent me here? Jer?*

"I will come."

How did I get here?

Everything faded to black.

Scarborough: Nicole and Owen

She must have fallen asleep while rocking Owen, because Nicole suddenly woke up. She got up slowly, careful not to wake Owen, and then put him down in his crib. The room was warm and she crossed to a window and opened it.

Outside, the air was crisp and clear, and she breathed in deeply. Suddenly a tiny sparrow hopped up onto the ledge and cocked its head at her. She smiled and made a soft whistling noise. The bird cocked its head to the side again and then flew to the back of her rocking chair. While she was enjoying the cool of the outdoors, he was clearly thrilled with the warmth indoors.

He perched for a moment and ruffled his feathers all up. Nicole smiled at him. It was funny how the tiniest creatures could still bring such joy to—

The bird exploded in a puff of feathers. Nicole blinked in disbelief, but the bird was gone. Bits of him rained down in the room. For one wild moment she wondered if it had been because she hadn't invited him in by name, and then she heard a sound that made her blood curdle. It was wild high-pitched laughter.

She turned slowly and saw Owen, *standing* in his crib, one finger pointing at the remains of the bird and his face twisted up in a grin of pure evil.

He killed the bird! My baby killed the innocent little bird! He is the child who will end the world. She knew then what she had to do, and it had to be done quickly, before she lost her nerve or before Anne-Louise or her father could stop her. She walked to Owen, grabbed him up, and headed for the hidden passage at a run.

She made it to the section of wall, slid her hand where she had seen Amanda move it, and then ducked into the opening. It sealed behind her, and she didn't bother summoning a light but just ran down the hall toward the inner sanctum. In her arms Owen cooed contentedly, and Nicole felt the tears streaming down her face.

You should have known, should have believed, a voice whispered in her ear.

Yes, she should have.

Hurry now before it's too late, before he stops you.

"I'm hurrying!"

She made it to the chamber and looked around wildly. She had not had a chance to examine it closely earlier. In the one corner there was an altar. It seemed right that she should use it. She ran over and placed Owen on its deeply gouged and stained surface. The blood of sacrifices past seemed to reach out to seize him from her arms.

To the left was a cabinet. She opened it and found candles, stones, and crystals for various purposes and a collection of athames. *I should do a purifying ritual, a ceremony to cleanse his soul and send him to the Goddess,* she thought as her hand moved toward the white candles.

Wicked: Resurrection

No time! Strike now before it's too late.

She raised the athame high into the air and turned toward Owen.

Anne-Louise wasn't sure what she was searching for among the books and papers of Sir William Moore. She had been at it for several hours with nothing useful to show for it.

I should get some tea, take a break, check up on Nicole. She started to move toward the door.

And then Anne-Louise spotted something that seemed wrong. Among all the neat rows of books there was a book shoved on top of some others and sticking out at an angle. It was wrapped in an embroidered silk cloth, and she instantly recognized the symbol for the House of Cahors.

A page was marked and she opened to it. She read about the destruction of the Cahors Castle in France and how many things of great monetary and magical value had been stolen, including a book of prophecies written by the dark wizard Merlin.

As Anne-Louise continued to read, she gasped out loud. There was a sudden popping sound, and she lifted her head to see the space in front of her literally rent in two as though it were a curtain.

Sasha tumbled through the hole and leaped to her feet as it sealed before her.

304

She staggered and looked fearfully around. Then her gaze fastened on Anne-Louise.

"Goddess," she breathed, "I'm alive." She raced into Anne-Louise's arms. "Thank you."

Anne-Louise held her covenate closely as relief surged through her. Sasha was here, and apparently unharmed. But how?

"Sasha," she said, "I didn't bring you here."

The mother of Jer and Eli Deveraux lifted her head from Anne-Louise's shoulder. "Then who did? I was about to die. Then the ground shook and a portal opened. Going anywhere was preferable to dying by the hand of Merlin."

A cold terror seized Anne-Louise. *"What?"*

"Where is Nicole?" Sasha asked, grabbing Anne-Louise's shoulders and giving her a shake. "We have to stop her before it's too late!"

"I don't know where she is." Anne-Louise frowned. "Stop her from what?"

"Owen. She's sacrificing Owen," Sasha said. "Anne-Louise, please believe me. We may already be too late."

"Goddess . . ." Anne-Louise breathed in horror. There was only one place a deed that terrible could be performed. She turned and raced toward the entrance to the secret tunnel, Sasha close on her heels.

As soon as they entered the tunnel, Anne-Louise began shouting. "Nicole, stop! Don't do it! It's a trap!"

Heart in her throat, she burst into the main chamber and saw Nicole swinging an athame down toward Owen. She threw a ward across the room to encase Owen, and the knife glanced off it.

"Nicole! It's a lie. Merlin's prophecies, every thirteenth one is a lie. It's backward to try to manipulate time, change history."

Nicole looked at her with glassy eyes, and for a moment Anne-Louise thought she might be possessed. Slowly Nicole lowered the athame and blinked at her.

"What did you say?"

But Anne-Louise couldn't answer her as she stared at Owen, who sat quietly for once, a halo of light around his head.

Mumbai: Jer, Eve, Eli, Philippe, Pablo, Armand, Amanda, and Tommy

Jer spun around, looking for Holly. One moment she had been there, and the next gone. A dagger whistled through the air past his cheek, and he heard a thud as it landed in flesh. He turned just in time to see Eve crumple to the snow.

The Black Fire flickered once and then went out. *It requires three to create it and three to keep it burning,* he realized. "Incoming!" he shouted, erecting a hasty barrier where the fire had burned a moment before.

Alex crashed through the barrier and slammed into

Jer. Jer was flung onto his back while Alex slammed his fists into his face, preferring, it seemed, to beat him to death with his own hands. Jer tried to push back, but two spectral knights in luminous armor pushed his wrists into the snow.

"Monster!" Alex bellowed at him. "How could you, a Deveraux, betray your own kind?"

He brought both his fists down onto Jer's nose. Pain shot straight into his brain; inside his skull he heard a crunch and knew his nose was broken. More blows shattered more bones, and then it felt as if his skin were being ripped away. He fought to keep his eyes open and saw the changing face of Alex Carruthers: in one moment the handsome man who had deceived Holly and her family; in the next the moldering corpse of the man who had bound Jean Deveraux's soul to that of Isabeau Cahors. Purple-blue skin hung off Alex's face, and worms crawled from his eye sockets.

"You should have agreed to thrall with Holly Cathers, and then handed her over to your family, the Deveraux. But we got her anyway. She's in thrall to *me*. The lady to my lord. Think about that as I kill you."

"She . . . ," Jer managed. "She is not in thrall. She saved me."

"Menteur!" Laurent shouted. "Liar!" He pummeled Jer's face like a savage. His rage was stunning; through

the haze of pain, Jer tried to comprehend it. Anger was the son of fear. What was Laurent afraid of?

"Always in my way, always!" Laurent broke into medieval French, and Jer understood it. He went back in time again, back . . .

Jean paused at the top of the stairs in his wedding finery and listened to his father speaking to Paul-Henri, Jean's younger brother.

"If he fails to get a boy on her, you can try next," Laurent said.

"But, *mon père,* to do that I must either rape her or murder him, or both," Paul-Henri protested. Mildly.

"Pfft. Have you learned nothing? You are French. Seduce her."

"But—"

"By the horns of the God, Paul-Henri, it's a political match. She doesn't love him. My spies tell me she weeps at her window. Her bitch of a mother is sacrificing serfs with abandon, forcing Isabeau to bathe in their blood, and for what? Courage! The ability to lie with Jean without screaming."

Jean smiled evilly. He would enjoy making Isabeau scream. And enjoy even more the prospect of killing Paul-Henri. Both, as soon as possible. He would be his father's only son.

★ ★ ★

Myrrh

"But you loved her," Alex/Laurent screamed at him. Spittle flew everywhere. "The spirit of Jean, inside you still, loved Isabeau. *Love?* You destroyed our family with your love! And even now you fight for the Cahors! Against your own blood kin!"

I am not Jean. I am . . .

Something sharp sliced his neck. Blood gushed, steamed, froze.

I am . . .

He was dying.

I would die for her. For Isabeau . . .

mais non, *no, not Isabeau . . .*

Isabeau was born so that Holly would be . . .

Wait for me, wherever it is the God sends me, he thought, as the world thinned into a red line. Then, *No, don't. Don't come there, ever. It will be hell.*

Scarborough: Nicole, Anne-Louise, Richard, Sasha, and Owen

Anne-Louise, Sasha, and Richard talked in hushed tones as Nicole laid Owen down for the night. She drank a cup of herbal tea laced with soothing herbs that Sasha had made her and sat beside his cradle, rocking him, seeing again the nimbus of light that glowed around his head like a halo. She set the red cup decorated with green ivy on his changing table and rubbed his cheek with her warm fingers. Marveling at the softness, she wondered who he was, really. Kari had said he would die if he left the house. Was that true, or just another of Merlin's lies? Kari seemed to see things differently now that she was dead, and Nicole wanted to ask her what she saw when she looked at Owen.

But Kari was gone. They'd searched for her, but no finder's spell or scrying stone had located her. Also missing was nearly all the money Anne-Louise had brought with her, which meant, at least, that Kari had run away—that she had not been abducted.

Nicole had thought she'd feel safer without Kari near the baby, but not knowing where she was, or why she'd gone, made Nicole more nervous. Now that she was a mother, it was so much harder to deal with her fear. She couldn't run away; she had to stand her ground and protect her baby. Fear could be a very selfish emotion; before Owen had come into her life, she had been self-centered in the extreme. Back then she'd run and left Holly and Amanda behind, breaking the power of the three . . . for magic was strongest when three witches conjured.

Three witches, three warlocks, three mages, three wizards. The triangle was the most stable of all conjuring images. After all, what was a pentagram but triangles within triangles within triangles? Trinities within trinities.

Nicole thought of how demanding she'd been with her mother, insisting on preferential treatment, and how contemptuous of Richard, her father, who had known his wife was having an affair—with Eli's father!—and had done nothing about it except look sad and depressed. But Richard Anderson hadn't left. He'd stayed . . . for his wife, and his children. Love endured all things.

She thought back to Cologne again, unsure why her mind kept going there. Musing, she reached for her cup . . .

. . . reached for her cup . . .

. . . reached for her cup . . .

It was no longer there.

And neither was she.

The Temple of the Blind Justices: Nicole

Nicole staggered in a little circle. She was surrounded by a white mist, and as it cleared, she saw that she was standing in the middle of a ring of Grecian columns that rose so high into the boiling clouds overhead that she couldn't see their tops. Between the columns men and women sat on white marble chairs wearing Grecian-style togas. Their eyes were milky white, and their faces were youthful and unlined. Some were as white as bone; others, golden-hued, mocha-brown, purple-black.

"Where's Owen?" she cried. "Where am I?"

"Nicole Anderson-Moore, you face the Blind Justices."

Her attention darted from face to face. She didn't know who had spoken. No one's mouth had moved.

"Where's my baby?" she yelled. She ran toward the closest man, smacking into an invisible barrier about five feet from him. She slammed her fists against it. "Owen!"

"The baby brought you here," the voice said again. Again, none of them seemed to have moved a muscle.

"What do you mean?" She rammed the barrier again.

"If you will calm yourself, we will tell you."

"Are you Deveraux?" she asked them. And something happened. Something shifted. She looked at each face in turn. Milky-white eyes stared back at her.

"We are not Deveraux, or Cahors, or any other name belonging to a man," said the voice. "We have moved beyond all that."

"Owen—"

"The name you gave him."

She caught her breath. "Does he have another name? Do you know who his father is?"

"That is for you to tell us. That is why we have brought you here. For confirmation."

"You . . . You think you know who it is," she said slowly, as her heart pounded. She felt dizzy, a little sweaty. "Tell me."

There was silence. "You have been brought here because this child was not meant to be."

Myrrh

She was speechless. Terror ripped through her. They were going to hurt Owen.

"Yes, yes, he was," she blurted. "Of course he was."

"Then you have aided and abetted in altering the balance," the voice said. "And for that crime you must pay."

Ise, Japan, 1281: Nicolette, Elijah, Louis, and Marie

Kameyama, the great cloistered emperor of Japan, prostrated himself in the black robes of a Shinto priest, forehead to tatami mat. A table held the sacred shining Mirror of the Goddess Ameratsu, his patron and heavenly consort. He prayed to Her without words, for She knew his heart, and he would never be so disrespectful as to address Her directly, even though, once a year, they communed sensually and brought blessings on Japan.

Outside the simple wooden shrine thousands of Kameyama's subjects prayed as well. It was the most massive vigil ever held, and belief that Japan was divinely favored surged through the petitioners like a living being; for had not Ameratsu driven back their enemies seven years before, with bad weather?

But this time there were one hundred forty thousand rampaging Mongols of the fearsome Kublai Khan, using new weapons and new battle tactics. With their four thousand four hundred ships, the barbarians fought not in the traditional Japanese way, one warrior targeting another, for honor and focus—but in enormous formations working together, like some strange superior being. The Japanese army fielded only forty thousand men, trained to respect the enemy in hand-to-hand combat—and they were dying for it. The sea surged red, with Japanese blood.

Japan had been saved seven years before by violent sea storms that had sunk half the Mongol fleet. Surely such weather had been created by the great Goddess Ameratsu. Surely, if She heard the pleas of her devoted followers, she would create such a miracle once more. Thus, the days and nights and days became one long prayer, sent up to heaven with incense, bells, and chants.

But the weather that day was fine, and the enemy was slaughtering Kameyama's men up and down the coast. Mongol arrows and Mongol blades mowed down loyal samurai like rice seedlings. Kameyama feared that soon the Japanese enemies of the imperial family would also rise against the Chrysanthemum Throne, when it was weakest.

And so, Kameyama prayed to his Goddess. And hidden in the shadows, the most powerful witch and warlock in the world worked to aid Ameratsu, in their own way. They were Nicolette of House Cahors, and her Deveraux husband, Elijah.

Myrrh

Kameyama didn't know everything about their magic powers, but he knew that Nicolette prayed to the Goddess, and Elijah worshipped the Horned God. Wind began to ripple like a river as the arcane words of the oldest language intermingled with Latin, Greek, and old French. He didn't know their spells and incantations; they spoke to him in Japanese.

The magical ones both wore formal black kimonos—they and their children, Marie and Louis—intertwined with crests of Pandion, the lady hawk, and Fantasme, the cruel hunter. There were also moons, for the Goddess, encircling the head of the Green Man like a halo of holiness. The blood of sacrifices sizzled onto white-hot charcoal simmering in black braziers, which Kameyama pretended not to know were there.

Elijah and Nicolette conjured the elements. Both parents were quite aware that despite the love they bore for the children—and love was the force of light—their spells were curses, dark and deep. They willed evil weather into the world—fierce lightning, wild and divine wind; they wished for the deaths of thousands. Perhaps later Cahors or Deveraux would walk in the light. The times in which they lived brooked no mercy. Kameyama was their ally, if not their friend—witches and warlocks had no friends among the non-magical. In most fiefdoms and demesnes, those discovered practicing the air were torn to pieces with pincers, their eyes burned out of their sockets, their babes ripped living from the wombs of their mothers.

Mercy was a dream promised by the Christian God, whose priests were the most merciless of all men. A dream promised, but forever denied—or so it seemed to those who did not worship Him.

And so, Elijah and Nicolette poured all their energy into defeat of their enemies, into death and destruction. While Marie sucked her thumb and watched the dead animals on the braziers turn to charcoal and Louis tossed a rat's skull from palm to palm like a juggler's ball, their parents brought evil into the world.

The sky began to howl, the wind to shriek. Nicolette heard the murmurs of the Japanese faithful outside the sacred shrine and wondered if they would begin to panic. Elijah was speaking words so evil that she wanted to cover their children's ears. But in those days there was more power in evil than in good. Let those who had ears to hear . . . *hear*. It was their legacy. Their children would be even more powerful than Nicolette and Elijah were.

A thunderclap split the sky, and lightning illuminated the room. Rain shot down like Mongol arrows, hard and cruel. Nicolette smiled and put her hand over her husband's. It was done. She closed her eyes and saw the clouds and the currents switching places;

Myrrh

Elijah lured chaos to come into the world, and to the Sea of Japan that licked the shore like a lover.

The wife of Elijah Deveraux promised delight and joy to Pan if He would blow His essence into the typhoon. Before arriving in Japan, the family had gone to India, and Elijah had promised the same to the Goddess in Her incarnation as Kali, the Goddess of time and change. The Magnificent One promised a world that bowed to Cahors and Deveraux. There was no pairing more deadly, no conjoined family more powerful. They were in thrall, lady to lord. Japan was nothing to them; they would travel back and forth in time and space, bending it to their will.

"*Maman, j'ai peur*," Marie whispered, tugging on the long sleeve of Nicolette's kimono.

"Fear is not for you. It is for them," Nicolette said.

Then the typhoon hit—a gale, a tsunami tidal wave of unimaginable fury. The elemental forces had been driven mad with magic, with demonic omnipotence. In a whiplash fury the shrine was gone, blasted into kindling; Kameyama's shout was lost as Nicolette was whirled in a circle, crazily, tumbling heels over head. She screamed for her children, and Elijah, screamed over and over, and saw images—

She saw a Cahors witch burned at the stake.

She saw a woman drowning as a dam broke and flood waters tore apart a town.

She saw a Deveraux man and a Cahors woman buried in a building as an earthquake shook it.

And then time froze inside the whirlwind and everything halted. Nicolette was surrounded by cool, white ether as she sank slowly to a cold white marble floor. Then, as the mist thinned, she saw Elijah across the floor, but the children were nowhere to be seen.

"Marie! Louis! Where are you? Elijah!"

Nicolette tried to run to him, and found she could not. She was rooted to the spot. She screamed . . . but no sound came out of her mouth. Elijah's dark eyes burned as his mouth worked. She could tell he was trying to free them both from whatever magic held them fast.

The last of the roiling fog vanished. White columns rose high above her, disappearing into mist. Men and women with milky eyes sat on white marble thrones. They were draped in white robes, and she was afraid to look at them.

"We summon thee, Cahors and Deveraux," a voice said, although none of their mouths moved. *"You destroy the balance. You affect time and space. This cannot be allowed."*

What? Nicolette thought, still unable to speak aloud.

"We are the Blind Justices. We preserve the balance between good and evil. And you are growing too strong. Cahors and Deveraux may not exist in harmony, or the world

will cease to exist. Henceforth, let your Houses war against each other. Let them battle and plot. Where there was love, now there is murderous vendetta."

Elijah, my love, Nicolette thought as each Justice in turn blazed in a nimbus of light. Then all the brilliance was sucked from the room.

"Cast out," the voice said. *"Cast out of the paradise of true love. Cahors, Deveraux, you may never enter it together again."*

No! Nicolette screamed. She stared at Elijah, willing him to stop them, slay them, call down the wrath of his God upon them. His eyes were burning; flames danced inside them. Ebony flames, black fire, and then . . .

. . . and then she saw a young woman, weeping tears of black fire; she was a child of the future; she was Holly, of the Cahors, and she loved Jeraud Deveraux.

Oh, my sister, Nicolette cried out to her. *Don't let this come to pass.*

Then she saw nothing as she fainted dead away.

Nicolette, Elijah, Marie, and Louis were never seen again. Deveraux blamed Cahors for the disappearance. Cahors knights snuck into Castle Deveraux and assassinated the six children of the reigning duke in an act of vengeance. The two families hated each other, with wrath that pushed past sanity; a rage as vast as that of Kali fed the hatred that tore them into factions and wars and hatred and bloodshed.

Across the continents and oceans, knowing sorcerers and wizards sought to keep it that way. If the Cahors and Deveraux hacked at each other's necks, they would hack at no one else's.

Scarborough: Richard, Anne-Louise, Owen, and Sasha

Richard paced, worried for his daughter and feeling more helpless than he'd felt in a long time. "Is it possible she went after Amanda and Tommy?" he asked.

Anne-Louise shook her head. "I don't think Nicole can open a portal by herself, and besides, I don't think she would leave Owen."

He knew she was right, but he didn't like it. Divide and conquer. It was an old battle tactic, and you didn't get much more divided than he had been in the last several months. Enough.

"Can you find the ones in India again, get a good location and open a portal, a two-way one?"

"Maybe I can open a portal," Sasha said. "It seems I'm getting rather good at that."

"Or someone is," he replied pointedly.

She hadn't told them very much about her encounter with Merlin. But it was clear she was terrified. He would let it go for the moment, but sooner or later she was going to have to tell them everything she knew.

Anne-Louise headed for her room, and a moment

later was back. "A strand of Pablo's hair; that will help us find them."

"You're wanting to go to them?" Sasha asked.

"No. I'm going to go and bring them back."

House Moore might have been a death trap, but at least it was one he was getting to know fairly well.

Mumbai

Armand turned around and killed a demon that had been trying to catch him unawares. Beside him a portal shimmered, and Richard Anderson stepped through. He was carrying a machine gun.

The man flashed him a wicked grin. "The cavalry is here. Now get the hell out," he said, jerking a finger over his shoulder to the portal.

"Pablo!" Armand shouted. In an instant the boy was by his side and they stepped through together.

Demons flew through the air and crawled across the ground in an attempt to follow. Richard fired on them and was pleased to see that the magic in the bullets had as great an impact as the bullets themselves.

"Dad!"

Tommy and Amanda ran toward him, half-carrying, half-dragging Jer between them. They passed through the portal. Behind them came Philippe carrying a young woman. Next to him was Eli.

The last time Richard had checked, Eli had been

on the other side. He swung his gun toward him. His finger tightened on the trigger, and he felt a small measure of satisfaction. He had always hated Eli.

"No! He is with us!" Philippe said.

Richard knew he could shoot anyway and claim it was an accident. He sighed and instead shot a demon who was chasing the three. They barreled past him through the portal. He took one last sweeping look but didn't see Nicole. He would have stayed, but he figured the others had answers. He'd go back to House Moore with them, and come back better armed—with weapons and knowledge.

Back in the Great Room at House Moore, Anne-Louise and Sasha were already tending the wounded. The woman had been stabbed in the chest, and Jer looked like someone had broken their fists on his face.

Amanda ran over to Richard and threw her arms around him. She kissed his cheek and then pulled away, wiping at her eyes. "Where's Nicole?" she asked.

"I was hoping you'd tell me," he said grimly.

ELEVEN

ROSEMARY

☾

Lives are lost and lines are changed
Time itself is rearranged
But we do not fear the night
For the sun god gives us might

Hiding now in darkness near
Pressing in is all our fear
Something stirs deep inside
Something that we need to hide

The Temple of the Blind Justices: Nicole

"How can you think I did this to myself on purpose?" Nicole shouted.

"You are a Deveraux lover." The voice echoed all around her.

"Not for a long time. Or didn't you notice we broke up. His dad murdered my mom, and he would have done the same to me. Owen, I don't know how he came to me. I don't even really remember being pregnant. It was like one day I wasn't and the next day

I was nine months pregnant. Like magic."

She could feel them stirring at that. Something else popped into her mind. "I believe someone has changed time." The thought had come to her a few times, but she had quickly discounted it.

The Justices reacted more strongly.

"How do you know this?"

"I don't. I don't know anything," she said. She felt tired, overwhelmed, weak. And more than that, she felt drained. "I need to go back to be with my sister. We're twins and I think we feed each other our magical power. Please. Let me go."

"Do you think you are the first daughter of magic to have a twin? You are not even the only or the most powerful twins in this time."

"What? Who are you talking about?" Nicole demanded.

"You were lucky to remain together. Not so with the others. Too strong, too much power. Together they tip the scales."

She stared at their unmoving mouths. Their milky eyes.

"Who?"

"Separated and changed, one hiding and the other never knowing her name."

"Why are you telling me this?" Nicole asked.

And then, in her heart, she knew why. They were

not going to let her go. That was why they spoke so openly.

No. I can't leave Owen and Amanda.

She took a ragged breath. "If you only plan on killing me, at least speak English. If your plan was so brilliant, prove it to me, tell me who you separated."

"One child in darkness hid in shame. The other child in light without her own name."

"What does that even mean?" Nicole asked.

"They are both Deveraux."

A chill danced up Nicole's spine. Deveraux twin girls. And she and Amanda were Cahors twin girls. That couldn't be a coincidence. But the others were more powerful than she and Amanda. *Add Holly, though, and no Deveraux alive can touch us,* Nicole thought. *The one raised in the Supreme Coven knew who she was but hid. Who was she afraid of? Michael? Sir William? The other one, raised in the Mother Coven with no idea that she was a Deveraux.*

And in her mind's eye she saw the battle in the headquarters of the Supreme Coven and the warlock Eve who knew Jer, who'd helped them, and who'd escaped herself. And then she saw another face, a woman with strikingly similar features and exquisite grace. Anne-Louise. Anne-Louise, who could cast wards far more powerful than any other. Anne-Louise, who had been raised inside the temple of the

Mother Coven because she'd been an *orphan.*

Nicole fell to her knees and retched. Anne-Louise who even now was with Owen.

France: Kari

Kari stood before the ruins of Castle Cahors. Evil permeated the air like a foul stench; she could feel the death throes of a thousand souls; a thousand thousand. There had been much death-dealing here, for political gain, and magical conquest.

I hear the dead, she thought, *because I am dead.*

She didn't know why she was there. It was like waking up into a dream, not waking out of one. The air shimmered, and she stumbled backward. The ground vibrated, tickling the soles of her feet.

Tu est là, said the voice. You are there.

"Yes," she said in English.

One such as you completes the circuit. One is here who will die if she comes to your time. And you have died.

"I died," she whispered. Someone else might have been terrified, but she felt . . . nothing.

It is not yet time. They are coming. Wait for them.

In her mind she saw an inn down the road. Behind her the French cab idled, waiting for her. She turned and climbed back in. An hour later she lay down on her bed in her rented room, and did not dream.

Three days later she was summoned again.

★ ★ ★

Dr. Nigel Temar stepped out of the shadows of the chestnut trees just as a young woman with brown hair approached the ruins of Castle Cahors. For one instant he thought she was Kari, but no such luck. And yet, his GPS system had finally begun to work, and it had signaled that she should be there.

Then the woman saw him, and looked as confused as he probably did. She cocked her head as an Asian-looking man came up behind her and took her hand.

"*Bonjour*," she said cautiously. The man remained silent.

"These are lovely ruins, are they not?" Nigel said. "In my guidebook—"

"They're not in any guidebooks, at least the ones we have," she cut in. "Do you know what they're called?"

Nigel licked his lips. "Castle Ca—"

He stopped speaking as he caught the flash of motion on the road, and realized a car was approaching. He watched as it rolled to a stop.

And Kari stepped out.

"Oh, God!" he shouted, just as the woman and the man yelled, "Kari!"

All three of them ran to her. The woman reached Kari first and threw her arms around her. "We've been so worried. What happened?"

"Where've you been?" Dr. Temar demanded. "Why did you leave like that?"

The Asian man blinked. "I know you. You're Dr. Temar, from the university."

"Yes," Nigel said. "And you're Tommy Nagai. A friend of Kari's. I've been looking for her. And my system . . ." He gestured to his tracker, a small basic black rectangle. He managed a weak smile. "My system *worked*."

"Probably because it's Wolf Moon," Amanda said. "When there's wild work to be done." She took a deep breath. "I'm Amanda Anderson. A bunch of us . . . hung out with Kari."

"Performed magic rituals, you mean," Dr. Temar said, "with Jer Deveraux."

"And you brought Kari back," Amanda said. "But not with magic."

The earth beneath their feet shook.

Hard.

"What's happening?" Dr. Temar cried. He grabbed on to Kari just as the ground he'd been standing on jutted upward, slamming them both to their knees. He heard Tommy shout; then Amanda began speaking in Latin, or a language more ancient and arcane. Dirt clouds spewed upward, and Dr. Temar's left leg dangled in thin air. His arms around Kari, he pulled up on his elbows and looked over his shoulder, to see a huge fissure zigzag through the wild grass.

"Kari!" he cried, pushing her out of the way. But the fissure cracked wider, sending shoots toward them, as if it were chasing them. He scrambled faster, grabbing her wrists and dragging her toward the road.

There was a huge *whoosh,* and then a roar like a sonic boom. He whirled around as smoke and steam rushed out of the fissure like tons of dry ice.

The air shimmered; the sky lowered, darkened. A deep blue-white glow burst out of the huge crack in the earth.

And in it, surrounded by a ball of icy light, a man stood. He wore a midnight blue magician's robe spangled with moons and stars, and a hood. His face was leathery, and old, and a white bushy beard hung down to his chest. His eyes were eerily blue.

The sphere vanished, and he stood facing the ruins of Castle Cahors.

"Merci," the man said to Kari.

Amanda stared at him. He looked familiar, like an image from a book . . . a book . . . *the book.*

Kari said, "Owen."

"Is he here?" the man asked. He squared his shoulders. "I demand him."

"Owen?" Tommy asked. "How do you know—"

"Who are you?" Dr. Temar said.

"Oh, Goddess," Amanda whispered. "I know who he is." She took a deep breath. "He's Merlin."

"Merlin?" Tommy said, his eyes widening. "Like in the movies?"

"Movies?" the man shouted. "Man, have you eyes?"

"Owen," Kari said again.

Amanda stared at the man. At Merlin. He couldn't be . . . and yet, where had they kept Nicole prisoner? On the island of Avalon. And what had she told them? There had been something there. Something ancient.

"I told you to bring him," Merlin said through clenched teeth. He was speaking to Kari.

She shook her head. "Did not hear."

He doubled his fists. *"Still* they thwart me! From the grave they taunt me! Melchior, Gaspar, Balthasar, I will end you."

"The Wise Men," Amanda murmured.

Merlin whirled on her. His face was contorted with fury. "Wise, indeed. Ruthless, cunning, immoral bastards. Where is the child?"

Tommy looked at Amanda. "What's going on?"

Suddenly Merlin smiled. He exhaled slowly, and his features softened. He pulled down his hood, revealing a mane of white hair, which he raked with his long fingers.

"Forgive me. I have been a long time away. Imprisoned. Unjustly," he added. His voice was tinged with insincere warmth. He reached a hand toward Amanda. "I sense much power in you."

Kari stirred. "Folklore," she said.

"Yes, yes," Dr. Temar cut in. "Merlin was imprisoned in the Crystal Cave. A fatherless boy whose name meant 'Falcon' became a great sorcerer."

"Falcon," Kari said. "Fantasme."

"The familiar of the Deveraux," Amanda added. She cocked her head, bracing herself for a magical attack. Waves of darkness rolled off Merlin. He was deadly. Dangerous.

"*They* imprisoned you," Dr. Temar said. "The Wise Men." Merlin raised his brows. "How could that possibly have come to pass?" Dr. Temar asked.

"Because . . . you were one of them," Amanda said. "You were astrologers, sorcerers."

"Zoroastrians," Dr. Temar added.

"Nonsense," Merlin said, shaking his head. "Now, if I might see Owen."

"That's why you're here. For him," Amanda said in a low, icy voice. "Somehow you got free and you want him."

"I want my son," he affirmed. "He is mine. I mean to have him." He began to make motions. Light and thunder blurred the air. Crows cawed. "And no one will keep him from me."

The sky went black as he disappeared. And everyone returned to House Moore.

The Temple of the Blind Justices: Nicole

Nicole had a vague awareness that time was passing. She did know that she was growing weaker, and she could almost hear the cries of her loved ones as they searched for her.

Then there was a stirring. "He is free," one of the Justices whispered.

Just one. They were separate, individuals. Something had changed.

"Who?" Nicole said, shooting to her feet. "Not—"

"The child's father," another one acknowledged.

Nicole shook her head. That terrible thing on the island, it had come into her room; it had somehow fathered a child with her. So many terrible things. How was that balance? From where she'd been sitting, the bad guys seemed to win a lot more than the good guys. She looked from face to face, seeking an ally, seeking a friend. They all sat in stony silence, immune to her pain.

Except for one. The one in the center chair was smiling. His robes were white, and yet there was a darkness surrounding him. Could they not see it?

She looked closer. He was tall, and his cheekbones were deep and hollow, like William Moore's. Where had she seen him before?

Her breath caught. Once she had caught Amanda sleepwalking, and Amanda had been standing and staring at a row of ancestral portraits. But not at the *row*. At the portrait of this very man.

She raised her arm and pointed at him.

"You! You're the one who has been working against us. You're the one who's been talking to my cousin and nearly caused me to kill my own baby." Rage made her shake. "You're still a Moore. Still loyal to your House."

"Is this true?" the rest of the Justices asked in unison, turning like one person to face the accused.

"No," he denied, blinking his white eyes.

And then suddenly the air around him was filled with images. Nicole and the Justices watched as time and time again he sabotaged the Cahors and manipulated them. Yes, changing time. Yes, summoning imps and sprites. Calling the yowic. Alerting Merlin that rescue was at hand.

"She is correct. You are not a keeper of the balance. Xavier Moore, as once you were called, you are guilty," the Justices proclaimed, rising from their marble thrones.

"No. She's lying. She's creating those images," Xavier Moore insisted, leaping from his own throne. "To frame me. To take attention off her own wrongdoing."

"Guilty."

"I am *not!*" he cried.

"*Guilty!*" They stretched out their hands, as Nicole had. There was a flash of fire.

He was gone. His throne was empty.

"What happened?" Nicole asked.

"*Guilty. The treacherous Xavier Moore tipped the scales. He exists no longer.*"

She exhaled. "Oh, thank Goddess. You know I'm innocent."

There was a rippling, as though they were murmuring, but not loud enough for her to hear.

"*You will be released. But we must find another to take his place.*"

"Who?" Nicole asked.

"*One who has touched evil as often as good.*"

Fear gripped Nicole. "You don't mean—"

And then she was gone.

And she was in House Moore.

And staring at her were both Philippe and Eli.

Philippe sat, holding Nicole's hand as he finished recounting his part of the tale. When he had finished, Richard leaned forward and spoke.

"So we know that Merlin was once one of the Magi and that the others imprisoned him. So the question is, how did they do it and how can we replicate it?"

"I remember very little about what I saw and felt

when we were at the Dom de Cologne," Pablo said. "I called out for Philippe . . ." He thought a moment. "They were buried with something. A device. An amulet."

"Good, Pablo. That's good. How do we retrieve it?" Richard asked.

"By force," Eli said, his jaw clenched.

The Frozen Wasteland: Holly

While she could keep herself warm, Holly seemed unable to find or conjure anything with which to feed herself. Her stomach growled angrily and she knew that she was in trouble. Her powers had been steadily waning, and she knew it was only a matter of time before they failed completely. And then she would starve. If she didn't freeze to death first.

Suddenly there was a brilliant flash of light, and when it passed, she was not where she had been. She stood in a circle, surrounded by columns and massive thronelike chairs. Was this hallucination brought on by her impending death? She turned slowly.

"Holly Cathers. We are the Justices. We maintain the balance in this and all worlds between good and evil. Our numbers are diminished and we seek to replace the one who is no more. We have chosen you."

She opened her mouth to ask what was going on, but suddenly she knew . . . everything. She saw Nicole standing in the very same spot. She saw the destruction of the Justice who had tipped the scales. She saw the balance, teetering on a fine point throughout all of space and time.

She shook her head fiercely. "No, you can't make me!"

And then standing beside her was the Goddess, in Her form as the Queen of Witches. Holly had seen her too often, had sacrificed too much to her not to recognize her in a moment.

"There is always a cost, a price to be paid," the Goddess said. "You have known this, and yet you have sacrificed to both the dark and the light. Now this is your destiny. If you deny it, all whom you love will be destroyed from the earth."

"You have to let me help them," Holly insisted. "They love you. Worship you. How can you threaten me with their deaths?"

The Goddess gazed on her, her face both beautiful and terrible to behold. Her eyes were very blue, her lips shell pink. And yet, as light changed and moved in her eyes, they darkened.

"It is no threat," she replied. "It is what will happen. You may help them by protecting the balance. Anything else, and you shall curse them."

Holly collapsed onto the marble floor. She had known there was a price to be paid, but she had never dreamed it would be this.

Jer, she cried out in spirit.

Holly.

She could hear him and feel him in her heart and her mind. So much silence for so long, and now there he was again. She closed her eyes and cried.

Comme je t'aime. Comme je t'adore.

"If you love him and do not wish him to die, then you must let him go," the Justices proclaimed. *"For all time, and all eternity. You will never, ever see him again."*

And that was how she knew that she had never completely given up hope that they would be together. For if she had, her heart would not now have been able to break.

Cologne, Germany: the Heroes

They had made it inside the cathedral unchallenged. That alone was enough to frighten Nicole. Though it cost her dearly, she had left Owen behind at House Moore, speaking privately to Sasha to guard him well. Sasha, not Anne-Louise. Sasha looked puzzled but agreed; and Nicole left without telling anyone what she'd learned while a prisoner of the Justices. She was fairly certain Anne-Louise didn't know that she was a Deveraux. And perhaps it was a lie, created by the traitor, Xavier Moore, meant to confuse them.

Dr. Temar and Kari had also been left behind at House Moore, although there had been secret debates about sending him and Kari away. If Merlin attempted to contact her again, the dead woman could act as a scrying stone for him, acting as his eyes and ears inside House Moore. But no one had the heart to abandon the two. Nicole knew that Nigel Temar had brought Kari back because he loved her. His attempt had gone terribly wrong, but who was she to deny the powerful pull of love?

Tears welled; she had to be here, in Cologne. She was one of the Three. And she reminded herself that Sasha could open a portal in case they needed to retreat. The situation was precarious at best; when had her life and the lives of her loved ones been truly safe?

Never. Maybe we can change that. With what we do this day.

They had taken two days to travel to the cathedral. They had avoided using any magic, to not draw attention to themselves or their intended destination.

As Nicole entered the cathedral, she couldn't help but contrast it with her last visit there. This time she wasn't alone. This time she was seeking something far more precious than sanctuary.

Together she, Amanda, and Pablo headed past the glittering altar and the box that was said to house the relics of the Three Kings. A pretty fantasy for the faithful and the tourists. Their finder's spell had revealed their real resting place—in a tiny crypt dead center in the nave of the cathedral.

Past cobwebs and skittering creatures they crept, hearts in their throats. Saints, queens, and knights lay in effigy atop stone coffins etched with Latin prayers for their souls.

She smelled spices—frankincense, and myrrh.

And then, there it was . . . a simple stone box, unadorned, save for a pentagram on the side.

The Star of Bethlehem.

Nicole looked at Amanda and Pablo. The others had fanned out inside the church at key places, watching and waiting, alert for their signal. If Merlin knew of the existence of this place, he would surely be coming. If the kings were really in the sarcophagus. If they had the means to send Merlin back.

Too many questions and not enough answers.

Using their combined magic, the three of them lifted off the lid of the sarcophagus. Nicole gazed down on the full skeletons of three men crowded together, wearing the faded tatters of what appeared to have been very ornate clothing.

Nicole's skin crawled. *Please, help us,* she begged the dead sorcerers.

"Look, around their necks," Amanda whispered.

Three tarnished gold discs hung on chains. Pablo nodded.

"Yes," he whispered, clutching both their hands. "Yes. I saw them when I collapsed. But I do not know how they go together."

Nicole clenched her teeth, reached down, and removed the gold disc from the one closest to her. Amanda and Pablo did the same. Then they looked at one another, and each of them hung a disc around their necks.

"Oh, my Goddess, I'm so scared," Amanda confessed.

The weight of the gold disc was like the weight of the world. Nicole nodded and took Amanda's hand.

"We're together," she reminded her. "I'll watch out for you."

"And me for you. And you," Amanda added, to Pablo.

Hastily they replaced the sarcophagus lid, and then hurried back to the front of the cathedral.

"We have it, but we don't know yet how to use it," Nicole said to Jer.

Jer just nodded as he glanced at the gleaming discs, then returned his attention to one of the windows.

"What's wrong?" Amanda asked in a low voice.

"We're in trouble," Jer said.

Nicole looked past him and gasped. There, just beyond the church grounds, was an army of nightmares waiting to destroy them—demons, wraiths, monsters. Nicole didn't even have words for all the horrors surrounding the cathedral.

"Why can't we just open a portal back to House Moore?" Amanda asked.

"The cathedral itself is heavily warded. We won't be able to open a portal until we get off church grounds," Armand explained.

"Owen," Nicole said faintly.

"We'll do what we can," Philippe promised. He glanced at Jer. "I am yours to command."

Preparations were quickly made. They conjured armor, weapons, and a few warhorses. The plan was to make it past enemy lines and open a portal at the first opportunity.

They rode out of the church doors and lined up just in front of the entrance, facing the enemy.

For one moment there was absolute silence, and then the earth itself seemed to groan as their enemies rode, flew, and marched toward them with Merlin leading the charge, seated atop a dragon.

Jer felt the fear that rippled through the line like electricity. No one moved, or breathed, as they watched the enemy advance. And then there was the sound of a single bullet, and the mighty dragon crashed to the ground, dead, a gaping wound where its left eye had once been.

"I'm sorry. Were we waiting for something?" he heard Richard shout.

"Charge! Attack!" Jer Deveraux shouted, and his voice echoed off the stones. Lightning blazed; a dozen shooting stars bulleted across the heavens, bursting red, green, white, and silver, as prayers and spells erupted toward the God and the Goddess. Horses and demons and ghosts raced toward one another. Weapons clashed and clanged.

In another time I was another warrior, Jer thought. *I led the charge again and again; I was feared; I was fierce; I was the young lion of House Deveraux. And a witch felled me. A witch brought my House low. I was a king and she—*

She is not here. She is safe.

I am Jer, and she is Holly, and we're our own people.

"Good-bye," he said in English.

Dressed in the armor and helmet of a knight, Philippe kicked his horse hard. From the opposing side a Deveraux wraith streaked toward him. A blur of bone, black, and scarlet, its unearthly shriek pierced his eardrums. Its dark green robe flared; black eyes stared from beneath its hood. It flared through the sky with a scythe raised over its head, the death-dealing weapon gripped in a hand of bone.

Philippe's warhorse galloped fearlessly, chuffing steam, and he aimed his magical lance at the apparition. He braced himself, knowing that although he could destroy the wraith, it could cut off his head.

He kicked the horse's flanks, urging it to greater speed. The lance weighed thirty kilos at least, and taxed his biceps and forearm; he willed the strain to another place and filled his mind with expectations of victory, and Nicole's image blazed brightly. He heard the rush of blood in his temples, overpowering the shouts and explosions surrounding him. He could see nothing but Nicole's face.

The wraith bore in on him, speeding faster than Philippe had expected. Lightning struck the scythe and rain broke the sky, pouring down like a waterfall. Closer, closer; the icy breath of death blew on him.

The scythe slashed down, slicing Philippe's horse across its neck, and the horse whinnied in agony. Its forelegs buckled, and as it went down, Philippe prepared to let go of the lance and leap off his mount. But at the crucial moment, he ticked his glance down, to find Eli on his back, blood pouring through his breastplate. If Philippe dropped his lance, it would hit Eli.

The wraith's black eyes met his, and Philippe saw his face in their obsidian reflection. He was going to die.

Nicole, he thought. *If Eli and I both die, who will protect her? It must be you, my Heavenly Father; and you, Mother Goddess. Give me something to shield her, save her. Let me never rest until she and Owen are truly safe.*

The cold blade of the scythe touched his neck. He would die praying to his Christian God, to his Mother. His lips moved.

And then: He saw.

He saw it all.

He heard it.

This is the ritual they must perform, the Ladies of the Lily three: Together they must put the amulet, piece to piece to piece, jagged, like their hearts. Worn down, like their souls. And yet, potent when merged and bound by true love of sister to sister to sister witch.

The words of the ritual danced in the air around him and flowed through him.

Let me outlive my death, he begged. *Let me tell them.*

And then . . .

The scythe came down.

In the Temple of the Blind Justices: Holly

"It is forbidden to return," the single voice of the Blind Justices informed Holly. But she knew the strains of that voice now: Loudest in her refusal was a Justice named Alariel, the Justice who sat to Holly's right. They all had names.

Holly stood before them, her marble throne vacant, and turned in a slow circle. She was dressed as they were, in white veils and robes, like a nun. White on white on white, blinding.

"I'm going," she told them. "Don't try to stop me. I am the most powerful witch in the world." Her heart was pounding, and she knew she sounded less like a grown woman in control of her own fate and more like a petulant child. She was so frightened and worried for her Jer and her cousins that she could barely speak.

"Not this world. We can stop you," the voice said.

"Then . . . don't. Please," she said, forcing herself to sound more reasonable. "Let me go to them, and explain. They're fighting for the sake of the balance, but they're distracted because they don't know what happened to me."

"You may not save them." That was Stephen St. John, once a mortal, like herself. *"You may not take sides. It will further upset the balance. This must play out on the mortal plane."*

"I won't save them," she promised.

And then . . .

Oh, my Goddess, the blood. The deaths. Eli! Philippe!

She was in a city, which she had not expected. It was Cologne. The cathedral loomed large against the moon, and the unseeing, unknowing citizens were nowhere to be seen. It was as if another city had been superimposed on the mortal one, and the battle played out there.

Pulled into an alley away from the chaos, Philippe's head lay beside his body. Eli was bleeding profusely beside him. Amanda held hands with Nicole. Her hand was clasped tightly around Amanda's as the two recited a healing spell, Nicole's voice cracking at every syllable with broken weeping.

Tommy and Richard stood with them, heads bowed. Then Tommy slowly raised his chin, and saw Holly. His eyes widened and his lips parted.

"Holly," he rasped.

The others looked up.

"Holly, oh, Goddess!" Amanda cried and tried to run to her, but Nicole blinked hard and yanked her back. Her eyes were almost swollen shut, and her lips were bleeding.

"Holly, help them," Nicole said, asking no questions, needing no answers as she swayed, but remained standing.

"She needs us," Amanda corrected. "We're the Ladies of the Lily. It's the power of the Three. Oh, Holly, where have you been? We've needed you so badly. Come on, quickly!"

Holly's twin cousins held out their free hands, intending to create their circle. She took a step toward them.

Then she remembered her promise. And the memory of every terrible thing she had done to acquire more power to save her covenates hit her like a fatal blow. She was more powerful than any of them, and because of it she was unable to help them.

"I'm sorry," she said, as skyrockets of light flared overhead and an explosion shook the ground. Light flared around her, sealing her into a protective sphere of light. "I can't. I can't do anything to help you."

"No!" Nicole screamed, falling down between Philippe and Eli. "Look at Philippe! And Eli is dying!"

A projectile slammed into the rock above Holly's head; fragments sprayed outward like shrapnel. The bubble around Holly intensified. Amanda and Tommy murmured an incantation, forming an invisible barrier between the group and the flying pieces of rock. Nicole threw her arms protectively over both men.

"What's happened to you?" Richard asked Holly.

"I—I'm one of the Blind Justices now," she said, and she knew that until she'd spoken those words, she hadn't really believed it. "We maintain the balance. I'm not allowed to interfere."

"*Interfere?*" Nicole said, raising her head. "I'm begging you to save Eli's life. And Owen! Oh, Philippe . . ." She caught herself. "Damn you, Holly, help us!"

Holly's heart was breaking. She could feel the sphere thickening as she stared through its light, casting her loved ones in a milky white glow.

"If it was *Jer,* you would . . . ," Amanda began, then trailed off.

Jer staggered into the alley, Eve's arm slung over his shoulders. His face was bloodied; Holly couldn't see any of his scars. Eve's expression barely changed when she caught sight of Holly. The warlock was worn down, shell-shocked. She eased her arm off Jer's shoulder and stepped away. Jer stared at Holly for a heartbeat. Two, three. And then he ran for her, through the sphere, and threw his arms around her. She held him close, breathing in the scent of him, the solid warmth, his love.

"Holly, by the God," he breathed, and then they kissed. Their lips touched; their mouths joined. He pulled the breath out of her, pushed it back, mingled it with his. Their hearts beat against each other. They held, believed, fused.

"I'm so sorry, I'm so sorry," Jer said in a rush. "Holly, I love you. Join me in thrall, the lady to the lord. Now. Here." He gestured to Amanda, Nicole, and Tommy. "Help us form a Circle. Eve, no offense, but you're a warlock, and—"

For a moment Holly couldn't even react. Then sorrow welled inside her, and anger pulled her down, down to the depths beyond where anyone should have to go, have to suffer . . .

All she could do was not react.

"Okay," Jer said, "Nicole, you stand there. Oh, God, if we can heal Eli, and conjure the Black Fire . . ."

Holly still didn't move. Jer grew still, gazed at her. "Holly?"

"I . . ." She started crying. Burying her face in her hands, her shoulders moved as she shook her head. "Can't."

"Holly, I know I hurt you," Jer said, "and it was awful for you, being with Laurent. But I'm ready, and our side needs it. I love you. And I know you love me."

"Jer," she said.

"She's something called a Blind Justice," Amanda said. "She can't 'interfere.'" She made air quotes.

"What? A what?" Jer asked. Holly could feel his gaze on her.

"You have to join in thrall with my cousin. We need Eli," Eve stated flatly. "We're going to conjure the Black Fire."

"No. You don't know if you can control it," Richard argued.

Holly lowered her hands. Jer stood before her with his blood and his scars, and he was the most beautiful man she had ever seen. Everything in her wanted to be with him, to be in thrall, to know that joy with her one true love.

Anguished, she put her arms around herself and wept. "You have to forget me, Jer. All of you," she managed. "Forever."

★ ★ ★

Jer blinked, staring hard at the spot that Holly had been standing in. She had just vanished. Was he hallucinating? Was he dead?

"What happened?" he asked.

Armand came up beside him. "She is a Justice. She is not allowed to help."

Three huge beings stepped forward. Their clothes, their very faces radiated light.

"She may not help, but we will," said the tallest of the three.

He clapped his hands, and in a swirl of light the cathedral, the battle, everything was gone.

And once more they were in the Great Room in the house of their enemy in Scarborough.

TWELVE

PEPPER

☽

Turn back the clock, turn back time
If you expect any reason or rhyme
For what we've been told is not true
The feud is old, older than new

Scrying, searching for the truth
We seek to reclaim beauty and youth
For there a secret dormant lies
That will free us all or else all dies

Scarborough

Sasha was relieved when the others appeared, but she soon joined them in mourning the loss of Philippe and Holly. She, Anne-Louise, and Amanda set about trying to heal Eli. The damage was extensive, though, and she wasn't sure that he would live out the night.

The only word Nicole spoke through it all was to invite in lawyer Derek when he showed up at the front gate.

Derek entered the room and stopped in his tracks

when he saw the ragtag assembly. "Jeraud Deveraux? How . . . What happened?" he asked.

His eyes flitted nervously between Eve and Anne-Louise.

"Good and evil, life and death, you know, the standards," Jer informed him sarcastically.

Derek ignored Jer and instead turned toward Eve. "Are you okay?" he asked, and from the way his voice and face softened, Sasha could tell that Derek was in love with Eve. Of course, they must have known each other. They both served the Supreme Coven.

Wistfully she remembered a time when Michael had looked at her that way. Something told her, though, that Derek was a far better man, warlock or no, than Michael could ever have been.

Anne-Louise was uneasy in her skin. The beings, angels maybe, that had helped them escape had not traveled with them to House Moore. Or if they had, she couldn't see them. Armand and Pablo sat together, grieving the loss of Philippe and praying for his soul.

She worked late into the night trying to stabilize Eli, and as dawn broke, he began to heal. She wandered into the kitchen for some coffee and found several others also awake—including Eve. The warlock seemed so familiar to her but she couldn't decide why.

Pepper

Eve's gaze was hooded, uneasy. "There's something about you," she said.

Anne-Louise nodded. "You feel it too?"

There was a beat.

"So, you two still don't know?" Derek asked.

Anne-Louise turned to him, somewhat surprised that he was still there.

"Know what?" Eve asked.

"You're twins," Nicole said from her perch on a kitchen school.

"Twins?" Eve and Anne-Louise echoed at the same time.

"Yeah, I got that from the Justices. Apparently the two of you together would be way too powerful so for the sake of balance they split you up at birth."

"*What?*" Anne-Louise cried. "Our parents—"

"They were Deveraux," Eve said, interrupting.

Anne-Louise felt sick. *Deveraux.* "You're wrong," she said. Then, as Derek sat unmoving, she added, "How do you know all this?"

Derek shrugged as if the answer were obvious. "When Michael Deveraux died, we were able to track down and see all the Deveraux family."

"Family finder's spell," Amanda muttered.

Jer straightened. "Guess I must not have been in dear old Dad's will, or else I would have heard from you guys."

363

Derek smiled. "He left everything to Eli."

Jer nodded.

"You're my sister?" Anne-Louise blurted out suddenly.

Eve nodded slowly. "Apparently." She moved first, and a moment later they embraced.

The Ruins of Castle Cahors, France

Merlin still had to be dealt with.

The Coven of the Survivors had all agreed that the final battle should not take place in Sir William's ancestral home. It was too much of a home field advantage. After a lot of discussion they all settled on the ruins of the Cahors Castle, where Merlin had re-entered their world. They would take the battle there.

Richard still wasn't entirely clear what had happened in Cologne. One minute they had been in the thick of battle in the city, and the next they had been transported to Scarborough. There they had been for three days, resting, healing. Eli had made a complete recovery, as had everyone else who had been injured.

But Philippe stayed dead.

With Sasha's help, Jer and Eli created a portal to arrive at the ruins of the Cahors Castle. The three figures—angels?—were waiting for them, and they helped Anne-Louise erect a protective barrier that would cloak their presence until they were ready.

Dawn broke. Richard knew it was the last one most of them would ever see. He stood apart from the others, savoring it, committing each color and hue to memory. After a few minutes Pablo joined him, and together they watched and breathed and tried not to let the coming ordeal take the moment from them.

"You think of fishing often," Pablo said.

Richard looked surprised, and then he smiled. "I suppose I do."

"I have never fished." Pablo looked very young, and very alone. Richard felt a rush of sympathy for him.

"We'll go when this is over."

"*Gracias.* I would like that," Pablo told him.

At last they turned and rejoined the others. Another final battle. It seemed ironic. Maybe there was no such thing as final battles, just ever more overwhelming ones. Richard feared that compared to the assault on the Supreme Coven headquarters in London this was going to be a nightmare.

Some who had stood with them then were dead now, but that didn't necessarily mean anything. He smiled at Kari encouragingly. Others had fought against them the last time. He shot a steely-eyed look at Eli, who returned it without flinching.

He wished Holly were with them. She was dangerous, unpredictable, but she was also powerful and completely devoted to his daughters, who could not be the three Ladies of the Lily without her.

It was almost time. Jer could feel it, hear it as though the ruins of Isabeau's home were speaking to him. He walked the front line, inspecting his troops.

Tommy and Amanda stood hand in hand, the lady to the lord. Nicole stood beside her sister, and beside Nicole was his brother, Eli. Witch and warlock, female and male, their magic would work well together. Eve and her twin, Anne-Louise, stood together, one a master of offense and the other a master of defense; the power the two of them were already generating was incredible.

With a call from Anne-Louise, Luna, high priestess of the Mother Coven, had been shamed into coming, and bringing witch fighters with her. Rose had come too. Even now they stood at attention, waiting for Jer's signal. Luna, Sasha, and Rose formed another trinity.

Still others were summoned from covens of the Goddess around the world, standing by as a second wave if needed. Though Jer believed if they were called for they wouldn't make it in time to do anything but bury the bodies.

Derek, having confessed to a closeted fascination

with Catholicism, stood with Pablo and Armand. They all wore crosses, even Derek, and Armand was adorned from head to toe with symbols from every religion Jer had ever heard of, and then some. If history held true, most of the demons would attack him first.

Behind these three men stood the three angels. It creeped Jer out, and he regretted his unkind thoughts about the European witches and their worship of the Christian God. The lead angel inclined his head slightly to Jer, not out of deference but indicating readiness. Jer wasn't sure how he knew the difference, but he felt it in his very bones, just as he felt how inhuman they were.

I guess there has to be a flip side to demons. After all, it's supposed to be about balance. There was naked fear in Derek's eyes as he, too, stared at the angels. Pablo and Armand had their heads bowed in prayer, and the angel nearest Armand seemed to be whispering in his ear.

Jer turned and kept walking, forcing his thoughts back to the rest of his people. When the time came, he would stand with Kari. They had cared for each other once and they should be able to work some powerful magic, even if one of them was dead. Who knew? Maybe it would create a fierce, unexpected kind of magic. On his mark, he, Eli, and Eve would manifest the Black Fire.

Cats wound their way in and around the line and

the groups. Jer didn't know how, but it seemed that every cat who had once loved or aided one of the ladies was there. Bast, Freya, and Astarte all appeared to be alive and well. Hecate and Osiris were well, though certainly not alive. Whisper, the Goddess cat, watched over them all.

In the sky above, Fantasme and Pandion circled each other warily, but kept watch for danger. The two wished nothing more than to kill each other, but the will of their masters kept them from joining together in battle.

Owen was safe enough with Nigel Temar. The man gave Jer the creeps, but he was a fine doctor, and he would act as base camp and surgeon, though Jer doubted his services would be needed until after it was all over. Jer had told Nigel to heal only, but not to resurrect. He saw how Kari was and he wouldn't wish that on anyone.

That left only Richard. Jer had been watching him all morning. The man was a marvel. As the only fighter who couldn't perform magic, his courage was that much more astounding. He had an ample supply of weapons, and Derek had helped him by enchanting all his weapons and ammo, then warding them with extra magic so that only Richard could fire them. Jer thought that last part had been especially brilliant.

Richard turned as though sensing he was being

watched and gave Jer a tight smile. *He's ready, maybe more so than the rest of us.* It was almost time to summon the dead. He shivered involuntarily and wished again that Holly were there. She was a lot more comfortable with leading ghost armies than he was.

"Jer?"

He turned and saw his mother smiling at him. The Goddess herself could not have looked more beautiful. He reached out and hugged her tight, knowing it might be the last time.

"Yeah, Mom?"

"There's a gift I wish to give to Richard, but I need your help."

"What did you have in mind?"

Richard rechecked his guns for the last time and then settled in to wait. As much as he wished Holly were there, he was pleased with the way Jer Deveraux had stepped up. The boy had finally become a man, and it was good to see. He had never thought much of him, all those years that Amanda had pined after him. All he'd been was a selfish, brooding child. Richard was glad to see that things had changed. He would have been happy to see one of his girls end up with this Jer.

"Richard?"

He jerked as he heard the soft voice speak his name. As one in a dream, he turned around. His dead wife,

Marie-Claire, stood behind him, a soft shimmer in the morning light. His chest tightened; his throat closed up. She was a ghost, but far more than just a memory.

"Marie," he whispered.

Tears streamed down her cheeks. "I am sorry, Richard, so very sorry."

For cheating on him with Michael Deveraux, she meant. For not realizing that beneath his peaceful exterior the warrior lurked.

He shook his head. "Don't waste time, sweetheart."

She nodded. "There are so many things I wish we could have shared. It was my fault—"

"No, it was mine. He was a warlock."

She caught her breath. "I loved you. I still love you. I will never stop."

"I love you, too, Marie."

"The girls . . ."

"I'll get them through this. They're amazing women. Like their mother." His voice broke.

"You have to live," she begged him. "You have to. Richard, come here to me."

He closed his eyes and felt the softness of her lips, smelled the fragrance of her breath, and let himself believe she was really there. Something passed between them, and suddenly he could feel electricity racing across his skin.

"What's happening?" he asked her after she pulled away.

She smiled. "I've given you my magic. I didn't know how to use it while I was alive."

"Marie," he said, and he felt different. Stronger.

"I'll be with you in the battle and afterward. When I have to go, I'll take it back."

He had no words, and so he watched as she turned and joined an army of ghosts assembling on the flat grass shadowed by the castle ruins. He recognized some of them—Dan and Kialish, from Seattle—but there were dozens who were unfamiliar.

He looked down at his hand, pictured a fireball erupting from it, and it did. He smiled as he hurled it at one of the old castle stones and watched the flames dissipate. In many ways this was going to be like the Australian Dreamtime that he had once had to rescue Jer from. What he could imagine, he could create. He shifted his machine gun to his left hand.

"This should be fun."

Nicole's hands shook. She stood between Amanda and Eli and held hands with them both. It felt like her world was collapsing around her and time was fluid. The Nicole who shared so much with her sister now was not the Nicole who had dated wild Eli. It was as though her past and present were colliding and she was caught in the middle, praying not to be crushed.

"Don't be afraid," Eli said.

"Easy for you to say," she whispered.

"Not really." He grinned sadly at her.

She turned so she could see his face. "What does that mean?"

"I've been afraid every day of my life."

She started to laugh, but then realized he was serious. "You do a good job hiding it."

He shrugged. "It doesn't pay to show weakness when your last name is Deveraux. That's the quickest way to an early grave."

"One of them, at least," Nicole said, thinking about what lay before them.

He caught her gaze, held it. "Philippe was a good man."

Fresh tears stung her eyes. "Yes, he was."

"I'm not a good man."

"No. But I think you could be."

His features softened, and he looked almost . . . gentle. Almost kind. Almost . . . like Philippe.

"I'm beginning to think that with your help anything is possible."

A blush she didn't think she was capable of anymore warmed her cheeks. "I loved Philippe. You get that, right? I loved him and I still do."

"I know. Did you love me?"

"Once," she admitted. "I wanted you."

He turned to face her and put his hand under her chin. "Do you still?"

And just like that she was fourteen again. She licked her lips as she gazed into his dark eyes. What she had once loved in them she had grown to fear. Now both had been tempered by time and hardship. "I don't know."

He nodded his head slowly. "Fair enough. If we live through this, Nicole, I'll regain your love."

She smiled. In some strange way she felt that Philippe had somehow rubbed off on Eli. There would be time enough later to think about that, though—about them.

She felt Amanda squeeze her hand, and she returned the pressure, realizing her twin couldn't have helped but overhear the conversation.

Jer turned his attention to the rest of the forces that had gathered during the night. Jer's army knelt before him as he finished his incantation of protection. They wore battle armor, forged from the memories of the Middle Ages and the magic of the modern world. Silvery black clung to their bodies like catsuits, and breastplates and helmets of alloy protected their brains and vital organs. They carried machine guns, and lances, and pistols and crossbows. Armand and Pablo held crosses, and Jer had to suppress a snort of derision at their quaint, superstitious belief in the Christian God.

Magical mists undulated among so many familiar faces as they rose and saluted him as their supreme commander. The ghosts of fallen warriors flickered in and out of being: Kialish, Eddie, Dan, Barbara, Tante Cecile, Silvana, Alonzo, Jose Luis, Josh, Marie-Claire, and Holly's father, Daniel. Cahors down the centuries, some with their minds intact, looking confused as they regarded their leader—a hated Deveraux. He couldn't be certain of their loyalty. He had created hundreds of golems and placed the names of Merlin, Laurent, and Catherine in their mouths. Three dragons circled overhead, casting silhouettes against the moon. He heard the baying of hellhounds, favored familiars of warlocks.

The ground thundered as terra-cotta warriors from China and zombies from Haiti joined Jer's massed troops. Lions, griffins, and manticores took up their battle stations.

The ruins of the castle stood stark and unforgiving against the night sky. In front of the crumbling stone and mortar, Nicole looked so out of place. Jer could sense his brother's honest, true love for Nicole, and it unnerved him. To think that a warlock once so devoted to the Black Arts could feel the emotion of love—there had to be a power at work that Jer could not control, much less comprehend. Would it turn on him?

Had it taken Holly from him, forever?

His gut churned. His mind raced. Like Holly, he had made terrible sacrifices, bargaining with pieces of his soul, for the power to protect his covenates. He bore his scars outside and in, but he knew that hers ran as deep. Perhaps the wounds that had caused them had overwhelmed her. He didn't know. All he did know was that if he was going to die tonight, it would happen because he loved her, and her people, and his own.

I should never have rejected her offer to be joined in thrall, he thought, clenching his scarred fists as cold wind slapped him. Raindrops pounded his bare head. *I threw away my only chance at happiness. Besides, it was stupid to waste that chance to protect our people. Our combined power could have stopped this from ever happening.*

He shook his head to clear away such thoughts. Regrets were for the weak. He looked again at Nicole and marveled at how she had changed. The sorrow on her face for her dead Philippe was terrible to behold. Philippe hadn't seen the crazy, wild girl who had hung out at their house, hoping to see some big bad black magic. Bad girls like bad boys, and Nicole had innocently thought that the Deveraux were like that. She'd had no idea they were bad *men*. There was a huge difference.

Holly had known that. Holly had seen that. And she had turned away.

Jer took a deep breath. It was time. They were as prepared as they were ever going to be. In his mind he could feel Laurent reaching out for him, trying to find him. His stomach twisted painfully. He reached out and took Kari's cold hand in his own.

"Everyone ready?"

There were murmurs up and down the line.

"Drop it."

Anne-Louise waved her hand in the air, and the barrier that the angels had helped her erect, which shielded them from the eyes of the world, collapsed.

"By the God, Jer," Eve breathed. "Look."

Jer turned, and saw Merlin, dread sorcerer, an enemy more powerful even than Duc Laurent, astride a white stallion that was decked out in equestrian battle armor. Laurent's black stallion reared beside Merlin's horse, fire gutting from its nostrils. As its hooves slammed against the ground, sparks skittered into the night sky.

Ranged behind them were demonic creatures, and wraiths, and centuries of Deveraux phantoms that had pledged their souls and beating hearts to the destruction of the Cahors. There were thousands of them. Among them Jer saw his own father, Michael, and he felt sick to his soul. Some were nothing more than skeletal shapes; gray flesh clung to others. The light of life danced in the eyes of some; others seemed even deader than Kari. Zombies. Legions of them.

At the rear, towering strangely over the vast army, sat the heavily veiled Catherine of the Cahors, the woman who had conspired to kill Duc Laurent, his sons, Jean and Paul-Henri, and every other Deveraux who drew breath. She wore black armor chased with silver, and black gauntlets held the reins. The bloodied heads of recent human sacrifices dangled from her saddle. He counted six on one side, seven on the other. In her terrible majesty she resembled the ancient manifestation of the Goddess known as Kali, the Destroyer. Kali wore the skulls of men around her neck, and at her waist.

Though her face was hidden, he knew that she was staring straight at him, with the deadly accuracy of a laser machine gun aimed directly at his heart. Laurent and Merlin both smiled, and he knew they barely restrained themselves from attacking.

Our lines are drawn, and they are strange, he thought. *Cahors and Deveraux have changed sides, mingled, separated. This battle is about more than our blood feud. What is it that I'm fighting for?*

An image of Holly blossomed in his mind, and his heart skipped three beats. For a moment he thought he was dying. He murmured another protection spell and touched his breastplate. Amulets were fused into the metal and sewn into the simple shirt he wore beneath his catsuit.

Holly, be well. Live forever, he thought, and found himself making a fist and kissing his extended thumb, as he had seen the Catholic followers of the Goddess do. He thanked Pan that Holly was not there. And yet, if he died today, without seeing her once more . . .

. . . then I will haunt her. Through time and space I will look for her.

A bolt of lightning zigzagged across the sky and pierced the ground a few feet in front of him. Shouts rose up as trees burst into flame. He braced himself and danced backward, scrutinizing the ground in case a portal opened. His side had heavily warded their territory against such things, but he knew he could make no assumptions about what the other side could and could not do.

Nothing happened. The rain doused the trees. The next blaze of lightning shot over their heads, charging Jer's hair with static electricity, but nothing worse than that. His massed army retained their composure, but he could feel their fear, their anxiety. They were wise to be afraid. The balance of power was not in their favor.

"I'll be pissed off if you die," Eli said gruffly. Then he smiled his hard, cold smile. "But I'll be more pissed off if *I* die."

Eve chuckled. "Deveraux to the end." Her face was pale, and her voice dropped to a hoarse rasp. "They have more people than we do."

"It's not how many, it's how powerful," Jer countered, but she was right. They were so incredibly, vastly outnumbered.

Then the ground beneath his feet rumbled again, and flames shot from the fissure. Black light poured from it like boiling smoke. Immediately Jer, Eli, and Eve formed fireballs and hurled them in a thick arc of flame.

The fireballs slammed against the giant black-scaled demonic form, all fangs and talons and spines. It was Sir William Moore, as he was now. Jer himself had watched the creature slash its way out of the human body of Sir William. Now it unfurled its wings and gazed at the trio. Chills skittered down Jer's back, but he kept his chin high.

"Sir William," he said in a booming voice, "I'm Jeraud Deveraux."

The demon's huge mouth split into a slathering grin. Bloody drool looped from his razor-sharp fangs as his wings flapped in the rain. His talons curled, uncurled. Huge eyes gleamed with fiery scarlet light.

"Sir William!" a voice shouted. It was Laurent. He raised his left hand, covered in a red metal gauntlet. "Well met! We await you, sir!"

The demon swept a stately bow in the direction of Jer, Eli, and Eve, showing his backside to Laurent. Jer's lips parted in amazement.

"I am here. I am on your side, Jeraud," he hissed, and his voice sent skitters up Jer's spine. "I will help you destroy your ancestors and their allies. *Merlin*. I will rip out his backbone." He drooled and clacked his fangs as if in anticipation of the carnage to come.

Jer straightened his shoulders, aware that Eli and Eve both had created fireballs, and were waiting for his signal to lob them at the demon. They would need stronger magic than that if Sir William changed sides.

His gaze ticked to the opposing army. As if she couldn't believe what she was seeing, Catherine lifted her heavy black veils from her face. Jer couldn't make out her features in the darkness; he had a feeling that was a lucky thing.

"I hated your father. I hate your family. The Deveraux have plagued the Moores for centuries." Sir William drew himself up on his muscular legs that resembled those of a warhorse. He towered above Jer, his brother, and his cousin. Sulfur and smoke stained the air.

"But I hate Merlin more." The creature's voice brimmed with loathing, malice. "I know what he is. What he can do to the world. And you won't like what he does to it."

"Then you'll fight with us," Jer said.

The demon lowered his head. "Yes, I will." His face split apart with an enormous, insinuating smile. "Today."

Merci bien, Jer said.

"I'll take on your enemies, but don't get cocky. I may be more than a man, but I'm still only one warrior."

"We're grateful for your help, Sir William," Eve said steadily.

"A Deveraux assassin, grateful," the demon sneered. He looked hard at Jer. "Gaspar, Balthasar, and Melchior did the world a huge service when they bound Merlin. All is lost, unless you send him back to the Crystal Cave. He will rip your world to pieces. *Our* world. Unless you defeat him now."

"That's our intention," Jer said boldly.

If only we knew how.

THIRTEEN

THYME

☾

Terror fills the darkest hearts
Tears are shed as we part
As it was, it again will be
Only in death are we ever free

Standing here among the slain
Tasting blood and fire and pain
Flesh will tear and hearts will rend
And now it ends, at last it ends

In the Forever Time

There is a moment after death when things can go one of several ways, when souls can mingle and reunite—or be forever parted. Fate throws the bones, and hearts are mended, or shattered. What tips the balance in one's favor? Is it Mercy, or Grace, or Justice—the names of the three brightest angels?

Or is it Love, the name of the One True Being?

Thyme

The Ruins of Castle Cahors, France

Jer threw up his arm as he stared at the forces allied against them. There were thousands of demons. If things went as he expected they would, they would focus their attack on Armand.

He had to trust that the witch priest and his allies could take care of that part. Richard and the witch-warriors summoned to act as his troops would have to take care of his part.

Jer gave the signal, and his own ghost army flowed forward to do battle with the dead of the other side. That left the flesh-and-blood enemies to deal with.

It's time, he thought. *All my life, I felt so unnecessary. Useless. This is my highest, best purpose. If I die today, I'll have lived well.*

He took a moment to send his thanks to . . . whom? He didn't know whom he followed any longer. He had stopped worshipping the Horned God long ago. But the Goddess was a stranger to him.

Thank you, Holly, he thought. *Thank you for loving me, and believing in me.*

He wished she were there . . . and was glad that she wasn't.

Wherever you are, be well.

"Now!" he bellowed, and the shouts of his side rose up around him like a blazing inferno of will.

The thunder of hoofbeats and heartbeats and chanting; the screams of banshees and phantoms and horrors; the shouts of men. The savage cry of Richard Anderson, echoed by Eli.

Jer threw up his hand, and a dozen throwing stars rolled off his fingertips and flew at the enemy, cutting through flesh and bone. And in the corner of his eye he could see that he was right, all the demons were heading straight for Armand.

He held on to Kari's hand for dear life as he sent wave after wave of deadly magic toward Laurent. Nicole and Eli surged forward together, heading for Merlin.

We can do this! We can win! Amanda thought as another of Laurent's foot soldiers exploded in front of her. Beside her Tommy was spinning like a madman, death flashing off his fingertips first as fire and then as daggers of ice.

They fought for hours; for five seconds; it all happened so fast that time blurred. Wind whipped around her, slapping her hair across her face. It was like a hurricane, a tornado, a kamikaze. It was of magical origin, and it threw her off her feet.

"Amanda!" Tommy shouted. He was being billowed about, as she was, like two leaves on the wind.

Duc Laurent stood in the middle of a maelstrom

of his own making and twisted his hands faster and faster.

As Tommy helped her back to her feet, Amanda threw a fireball at Laurent. It didn't even get close, extinguished by the vortex whirling around him. Tommy sent several ice daggers toward him, but they were pulverized into dust by the winds that were gathering strength.

Amanda saw Jer rushing toward his ancestor, and she sent some shields to protect him as he ran. He had almost reached Laurent when an earthquake threw everyone on both sides to the ground. The ground rumbled, and the whole world rippled.

Amanda flipped over as the earth heaved beneath her. Then a hundred feet away it split open and a high-pitched keening sound tumbled forth. Smoke and fire appeared in the crevice, and then a figure ascended.

The Horned God rose into the sky and roared in rage. He was dressed in gold and green, in his image of Green Man. Majestic, terrifying, he seemed to gather leaves and grass and insects into his robes as he stepped forward. Upon his head he wore a crown of antlers, and from his eyes fire erupted.

He turned toward Amanda and she scrabbled backward across the rough ground. He stretched forth his hand, and next to her Luna fell to the ground dead.

Amanda screamed and continued to back up, trying

to get away, praying that his eyes wouldn't fall on her.

An earsplitting wail ripped the air, and next the Goddess shimmered into existence, wearing black robes tied with silken cords of moonlight. She threw what appeared to be a moonbeam and it landed around the head of the demonic Sir William. She flicked her wrist and the ropelike beam snapped taught and beheaded him.

"No, you can't!" Rose cried, throwing herself forward. "That's not who we are, that's not how we worship."

The Goddess turned and caught Rose by the chin and then calmly broke her neck. As if to mock her own actions, she wore the guises of the Lady Virgin, in white robes and blue, and with a diadem of stars.

Amanda started to shake uncontrollably. The Goddess had just killed one of her followers. Sir William had been their ally. Nothing could save any of them now if *Notre Dame* and the Horned God didn't care who they killed. She touched the amulet around her neck. Merlin was suddenly the least of their worries.

Then the Horned God and the Goddess set their sights on each other. The Horned God changed His aspect, becoming the patron of the Deveraux, as if to thumb his nose at the treacherous family who had shifted allegiance to his nemesis: His head was that of a goat, twin curled horns spiraling to either side of crescent-shaped eyes. Below the goat's fringed beard, the fanned hood of a jaguar served as a neck. The torso belonged to a jaguar, and the front legs and paws to some unnamed beast of prey with talons fully half as long as his body. His hind legs and tail were that of a crocodile.

The Goddess changed too, becoming Kali, the Goddess of Time and Change: mud-colored, four-armed, naked, Her tongue extending to the center of Her chest. She wore nothing but clacking necklaces of human skulls, anklets and bracelets of bones.

From her tongue and open mouth, flames and fireballs shot toward the Horned God, followed by daggers of ice. Lightning bolts emanated from his eyes, raging around Her, smashing the ground, the trees, the skies.

Cataclysm. Chaos. Apocalypse.

The Goddess changed her aspect: Athena, Bast, Durga, Circe, the Virgin, blurring, becoming one, many, legion—

"Stop! Oh, please, stop!" Amanda screamed as she threw herself behind one of the ancient stones of the castle. It exploded in front of her. She threw her hands up in front of herself and turned her face—

—just in time to see a fireball whoosh toward Eli's chest.

"Look out!" she shrieked.

★ ★ ★

Eli jerked sideways just as he heard Amanda's warning. The fireball only grazed him, which explained why he was still alive. He threw off the smoldering remnants of his shirt and looked down at his chest . . . at where the protection symbol should have been . . . which was now just a patch of charred flesh.

"No!" he screamed.

It was too late. Eli Deveraux started the scream, but Jean Deveraux finished it.

"Isabeau!"

He turned and saw the Cathers witch Nicole, just as her face changed and the features of his Isabeau took control.

"Traitor, murdering bitch!" he shouted as he ran to her.

She did not run, but stood her ground, the proud fierce Cahors daughter at the last.

His lips found hers, and the familiar curves of her body melted into his. The battle raged on around him, but he did not care. There was only this moment and her and the love and hate that filled him and made him tremble.

Ma femme. Ma vie. My woman, my life.

They tumbled to the ground, and their bodies joined.

Ma mort. My death.

Thyme

And then Jean looked at her, his bride, his love, his enemy. He drew his athame and rammed it into her heart just as her blade pierced his. He collapsed on top of her, and their blood ran out of their bodies, mingling in death just as it had during their wedding ceremony. Blood to blood, flesh to flesh.

"I have fulfilled my vow. I have killed you, witch," he whispered with his dying breath.

"And I have killed you, my husband, my love," she sobbed in response.

Around them the battle raged. Warriors fell. Phantoms exploded. The earth began to crack apart.

Nicole died first, and Isabeau was forced to let go. She floated a moment above the body, her spirit waiting. She watched as the light left Jean's . . . no, Eli's eyes. Then his body died and Jean came to her.

"Isabeau," Jean whispered. *"Nous sommes libres."*

We are free.

Free as birds.

It was over at last. The curse that had bound them to the earth and to each other was gone. And it was time to leave. But Isabeau knew she would not be leaving alone. It wasn't a curse only that had bound her to Jean. She would go anywhere as long as he was there. She was his and he was hers.

Whither thou goest . . .

. . . eternally.

★ ★ ★

Amanda screamed in horror as she crawled over to the body of her sister. Nicole's eyes were open, vacant. "You can't die!" she shrieked, shaking the body. "Niki! You have to live for Owen, for me."

There was no response. With tears blurring her vision Amanda turned and saw where Derek had taken refuge behind a large stone. She half-crawled, half-ran to him.

"We need Holly!" she shouted into his face.

"Holly's not here; she's in the Temple."

"She still has a real body. The Temple has to be a real place, too! Find it. You know how to find everyone! Find her!"

"There's no way to find the Temple, even if she *is* there," he shouted back.

She grabbed a fistful of his hair and yanked his head around so that he could see Nicole's broken body. "She's dead, which means her legal will is activated. So, tell me, Derek, where all her relatives are."

Understanding lit his features. He pulled some satchels out of his pockets and began mixing the ingredients together on the ground. While he worked, Sasha joined them.

"We need Holly," she said.

"We're trying to find her," Amanda said.

"Even if we can find her, I don't know how you

Thyme

think you're going to get to her," Derek said.

"Leave that to me," Sasha said.

A moment later they had their answer, and in the blink of an eye Sasha was gone. Moments later she was back and Holly was with her.

Holly looked around her at the destruction and at the Goddess and the Horned God as they battled each other. "Not supposed to interfere," she muttered as one in a trance.

Amanda slapped her hard. "Open your eyes, Holly. People are dying. The Goddess killed one of her own followers. How is this balance? How is this anything but chaos?"

Holly turned, and her eyes found Jer. A dozen spectral warriors circled him, trying to break through a magical barrier he had erected around himself. From the way he was hunched over, he was either badly injured or protecting something.

Owen. Jer was cradling Owen in his arms, trying to protect him. Holly knew that he would fail and both of them would die. She knew she should care. She *did* care.

She turned to Sasha just in time to see her eyes roll back in her head as she toppled forward into Holly's arms, a dozen ice daggers in her back. Holly dropped the body and stared at it for a moment. Jer's mother, lost so many times, was now truly dead. And for what?

381

Cut down not by an enemy but by the deity she had worshipped.

Holly turned and raised her arms. "Stop!" she cried.

All sound ceased. The God and the Goddess turned toward her, weapons at the ready. "I bind you both!" she said.

Clouds coursed across the sky. The sun winked out, covered by the moon, and the world hung breathless as the two titans froze in place.

And Kari, the dead girl Jer had once loved, turned and faced her. Her mouth dropped open.

"It does not end with this." A strange, echoic voice emanated from her unmoving mouth. It was like the Justices, but it was not they.

"This was never about Jean and Isabeau or Laurent and Catherine or any of us. It was always about them."

Kari's arm slowly raised as she pointed to the Horned God and the Goddess.

"The old ways, in ancient times, were about balance. The two of them were worshipped together as equals, husband and wife, brother and sister. Many people still worship them that way. But something happened, and they weren't content to be equals. So they started their feud, luring magic families into choosing one side or another. And we're the ones who pay in their little war."

"Deveraux chose the God and Cahors chose the Goddess," Holly said.

"No! Both chose the God, but together they were too power-

ful, the balance tipped, the Justices intervened. When Cahors and Deveraux began to fight each other, Cahors changed sides."

"How do you know this?" Holly demanded. "Who are you?"

Kari turned slowly and pointed to the armies of ghosts. *"They tell me. They bear witness to it all."*

Holly saw it then: a blazing force that towered above the will of the Justices. Balance was all, balance must be kept, and the God and Goddess were not doing as they should, not killing whom they should.

"It is up to you," said the voice—the voice of the One Higher, the One Whom Holly truly served.

Holly humbly bowed her head. Then she raised her arms and pronounced the last judgment.

"God and Goddess, I bind you and I banish you from this field of battle, and you may not return. Ever."

Jer raised his head just in time to see the Horned God and the Goddess vanish. He then turned to stare at Holly, who stood magnificent in her white robes with her hair flying around her head and her eyes glowing bright. Maybe they were all saved.

Then she lowered her arms and turned away, and Laurent's knights broke through his barriers. "Holly, help us!" Jer shouted.

He didn't think she had heard him, because she kept walking away.

"Holly, please! Don't leave me."

She stopped and turned slowly. "Why do you ask me to tip the scales?" she asked, her voice hollow.

"For the only thing that is more important than balance," he said.

"And that is?"

"Love. Holly Cathers, I love you, and I will chase you through this world and the next."

And then she smiled. "You won't have to," she whispered.

She threw up her arms again and the warriors that surrounded him collapsed into dust. Richard rushed forward and took Owen from Jer.

Isabeau and Jean were moving. She didn't know where; she just knew they were moving on. She heard screaming and glanced down at the bodies of their hosts crumpled below.

"We owe them our freedom," she said to Jean.

"I have some unfinished business. Will you wait for me?" he asked her.

She nodded and glided close to the bodies.

"*Merci, et adieu, mes braves.* For what you have given us, I will you to live." With spectral fingers she touched first Nicole and then Eli. They each awoke with a gasp.

Isabeau turned away and looked for her husband.

★ ★ ★

Thyme

Jean strode across the field of battle with the strength and glory that had been his on the day he'd taken Isabeau as his bride. All who looked upon his face fell back in terror. He gave them not a second glance. There was only one whom he sought.

And then he was upon her, Catherine, of the house of Cahors. Her spectral form was nearly as imposing as her real one had been. She turned, and when she saw him, fear flickered in her eyes. He conjured a vial of fine powder in his hands, a special concoction he had been working on for centuries. He had often thought about using it on himself, but this was a far better use.

"To hell with you," he spat, and threw the powder on her.

She screamed in torment, and a moment later she was gone.

Gone.

Forever, damn her to hell.

He turned back to find Isabeau, and was stayed by the hand of Duc Laurent, his father, somehow alive and in the flesh. That was one trick the old man had never shared with his children.

"Jean," Laurent began. "Unmanned by that—"

Before he could complete his thought, Jer Deveraux, his many-times-grandson, walked up behind the great duke and savagely ran an athame across his throat. Blood gushed; the duke fought to close the wound, and instead fell forward, dead. Blood pooled around his inert body, and soaked into the grass.

For a moment Jean and Jer stared at each other. Many times they had shared the same body without ever meeting.

Jean bowed his head in deference, and Jer saluted him in turn. They stood for a moment, and then Jean smiled.

"Take better care of your witch than I took of mine," Jean said.

"I will," Jer vowed.

Jean turned and saw Isabeau, waiting patiently. He went to her, wrapped his soul around her, and together they left behind everything they had ever known.

Nicole pulled the dagger from Eli's chest and screamed as he did the same for her. The wounds healed instantly and they lay, trembling, exhausted, and terrified in each other's arms.

She remembered it, all of it. And she knew also that the first time she and Eli had been together, Isabeau's presence had been inside her, so that her own memories had been fuzzy. Jean and Isabeau had tried to possess Eli and her long before they had turned their attention to Jer and Holly. Eli's protective marks had worked.

She began to cry. Eli wrapped his arms around

her and they held tightly to each other while the battle continued to rage around them.

When she felt hands grabbing at her shoulders, she tried to shrug them off.

"Nicole!"

Amanda and Holly stood above her, each holding a piece of the amulet. The pieces had been given to the three Cahors witches in preparation for this moment. "It's time," Holly said.

With Eli's help Nicole got to her feet. She produced her piece of the amulet.

"We still don't know what to do with them," Amanda said, her voice tired and frightened.

"I think I know someone who does," Eli said, his voice cracking.

Nicole turned to look at him, and there, next to him, was the ghost of Philippe.

"Philippe!" she cried, weeping, holding out her arms.

"Nicole, I gave my life for this one piece of knowledge that can save you," he said.

Nicole could hear the sounds of people dying, and she knew without having to look that Merlin was not far away. "What do we do?"

"Place the amulets one on top of the other with yours on the bottom and Amanda's in the middle. Holly's piece must lie on top. Then twist the top one clockwise and the bottom one counterclockwise."

They did as he said. Amanda, Nicole, and Holly, the Three Ladies of the Lily. Overhead, the sky grew darker; then jagged pieces of crimson showed through, as if the world were bleeding.

The discs slid into place with a click and the thrum of power pulsed through the discs.

"It takes three to make it work. Listen, here is what you each must say in turn."

Nicole tried to listen over the pounding of her heart and the sounds of death all around them. The ground rumbled again. She felt light-headed, sick.

Philippe's image shimmered in the air. "Hurry!" he urged. "Merlin is going to change everything. If you cannot stop him, death will come to millions."

And she saw what would happen: all over the world, people dying—old people, babies, animals, plants. The world would be ravaged, and once every-thing was dead, Merlin would start over, fashioning it as he wished. That was his insanity, his evil. He had gone so long ago with his brothers to see the Christ child, not to worship Him, but to bind Him with sil-ver, so that He could never save the world that Merlin intended to destroy.

She saw pillars of fire; saw tortures; heard screams. Merlin was a madman of incredible power. An evil being.

Perhaps he was even Satan, made flesh.

Nicole stumbled over her words, but Amanda picked up the string of Latin and continued fluently. Holly opened her mouth to speak, and a fireball exploded in her face.

She crumpled to the ground with a cry, and Nicole turned to see Merlin galloping toward them as if in slow motion—glowing, laughing, and growing larger.

"You must start over!" Philippe said, flickering more.

Nicole took a deep breath and then yanked Amanda down beside her.

"I can't see," Holly whimpered.

"You don't have to see," Nicole said, guiding Holly's hand to the disc.

"What's the matter, ladies? Having trouble remembering a simple spell?" Merlin laughed. Each laugh broke pieces of the sky, and the moon began to spin like a top.

Kari threw herself against Merlin, knocking him off balance. Nicole began her part of the spell.

Merlin stabbed Kari through the heart with his athame, but she remained standing. A look of surprise crossed his face.

Amanda took up her part of the spell.

"Dead," Kari said. "Me. You."

"How dare you," Merlin said. "I am not dead. I'm eternal, like Him."

Merlin swiped at her with his blade and took off her arm. Dead, decaying blood rained down onto them all, and Nicole began to gag.

Holly began her part of the spell.

And then Merlin cut off Kari's head. It fell onto the ground next to Nicole and the dead eyes looked up at Merlin.

"Thank—"

And then Kari, the dead girl, was truly dead again.

"Divine One, make me an Instrument, a Saving Force. Make me into Peace. Make me into Power.

Make me in Your Image."

Merlin turned toward Holly, raised his athame, and she said the final word.

"Selah."

Light blossomed, shimmering, a mushroom around Merlin. He raised his hands to cover his face, shouting, as the light became a funnel of incandescence and tossed him into the sky. Higher it rose, and higher, lifting him into the darkness, which became light as the whirlwind streaked toward the moon. And higher.

And then, in a flash of white light, the funnel was gone.

And so was Merlin.

And so were the forces of the enemy.

In the twinkling of an eye.

For a moment all was still.

Then Nicole jumped to her feet, and faced Philippe. He smiled at her.

"I knew you could do it," he said. "I have always had faith in you, Nicole."

"I love you," she said, tears streaming down her cheeks.

"I love you, too. I will always watch over you as long as you walk the earth." His smile faded slowly, and then he was gone.

Amanda helped Holly to her feet. Together the three turned. The enemy had vanished, utterly.

Jer walked toward them, and slowly the ghosts who had come to fight on their side began to leave as well. One, however, walked beside Jer. He looked familiar, though Nicole did not know him.

"Holly, dear," the ghost said.

"Daddy?" Holly asked, moving around Nicole as she burst into tears.

"Don't cry, baby. You've done well. Your mom and I are at peace and you and I will see each other again." He seemed to shift slightly, grow more solid as Jer put a hand on his shoulder. Then Danny Cathers stepped forward and hugged his daughter good-bye.

Nicole turned away, crying for them both. Then her heart caught in her throat. Thirty feet away, her mother was kissing her father. She wanted to go to them, but something deep inside told her that her father needed the moment more than she did. She nudged Amanda, and her sister turned to look and then began to cry too.

It was hard to believe that it was over. So much blood spilled, so much destruction. Nicole didn't know how she was going to adjust to peace, but she was looking forward to trying.

After Holly's father left, Jer gave her a swift kiss and promised to be back with her as soon as he'd checked on their people. He walked the battlefield and surveyed the damage.

Kari, Sasha, both were dead. Hot tears burned in the back of his eyes for them both. Rose and Luna of the Mother Coven were gone as well. He already knew that Dr. Nigel Temar was dead: Jer had taken Owen when he'd seen that the doctor had sustained a mortal wound.

Owen and Richard were both safe. Anne-Louise was bloodied but alive. Next to her, her sister, Eve, seemed to not care that both her legs were broken as she sat on the ground kissing Derek. Jer found Pablo and Armand, both alive but hurt and being tended to by the three angels—Mercy, Grace, and Justice. Around them lay the bodies of hundreds of demons.

Thyme

Jer turned back at last toward Holly and her cousins. Eli was standing protectively over Nicole while Tommy was holding Amanda as she cried. Slowly they all drifted together.

Hours later the survivors gathered in a private room in the Temple of the Mother Coven, after having washed up and had their wounds looked to. Anne-Louise couldn't help but feel a little amused at the looks of discomfort on the faces of the four warlocks in the group. Now that they had seen the true natures of the Horned God and Goddess, though, they needed to put aside such distinctions and fighting among themselves.

She cleared her throat. "Obviously the events of today have changed much, not only in our own lives but in the lives of all practitioners."

"Who will be the new high priestess of the Mother Coven?" Amanda asked.

"Apparently I am," Anne-Louise said.

She was met by smiles. "I think that is a very wise choice," Armand said.

"Congratulations, I think," Eli said.

"And just how will those in the Mother Coven cope with the high priestess being from a warlock family?" Jer asked.

Anne-Louise smiled grimly. "As with all organizations, we adapt or die. In the modern world it's not about names and families; it can't be. It's about individuals. I believe that you make your own fate no matter what cards you've been dealt."

"Well said, sis," Eve teased.

Anne-Louise looked at her and Derek. "The two of you are welcome to join this coven if you so choose."

"I think we're going to have to think about it," Derek said for both of them. "I'll be honest, though. Right now all I want to focus on is this lovely lady here."

Eve blushed. "We're not going anywhere, Anne-Louise," she said firmly.

Anne-Louise inclined her head. "Thank you. It is not going to be easy, but with help I believe we can change a lot of things that need to be changed. So, my question to all the rest of you is, where do you go from here?"

Armand smiled. "I'm going to return to the priesthood. There are rumors that the Vatican plans to reinstate their exorcism training programs. They're going to need help."

"I can't think of anyone I'd rather have protecting the world from demons," Holly said earnestly. She kissed him on the cheek. "Without you I would have died."

"We all would have," Richard said.

"I have to go back to the Temple. I'm still a Justice,"

Holly said, clearing her throat. She was blind now, like the others Justices. It was a small price, but still, it was a price.

Anne-Louise felt for her. "If it hadn't been for your intervention, the prophecy wouldn't have come true. Owen did save the world, because you were moved to help in order to save him."

Holly nodded. "That's true, but to be fair, he wasn't the only one I wanted to save."

Jer leaned forward and kissed Holly. "I'll be going with her. I've spent too much time running away from who I am and who I'm meant to be with."

"Glad to see you've stopped being an idiot," Nicole said, rolling her eyes.

"Let's be fair," Eli drawled, "most Deveraux men are complete idiots. I'm not happy to be here. I won't lie about that."

Nicole turned and glared daggers at him. "What's stopping you?" she asked, shifting Owen in her arms.

Eli said. "You. That kid needs a father and you need a husband, and seeing as how all the competition seems to have disappeared . . ."

Nicole slapped him, and Eli grinned. Anne-Louise shook her head. That was one marriage that was going to be turbulent. However, she could tell that there was genuine affection there and she saw hope for what Eli could become in time.

"And what of the House of Cathers?" Anne-Louise asked, looking pointedly at Amanda.

Amanda flushed. "Actually, it's the house of Nagai." She laced her fingers through Tommy's.

Tommy smiled at his bride. "We want our home to be a sanctuary for all who need it. A kind of safe haven for those who practice magic."

"And those who love them," Amanda said pointedly.

"I think that's a wonderful idea," Anne-Louise said. "I hope that we can send some of our covenates to you from time to time."

"Of course," Amanda reassured her.

"But not for a couple of months," Tommy hastened to add. "Amanda and I are planning on a real long, real private honeymoon."

"And a well-deserved one at that," Anne-Louise said. "I believe you should spend your first year in partial isolation while you adjust to each other and your new life. At the end of that time, I'll be in touch."

"It's a deal," Amanda said.

While the others talked, Richard stood off by himself, watching. Everyone had something or someone. Everyone except himself and Pablo.

Pablo turned to look at him and then quietly got

Thyme

up and walked over to stand next to him. Richard studied the boy. He was so young and he had lost so much. He would need someone to look out for him. He wasn't likely to follow Armand and join the priesthood, and both his daughters already had their hands full. He smiled to himself. As much as he loved having daughters, he'd always wished he could have had a son, someone to take fishing.

"Canada," he said to Pablo. "There's some beautiful land up there, wild, unspoiled. And I know some great places to fish."

Pablo hugged him hard, and Richard's heart ached for the boy. No real family, no chance to be just a kid. He'd make sure that changed. "I was thinking, if it would be okay with you, I'd like to make it official, adopt you legally."

"Will there be a lot of fishing?" Pablo asked, his voice uncertain.

"All the fishing you can stand . . . son."

And then they were both crying.

It was nearly time to go. Holly could feel the other Justices pulling at her mind. She saw now that she had been meant to come, meant to change things . . . meant to understand that there was a Greater Power than the Horned God and the Goddess. Now she could truly serve the One as the Head of the Justices, their leader.

And to think that less than three years before, she hadn't even known she was a witch.

She stretched out her hand. Even though she couldn't see Jer, she could feel his presence. The touch of his hand sent delicious shivers through her. So much death and loss. But they were together now, and in her heart she knew that it had all been worth it.

"I have a lot to make up to you for what a moron I've been," Jer whispered in her ear.

"Yes, you do," she said back.

He kissed her, and the promise in that kiss made her sigh.

As Holly and Jer made to leave, Nicole and Amanda bid them good-bye. Nicole's throat was tight and her eyes burned with tears, but she knew it was the best thing. And with Holly looking out for the world, things would be much better.

Once they had gone, Derek approached Amanda and Nicole and pulled them off to the side to speak with them.

"Is this about the will?" Nicole demanded. "Because as you can see, I'm not dead."

"Actually, you were dead. And Amanda—"

Amanda huffed at him. "I already told her I had you use that family finder's spell so that we could contact Holly."

Nicole smiled. Comrade-in-arms or no, Amanda was just never going to like Derek. Maybe it had nothing to do with the fact that he was a warlock. Maybe she just had a thing against lawyers.

"Well, about that, there is something that I did want to discuss with you girls."

"What is it?" Nicole asked.

Derek took a breath. "I did perform the family finder's spell, and when it's cast, it looks for family . . . all family."

"And?" Amanda asked.

He moved his shoulders as if to soften the news. "There are other Cathers out there."

Nicole shared a stunned glance with her sister.

"I guess the question is, do you want to find them?" Derek asked intently.

Nicole looked again at Amanda and then back at Derek. She shook her head. "Definitely not."

And then she sighed, and braced herself. After all, family . . . was family.

In the Forever Time, Restored

In the eternal greenwood, just outside the Temple of the Justices, the dawn rose like a miracle, and blessings sparkled on grass and leaf like dew. To the trilling of larks, the lord and his lady rode their magnificent stallions, side by side. Pandion alighted on Holly's arm, and Fantasme's bells jingled as he soared high among silvery clouds, piercing the sunbeams, then circled back around to land on Jer's shoulder.

For a span of heartbeats, for several revolutions of the planet, the balance was safe—at least long enough for a morning ride. As the horses chuffed, the magical falcon and the enchanted hawk lofted from master and mistress and flew together to their nest. There, three tiny nestlings chirped for their breakfast, and the proud father and sweet mother set about caring for their young.

Jer smiled at his one true love. And Holly, though she could see nothing, saw Jer's smile. She reached out a hand and traced his cheek, her fingers marveling at the smooth, unlined skin. Her love had taken away his scars.

Love is blind, she thought. *Love sees all. Oh, Jer Deveraux, I love you with all my heart, and with all my soul. And I will love you forever.*

"What are you thinking about?" His voice was soft and gentle. Happy.

"What do you think?" she replied.

Jer brought his horse closer to Holly's, and he leaned from the saddle. He gathered her up, and kissed her with all the joy and passion the universe could summon.

Then something shimmered, something happened,

and light blazed across his face. Holly's head was wreathed in golden light, and behind her, on a hill, sat a shining castle. Its spires and turrets gleamed in the rosy morning, and he heard flutes and drums, and smelled cooking meat.

"A gift, in thanks." It was the Justices. He caught his breath.

Holly said, "I heard it too."

"Take your ease," they said, *"and then, return."*

Jer settled her in front of him on his saddle and they cantered toward the castle. Pandion and Fantasme urged their chicks to flight, and all followed the lovers . . .

. . . to Scarborough Fair.

Remember me . . .

. . . Parsley, sage, rosemary and thyme.

USA Today bestselling author **Nancy Holder** has received four Bram Stoker awards for her supernatural fiction. She has served on the board of trustees for the Horror Writers Association. Her work has been translated into more than two dozen languages, and she has more than seventy-eight books and two hundred short stories to her credit. Her books for Simon Pulse include the Wicked series and the novel *Spirited*. She lives in San Diego with her daughter, Belle, and far too many animals. Visit Nancy online at nancyholder.com.

Debbie Viguié is the author of several Simon Pulse books, including the Wicked series, *Midnight Pearls*, *Scarlet Moon*, and *Violet Eyes*. Debbie has been writing for most of her life and holds a degree in creative writing from UC Davis. When Debbie is not busy writing, she enjoys traveling with her husband, Scott. They currently live in Hawaii. Visit Debbie online at debbieviguie.com.

More Book for Your BUCK

Check Your Pulse

Simon & Schuster's **Check Your Pulse** e-newsletter offers current updates on the hottest titles, exciting sweepstakes, and exclusive content from your favorite authors.

Visit **SimonSaysTEEN.com** to sign up, post your thoughts, and find out what every avid reader is talking about!